# [Nameless]

## Volume 1, Number 2: Fall/Winter 2012
### +++++ *Twilight Worlds* +++++

*Keith Kennedy * S. T. Joshi * Paul G. Bens, Jr. * William F. Nolan * Kris Kuksi*
*Earl Hamner, Jr. * Michael Aronovitz * Adam Bolivar * Wade German * George A. Romero*

### Editor-in-Chief/ Art Director
Jason V Brock

### Managing Editor
S. T. Joshi

### Design, Web, and Layout
JaSunni Productions, LLC
(www.JaSunni.com)

+++++

### Visit us online:
www.NamelessMag.com

+++++

### Written Contributors
Michael Aronovitz
*Paul G. Bens, Jr.*
Adam Bolivar
*Jason V Brock*
Sunni K Brock
*Matt Cardin*
Michael J. Clarke
*Ellen Denton*
Sam Gafford
*Wade German*
John D. Haefele
*Earl Hamner*
JC Hemphill
*S. T. Joshi*
Rahul Kanakia
*Keith Kennedy*
Kris Kuksi (+ Photos)
*William F. Nolan*
David Perlmutter
*J. J. Steinfeld*
Kaye Vincent
*Don Webb*
+++++

### Contributing Artists/ Photographers
Jason V Brock
*(Cover [utilizing elements by Kuksi] + Misc. Int. Images)*
Richard H. Fay
*(Art [Shedroid on Tentacles], pg 216)*
Kris Kuksi
*(Art, pgs 157, 159-161)*
Ron Sanders
*(Art [A Glass Darkly], pg 66; [Hither], pg 145)*
Steve Sorrentino
*(Image [S. Grendon], pg 90)*
Brenda Whiteway
*(Art [Sand Being], pg 38)*
James Wymore
*(Cartoons, pgs 44-45)*
+++++

### Special Thanks
Leslie Barany
*H. R. Giger*
Kris Kuksi & Family
*Our Advertisers & Contributors*
Our Readers & Subscribers
*Joe Parrington*
PETA
*Rod Serling Memorial Foundation & Family*
George Romero
+++++

### In Memoriam
Charles E. Fritch
*This issue is dedicated to his lifelong work in the field.*
Rod Serling
+++++

### Printing
Lightning Source
+++++

++ [NameL3ss] ++

+++++

[NameL3ss]

++ [NameL3ss] ++

(ISSN 2169-1681 [Print]; ISSN 2169-1673 [Electronic]) Print Single Issue Suggested Retail Sale Price: $19.95 USD (Single Issue MSRP: $24.95 USD) and includes the E-book version; prices and subscriptions/ shipping vary by region, and are subject to change without notice. *Published irregularly (Biannually: SPRING/SUMMER & FALL/WINTER) by CYCATRIX PRESS: 16420 SE McGillivray Blvd., Ste. 103-1010, Vancouver, WA, USA 98683.* Copyright ©2010 and beyond by JaSunni Productions, LLC, *and where specified elsewhere in the issue. All rights revert to the authors/artists upon publication. All design elements (including the overall layout and the distinctive* NAMELESS *logo) are* copyright ©2010 and beyond by JaSunni Productions, LLC. *Nothing shown can be reproduced without obtaining written permission from the creators. All cover images, whether book, magazine, CD, or DVD, as well as film posters, image captures, promotional images (headshots, behind-the-scenes, etc) and creator photos remain the copyrighted property of their respective owners, and are used herein with permission, or pursuant to Fair Use Guidelines: Every reasonable attempt has been made to contact image and content rights holders, and identify same; if there are inadvertent omissions, we apologize.* Go veg: Save your life, and save theirs! Advertising rates available. Discounts for bulk and standing retail orders. Direct all inquiries, address changes, submission queries, subscription orders, and so on to: info@namelessmag.com

# WANTED

## $10,000 REWARD

### MUSEUM HRGIGER

# + + ~~T4bLe~~ +f ~~C0nt3Nts~~ + +

Visit us online for more
**exclusive content:**
*www.NamelessMag.com*
+++++

"I object to violence because when it appears to do good, the good is only temporary; the evil it does is permanent."
--Mahatma Gandhi

"Nonviolence doesn't always work--but violence never does."
--Isaac Asimov

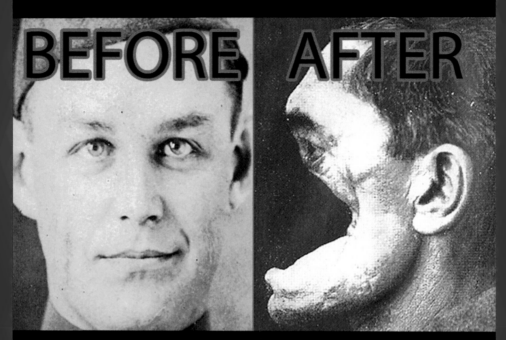

BEFORE AFTER

Guns=Weapons=Violence=Suffering=Evil

Not everyone *dies* from gun violence. Think about it.

as represented by the wretched NRA and the gun/ammo manufacturers, whose *raison d'être* is to create *more* weapons and ammunition, and who try every method they can to thwart even the statistical analysis of the true destructive impact of these WMDs (I mean, surely modern guns qualify as so-called "weapons of mass destruction" . . . guns have likely killed more people than any other single weapon class in all of human history), going so far as to *prohibit by law* the mere collection of Center for Disease Control data on morbidity and mortality by firearm. Besides, if the Right was so concerned about mental illness, they would have prevented Ronald Reagan from gutting the system in the 1980s (ironic that he was then shot by a mentally deranged person!). Regardless, it is not solely a mental health problem (for example, there is no evidence that the Newtown Massacre was anything other than a deranged *act*, versus a deranged person committing a terrible *act*; there is a difference).

In addition, to equate a war action (which I am against) such as the use of drones with Newtown is a logical fallacy: "Obama kills with drones!" is a rallying point for the Right, and it's a stupid one. That's analogous to saying GIs killed civilians in Europe to stop Hitler. Yes, that happened, but it falls under "unintended consequences." Recall that Obama inherited a war in two countries. One should blame the Bush-Cheney Administration/Axis for drone usage, *not* Obama. This is just one of many such mind tricks that people do to distract attention from the real problems in society: Conceptually, these arguments waver somewhere between the No Man's Land of "intentional misinformation" (AKA "disinformation)" and "self-delusion."

With regard to what I see as the *real* problem, the Right wants that to be obscured: access to too many guns that are too powerful, and too easy to obtain. It's that simple. One answer to this is as follows: reasonable restrictions, not prohibition of weapons; there is room for debate. It seems the Right only has one speed: unfettered access to as much firepower as possible, damn the consequences, intended or not. It's predicated on another logical error, I believe (logic is not something the Right is good with; they prefer emotionalism, though they are disingenuous about it): that the citizenry needs (as previously referenced) to "protect itself from the government." If one feels that way, then go to a place where there's *no* government. That's the only way that works: One could never take on the full might of the US military (sorry, the government and the military are commingled at this point). It's not possible, no matter how many or what type of arms one has; one would need *tactical nuclear weapons* even to make a dent, and the Feds would *still* win. Enough already with that: It's a tipping point that was passed in the Civil War. If the *entire South* failed to defeat the Federal Government, then what makes someone today think *they* can?

Militias are a last bastion for the weak-minded, I feel: They are usually anti-Left, and often racist.

Besides, we are in the society we've created—and whether that means popular cultural violence is feeding into the mix or merely a reflection of it is still (and likely to remain) an open question. But that doesn't mean we can't improve it. Fund health care for all, including mental health care. Stop being led by guns. Regulate and control drugs. And tax them. Regulate and license the Right-wing fearcast. There are many other illogical points concerning guns, mental health, poverty, Southerners, et cetera, that I won't address, as they are, generally speaking, moronic to the point of lobotomy. If you are not anti-gun by this point, or if you fail to grasp the real issues here, then you're a dupe, sorry. The Right is going to say all kinds of things: It's all hype from the economic side, basically—from the aforementioned gun lobby, the manufacturers of munitions and arms. Don't be fooled into inaction: Now is the time to take a stand.

I think we should dispense with "real" ammunition: Make only rubber bullets. Microstamp them, too (and the gun parts internally, just like a car VIN). Limit magazine sizes (ten bullets or less). Embed radioisotopes in the metal

## ++After Newtown++

Seems you can't go anywhere these days without possibly getting your ass shot off: A theatre in Aurora, CO; a shopping mall in Clackamas, OR; a school in Newtown, CT. It's true, too: Of all the mass or spree shootings *ever* in the US, there have been (at least) sixty-two since 1982; twenty-five of these have occurred since 2006, and seven of those happened in 2012 (interestingly, the Assault Weapons Ban was retired in 2004; the vast majority of these shootings were carried out with firearms that were legally obtained, including Newtown; it is escalating, with a mass shooting every five days on average).

So here it is: I am opposed to *all* gun ownership. For criminals, hunters (I'm an ethical vegetarian), the police, the military, for anyone. Sue me. In addition, I think Ted Nugent is a bloviating moron (his music sucks, too). And don't bore me with the silly notion that "when guns are outlawed, only outlaws will own guns!": That is sheer idiocy. "Outlaws" (how ludicrously "Old West/ Frontier" romanticized by the Right!) will use whatever they can: guns, knives, anything. The problem is that guns make *any* fight an unfair one. Don't take my word for it: Just look into the stats about using a gun to "defend" your home or family. A person is far more likely to be killed or injured by a gun in their home (whether or not a criminal is involved) than if there isn't one. Suppose the "perp" didn't bring a gun, then gets yours? (And why *would* they bring one? Then it's a possible felony for premeditated attempted murder if caught instead of an "accidental shooting" from a legal standpoint.) To say nothing of the marked increase in suicides and accidental shootings when a firearm is readily available...

Furthermore, I think the Second Amendment ("A well regulated militia being necessary to the security of a free state, the right of the people to keep and bear arms shall not be infringed") is an outdated and *grossly* misinterpreted anachronism that is essentially useless against a modern so-called "tyrannical government" (for example there are *no* prohibitions/limitations on owning rocket launchers or even flame throwers, as the technologies didn't exist when the Amendment was drafted... Where do we draw the line, if ever?). It was written at a time when our newly-founded country still relied on people to meet-up in loose confederations, far from a centralized governing body, in order to protect their ideals. Times have changed: There is a "well regulated militia" now, several branches of it, in fact. And as far as legality or interpretation are concerned, the Supreme Court isn't infallible: They are humans that can be compromised, or just make errors in judgment (such as the recent Citizens United decision). Besides, social media ('Twitter,' anyone?) is far more effective at rallying the populace to a cause than the barrel of a gun, just consider the events that led to the downfall of governments in Egypt and Syria: Folks responded to the calls for change from the Internet, from viral cell phone tweets (and then there are the images and videos shot from those camera-enabled mobile phones—the power is truly in the hands of the people now, and there is no turning back). Also, with respect to firearms, Republicans (and some Democrats) are not genuinely concerned about the mental health aspect of this social issue: They are beholden to the gun lobby, to make them visible to FLIR and other law enforcement technologies. Ban automatic and semi-automatic weapons of every stripe (semis are too easy to covert to fully automatic). Strict background checks and mental assessments; required gun safety training. Biometric locks on all weapons, and a database of every purchase, with a two-week waiting period on each sale, after the clean background check and permitting process is completed. Also, there needs to be a limit on the total number and type of weapons each individual can own, and the amount of ammo, and there should be mental/psychological evaluations every five years if one is to be considered a "responsible" gun owner; this could be accomplished with a magnetically-striped gun license, complete with ID photo and signature, just like a driver's license; track folks down if they fail to appear for re-evaluation, and take their guns away when you find them.

As well, there should be other common-sense considerations, such as no sales to convicted felons, the mentally ill, or anyone under the age of 28, and an immediate cessation of mail and Internet sales in the US (including from sites overseas). Impose high taxes on firearms and ammunition. Penalize the arms makers by making them criminally and financially liable for the mayhem introduced by too generous access to weapons and ammo (I mean, it costs money to stitch faces back on, to dispense wheelchairs, and to wipe splattered child brains off of recess areas). Additionally, there needs to be a large-scale, "no questions asked" buy-back program: After they are checked for use in a crime, laser scan and store the weapon impressions electronically, then melt them down. All good ideas.

While it is true that "guns don't kill people, people do," (though *people with guns* kill a *lot* of people) it should be noted that, thus far, guns are *not* US citizens with rights. Also, I would posit that the clause "life, liberty, and the pursuit of happiness" *does* preclude being randomly shot to death, since it includes at least two of the rights granted in the Declaration of Independence. I welcome the day that there are no firearms in the world: We should be building up our brethren, not annihilating them.

One thing is certain: This is a war. A war of political ideology between the Left (Democratic - the people), and Right (Republican - big business).

However, this war should not be waged with armaments, but with words, and firmly *against* financial interests controlling the United States government. Remember (Republican) President Eisenhower's sage advice: "In the councils of government, we must guard against the acquisition of unwarranted influence, whether sought or unsought, by the Military-Industrial complex. The potential for the disastrous rise of misplaced power exists and will persist."

—*Jason V Brock*
*Vancouver, WA*
*December 2012*

# Good Ole Chuck. . .

He was a wonderful friend.

He was a talented writer.

He was a dedicated editor.

He was Charles Edward Fritch, born January 20, 1927, in Utica, New York, where he grew up watching movie serials and reading science fiction.

At the age of ten he filled a notebook with ideas for stories and studied the stars through a telescope from his bedroom window.

He was a born writer: "I think if you're going to be a writer, you'll write—and nothing will stop you. I kept writing. I loved science fiction so I wrote that and finally started selling it."

Indeed he did. More than 52 stories and two collections in the genre. He wrote many fine stories (among his best: "Big, Wide, Wonderful World," "The Cog," "The Castaway," "Night Talk," and his last one, printed in 1999, "Different"). My favorite Fritch title, reflecting his wild sense of humor: "If at First You Don't Succeed, to Hell with It!"

We had some great years together, especially in the 1960s, when we gleefully attended Expo '67 in Canada.

Chuck came out to California, to Los Angeles, in 1952. We had exchanged letters (over my *Ray Bradbury Review*) when he was still living in Utica. I introduced him to Charles Beaumont, and Chuck became a staunch member of "The Group" (Beaumont, Bradbury, Richard Matheson, Robert Bloch, et al).

I have been crying from time to time over the last couple of days—ever since I learned of Chuck's passing. *So many* fine memories!

He died on October 11, 2012, and the world is a darker place without him. He was a good man in every way; with a wonderful sense of humor (he'd send Christmas cards in July!). I'd kid him about his middle name, "E," and he'd say: "I *need* it—to separate me from all the other Fritches!" His signature was very small and we'd have "contests" to see who could write his name the smallest. He loved puns, naming his second collection *Horse's Asteroid*. I begged him to change it ("Chuck, it has no *dignity!*") but he smiled and ignored my plea.

We collaborated together on a story, "The Ship," which wound up in *The Magazine of Fantasy and Science Fiction*. It was a gentle parody of Ray Bradbury.

*Nolan and Charles E. Fritch.*

We worked together in the same office in the 1950s in Inglewood as job counselors for the California Department of Employment.

With the Group, Chuck was "the quiet one," saying little but soaking up the conversation about stories and editors and publishers. We'd be up all night, reading our latest stories to each other.

I used his stories in five of my anthologies in the 1960s and printed his last story, "Different" (a superb tale), in *California Sorcery*, my "Group" collection in 1999.

He knew I was into doing bibliographies on my writer friends, and in late 1951 he mailed me "The Complete Fictional Works of Charles E. Fritch." It had just *one* entry, "The Wallpaper," his first story sale.

We worked on the SF magazine *Gamma* together in the 1960s, with Chuck as publisher and I as managing editor. He also published a mystery magazine, *Chase,* during that period. (I appeared in the first issue under *three* names!)

Of course, as an editor, he took over *Mike Shayne's Mystery Magazine* in 1979 (extending into 1985), doing a great job of bringing new writers into print.

He also wrote several novels about tough private eyes, from *Negative of a Nude* (1959) to *7 Deadly Sinners, Strip for Murder,* and *Fury in Black Lace.*

He enjoyed using several pen names beyond his own: Chester H. Carlfi, Eric Thomas, Christopher Sly, Troy Conway, and Charles Brockden.

In World War II, Chuck served as a paratrooper, returning to earn a major in psychology from Syracuse University.

As a writer, he was proud of having his work showcased in such anthologies as *The Year's Best Horror Stories* and *100 Great SF Stories*. One of his best tales, "The Misfortune Cookie," was adapted for *The [New] Twilight Zone* in 1986.

Chuck loved to show off his wife, Shirley, who looked like Elizabeth Taylor, having her make a grand entrance at parties while he chuckled at the crowd reactions. They were married for nearly 50 years and brought up four children together.

Sad to say, due to his illness, Chuck and I lost contact over his last thirteen years.

He was very happy for me when a story I'd sold to him, "A Real Nice Guy" (for *Mike Shayne*), ended up in the *Best Detective Stories of the Year*. And that was exactly what he was—a real nice guy. Good ole Chuck.

His friendship meant a great deal to me.

I loved him.

I'll never forget him.

—*William F. Nolan*
*Vancouver, WA*
*November 2012*

# thE Clock TowEr

## By Keith Kennedy

## I.

I am not an uneducated man; I know how these things go. The mad ravings of unimportant men are oft lost in the annals of history. That is why I write this account in the reddest of red, so that perhaps, this one document, this particular raving, may stand a better chance of one day finding eyes, and maybe even—though it seems now to be hope beyond hope—a voice.

Through a venerable and considerate sense of antiquarianism, I have always tried to do what is right by those around me. I believed since youth that one mistake—however grandiose or subtle—ought not be enough to tip the karmic balance against a man. The tale I now recount represents a contrary opinion.

And so, after experiencing great trepidation and fear of some otherworldly reprisal, I have finally become resigned to my fate, and I must begin.

I had always walked the same route, and by sheer fate it was written that Elise would pass me by, every morning, near Dyer Street. She would smile shyly and incline her head, and I in turn would incline mine, trying to keep my feelings hidden behind a clear, uniform gaze. But oh, how I wanted her, with every nuance of my being. I dreamed of her every inch pressed against me from the moment I first saw her. It was as if, since the tragic passing of my wife, I had been storing the sexual energy somewhere in my chest and now it was being let loose, wave after torrid wave, into my heart and my head and all the way down into my toes. And yet I managed just a quick nod, every morning, and kept the beast tamed.

Further along my morning walk, I would come across another constant. Daily, The Brigade, as they were known in the town, would be represented by a half a dozen members outside the clock tower. They would have buckets, which they would fill with water from the pump in the square, and, through a rough assembly

line, douse the stones before the barred entrance of the tower. On some mornings I thought I saw a darker fluid being washed away, but other times I could not be sure I saw anything. The possibility of seeking any further information was dashed away abruptly by the stern eyes of The Brigade and the way their heavy-set shoulders backed their countenance.

Despite these contrary experiences, eye contact of a flirtatious and then threatening nature in turn, my morning sojourn was always a pleasant one. I loved walking through the quiet streets and eventually coming to the gorgeous clock tower, admiring it from the square, then turning east and heading for the market. There was a spot on the far side of the square where I would often sit and admire the huge monolith that was the pride and joy of our little hamlet.

By all accounts, the clock tower had been built during the plague years, near the beginning of the Great Mortality, and, despite the breadth of pestilence, had been carefully maintained, kept pristine by the determined hands of our forefathers. Being so, the clock tower had become quite a symbol of survival to us all, especially due to the huge numbers we lost during and even after the plague. Our town was hit harder than most outside the larger communities, and many of our ancestors lived out lonely and difficult existences because of their misfortune. But with the clock tower as inspiration to some and a rallying point to others, we managed to regain our happy little place in the world. Though still struck regularly by misfortune—perhaps even more than was normal, some rumored—we were able to keep our heads high in the air.

The tower itself was constructed of a pale marble that some say was brought all the way from Rome. Through some trick of design, the marble topped the huge structure, but only surrounded the masonry all the way to the bottom. Around the edges of the only aperture, the small door on the backside of the tower, could be seen where the stones and marble met, in a strange overlapping pattern, like a miniature version of the cyclopean designs of so many ancient ruins. The lack of mortar between stones and layers was a mystery to modern architects, and it was commonly jested that the builders most have used honey to solidify the work, which explained in that small town way how we were so beset with flying insects—bees, wasps, and large flies—throughout the hot summer months.

I and others of like mind figured that it was in fact Italian builders that had constructed the tower, though many of the elder locals would scoff at this notion, throwing us great, devastating glares to exemplify how annoyed they were at the thought of our own kin not having put their very sweat and blood into our beloved clock tower. I, as a gentleman, never pushed the subject.

And why should I? I loved the clock tower as much as the next man or woman. My wife and I, as many before us, were married under its lined marble façade, the darkened clock face witness to our greatest joy.

And our daughter, of course, when barely old enough to breathe the air, was brought to see the clock tower, or perhaps brought so the clock tower could seer her. Druicilla, my precious child and sole remembrance of my wife. Oh, how they were alike! Their dark cascading hair and pure, green eyes; the brightness in their skin and that tiny, pointed nose, as if stolen by some gambit from a fairy in the woods.

I would walk home from the market and she would be up, functioning as woman of the house, though not old enough to marry by some years. She had always been that way, helping wherever she could, kind hearted as her mother had always been. She was my life's joy and my whole world revolved around her care.

But, as I mentioned, there came a mistake.

## II.

One morning I awoke in typical fashion, early and alert, and upon touching Druicilla's forehead with love noticed an irregular heat. I woke her, rather fretfully I must admit, and fawned over her for a short time before she convinced me that, although her head hurt, it was nothing to be concerned about, and I should take my morning walk. Unsure of whether I should go, she set me straight, asking me what I would do, just sit and watch her sleep? So I left, though concern weighed heavily on my heart.

As I passed Dyer Street, I was attempting with some effort to calm myself. How ridiculous to gather such drama about myself over a fever. In this state, trying to feel calm and not be an hysterical father so as to set a good example for Druicilla, I did not even notice the absence of Elise.

I perched in my typical place across the square, again telling myself to relax: as my daughter's only example, I must instill composure and control, so she would become a strong, genuine woman, not one of temerity and flights of fancy. While this strange conflagration of philosophy and emotion swept over me, I hardly noticed Elise approach on my left. She was, in fact, seated beside me before I had any sense I was not alone. When I turned, I felt that my heart would leap out of my chest from sheer proximity to the young woman. She smiled, full and open, and I felt a gut-wrenching tear somewhere within my ribcage. I wanted this woman with all my being, but I had kept her at arm's length for fear of how it would affect Druicilla. My daughter had always, and must always, come first, and yet, in the face of my stresses and with the lovely Elise so near, the effect that evolved was one of intoxication. In

hindsight, I had clearly lost some of my faculties, for with what had been on my mind only moments before, I should have been more fortified than ever to keep this woman and the reality of interaction at a great distance.

And yet, what happened felt wholly inevitable to me at the time. The Brigade had just cleared off and, without a single word, Elise looked around her and slid her fingers into my hand. She stood, and I, as though in a dream, stood as well. She led me, quickly, across the square and to the door of the clock tower. She sensed my hesitation as we approached and responded with a simple squeeze of my hand. When I again planted my feet, knowing that we were forbidden from entering the clock tower, she finally spoke.

"I want to show you something," she said, her voice a sweet, dangerous whisper.

She pulled me to the door and, strangely, opened it without incident.

We closed the door behind us and were in a rich, lustrous semi-darkness, to which my eyes quickly began to adjust. I looked at her briefly, but my eyes, along with hers, were drawn upwards by a ray of addled light sifting down through the cogs and gears—splashing and shimmering yellow heat across the somber, burnished face of the machine.

I looked back to Elise and she was beautiful, her brown hair turned golden by the reflected sun. I desired to reach for her taut neck, but instead again followed her gaze.

Somehow, from unseen heights, the sun had found its way inside the clock tower and was bouncing and blanketing the cold metal with its joyous, morning rays.

And yet the light was contained and overwhelmed, held in check by the crowded gears so that only a sprinkle, like glowing dust, reached us at the bottom.

At this strange moment of beauty I felt an undeniable chill as well, and the idea of this darkened place somehow swallowing and overcoming the light of the sun, so that only a tiny stream was allowed, became very unsettling. I suddenly felt the urge to flee the place and made my feelings known.

"We should not be here," I said, my voice much louder than I had intended. At this, Elise reached out and took my hand in both of hers, placing my hesitant palm on her chest. Her head was tilted downward now, and, without raising her chin, she looked at me, eyes piercing.

"But don't you want . . . ?"

That was as much as I heard, for the last of her words were engulfed by my pressing mouth. I knew, throughout the entire entanglement, that what I did was somehow wrong, but I could not summon the reason to

believe such a ludicrous thought. She was like nothing I had ever felt, younger and more taut than my wife had been when first I lay with her. And she resisted, in small ways, pulling away at one moment, then thrusting herself passionately forward the next. We did not even have the opportunity to remove our clothing, and I took her there, standing beneath the trickle of sunlight under the heavy, golden gears of the clock tower. When I entered her, she inhaled sharply, and I heard a whisper of sound as her maidenhead splashed on the stony ground. I thought little after that.

### III.

It was less than a week later that I stood in the cemetery, bearing witness to a pale wooden coffin being lowered into the earth. My heart had only five days to sing and feel guilt in turn before word of Elise's death. But I had known before I heard, for that morning, at Dyer Street, she and I had not exchanged smiles. Instead, she looked past me and my visage showed only concern. My fears, begun but days before, were fully founded, as her eyes were now surely sunken, and her cheeks drawn and gaunt. The Brigade found her next morning, lying peacefully before the clock tower.

After the funeral, I visited Carmine, a large, elderly gentleman who was the closest thing to a physician we had in our small town. He informed me, as I had heard from other sources, that the woman had died of natural causes, or possibly a stoppage of her heart. I recounted my fears and concerns over her changing appearance the last few days, but he could not say for certain that loss of weight or gauntness was in any way a symptom of what had ended her life. I did not, however, recount the coupling that had gone on a week prior, for I feared I had in some way caused her death.

There was something strange about the whole experience with Carmine that afternoon. Normally a jovial fellow—though not expected to be on this sad day—his demeanor was quite strained the entire time I questioned him. Firstly, I had never seen a man realign his eyeglasses so many times during one conversation, though I was only inquiring about routine things, nor was there any responsibility being laid at his feet. Yet he acted as if there was something he would not or could not tell me. With that lasting impression, I chose very quickly, despite my recent lack of good judgment, to act.

Under cover of darkness, and after placing my hand lightly on Druicilla's forehead, I made my way to the cemetery. As I dug up the new grave I had the most horrible thoughts, surely brought on by my surroundings. Had I not gotten entirely what I wanted? The forbidden fruit of this young, beautiful girl was given to me freely, and yet I suffered none of the consequences. Druicilla was unharmed, save for a persistent fever, and I had gotten my deepest desire fulfilled. So why this infatuation that something was so wrong?

I knew why. As I dug fresh, damp earth off the grave of a young girl, I knew. It was that feeling, that cold closeness I had sensed despite the light of the sun. Something in the clock tower, something I had done, had played into the death of this beautiful girl.

After too long, my spade hit wood, and I clambered into the grave. My hammer did its work, and I soon penetrated the lid of the coffin. Beneath lay my greatest fears realized.

Elise was no longer the beauty she had been mere days before. Her face was shrunken and wrinkled, and her flesh dry as a bone. Her eyes, though giving the impression of protrusion, were in fact empty of fluid, and it was only the sunken pits of the cavities that created the strange illusion. Her arms and hands, as far as I could see toward the base of the coffin, showed similar effects, the skin crumpled and broken, all hint of moisture gone. She looked as a skeleton would, only wrapped tightly in fine parchment.

I reached out with my hand and gently touched her face, breaking away a section of dried flesh. This caused a short chain reaction and the skin fell away as if under a breeze, exposing first her skull, then her cheek and finally her grinning teeth.

I refilled the grave with incredible rapidity and returned home, a different man than when I had left.

IV.

The next morning, I found myself staring for some time at the clock tower form my perch across the square. The members of The Brigade were there, but having cleaned the stones around the base of the tower, they seemed hesitant to leave. Perhaps it was just paranoia, but I swore I caught them glancing over at me from time to time, more often than would be considered normal.

I was about to give up on what had become a test of wills when I heard someone's voice coming from the alley to my right. It was Carmine, and he looked panicked, and his eyes wore blackened haloes as if he had received no sleep the night previous. I rose to go toward him, and he beckoned to me to be quick. As soon as I reached the alley he turned and was off in a hurry, gesturing for me to follow.

"What happens when life prospers?" he said beneath his breath. I could smell it now, the booze.

"I'm sorry?"

"What happens?" he repeated, now glaring at me as if the answer was somewhere deep in my skull.

"Carmine, I don't—"

"Ssh, shush, never mind," he said, waving at me with utter impatience. "I heard your daughter had a fever? Shall I come by?"

"Well, she keeps telling me it's nothing and that she feels fine. She made me swear not to bother you, but I suppose since you've come to me . . ."

"Fine, fine," the large man said, looking twice over his shoulder after each word. "You haven't seen my glasses, have you?" he asked, then shook his head to dismiss the question. "Yes, I'll come see her, but I fear I'll not be accomplishing anything in such a visit."

"What do you mean?" I asked.

Carmine stopped, panting from the exertion, and looked around with blatant conspiratorial fervor. "It is you who must help your own kin."

Now I was beginning to grow frustrated, not accustomed to this cryptic type of interaction. "Really, Carmine, I don't understand what you're talking about."

"What happens, do you think? Hmm? When there's no one dying? When the world is a happy little place? When there's no war, or plague or misfortune? No blood, no death?"

He continued on with one more phrase, a phrase that haunts me to this day. It was so strange and yet so accurate to my own fears that I turned and fled the man and his wild, dark eyes that very minute.

I tried to stay away from the clock tower for the rest of the day, even intending to avoid it for the rest of my life if necessary. Plots of moving to another place raced through my head, and yet I could not condone such drastic activity based on fear alone. And there was Druicilla to consider, of course. Not only her health, but to alter her life so greatly because of my emerging madness? And I hoped that, I recall. Hoped it was simply madness.

V.

My battle ended at twilight, and I succumbed to the pull of the clock tower. Looking over my shoulder at every street corner, I made my way to the old beast under the cover of encroaching night. As I pressed my back against its cold marble, a strange thing flared into my mind, like a memory, but passed on through ages. I saw people through time, through various states of war and death, and the one constant, the only constant, was the reverent look on their faces as they

gazed upward.

Not surprisingly, the door opened easily when I tried it, and I entered the tower.

There was no sunlight now, but something of the twilight remained, and there was again a small amount of light in the cylindrical base of the tower. I looked up, realizing that the golden coloring on the gears had not in fact come from the filtered sunlight; the gears themselves were golden, bright and grotesque in the gathering dark.

It struck me now just how many gears there were. Dozens upon dozens filling the tower as far up as the eye could see; all golden, all running with a smooth, mesmerizing efficiency. It should have been amazing, an almost magical place; but it wasn't. The sliding of the metal, the way cogs met other cogs, the way they joined each other with complete precision; it was sexual and malevolent. The whole machination was an orgy of sinister timing and friction. To look up into that cacophony of silence was to understand the point of its existence. It was made to go on and on, constructed to keep moving and turning; but for what?

I shook my head, knowing there were things here, concepts and rules, philosophy beyond my learning. What I knew for sure was that it had to stop. With visions of flame and destruction in my mind I turned and plunged for the door, but it was locked somehow. I checked around the edges of the door, but I could find no seam. The door was simply no longer passable.

I turned back to the blackness and saw the last of the day alight on the floor in the center of the room. I walked, as if mesmerized, toward the dark patch on the floor, the stain that Elise had left behind. I knelt and brushed my fingers against its rough surface, dragging up flakes of blood with my fingertips.

And I knew. As if I had always known but it had been supplanted by life; by knowledge, by history, by joy and routine. I knew the truth of the clock tower and wherein its malevolence lay.

The clock tower gave you what you wanted.

I looked at my hand and there was no blood. On the floor, no stain remained. I turned, composed, and walked slowly to the door. This time, I was allowed passage out into the world.

As soon as I cleared the door, I ran. It had not defeated me. I had held my emotions in check, but now I planned my revenge and it was one of flame and blood. I would tear the tower down, stone by stone, golden gears rent from one another, one by one. As I ran through the night, Carmine's final phrase that morning, that one phrase, sang in my head and fueled me.

## VI.

I arrived back home, thinking nothing of what might await me. The evil of the tower had played itself out before me, and I had not the time to indulge in a father's worries that day.

Carmine was there, in my house, looking as haggard as he had that morning. I instantly recognized the posture of a man who had been crying, having sat in such a position for many years after the death of my wife. Beneath Carmine's blackened eyes, I saw the all too familiar wetness.

"What? Did you check her? Is she okay?" I ran past, not waiting for his answers.

Druicilla lay upon her bed, the blanket pulled to her chin. She seemed to be wearing a wooden mask, so dry and taut were her features. Her skin was as pale as the marble of the clock tower; her skull shone through her face as if she were simply covered in a light, diaphanous cloth. I broke down then and found myself on my knees sometime later, splashes of tears on the floor beneath me.

"It's what you wanted," a voice came from behind me.

I turned and saw Carmine in the doorway.

"Since Mariah died, it's what you wanted," he continued. "Freedom to do what you choose, freedom from this responsibility of fatherhood, freedom to pursue life, as you did with the Porter girl."

"I didn't want this," I yelled.

"The clock tower only gives you what you want," he said. He turned and left before I could say more; nor was there any more to say.

I lay on the floor for a long time, until sleep finally took me.

## VII.

I said nothing, let alone taking fire and courage to the base of the clock tower. I knew, from the minute the beast had shown me the stain on the floor, that it had been my doing. Evil as old as that cannot reach out and grasp you; it needs denizens, fools willing to offer themselves up, willing to spill blood and passion and desire at its feet.

And so I leave you with the tale and the tale alone, but there is of course one last thing to disclose. The thing that was said, the words Carmine uttered as if he were responsible for writing them in blood, his face revealing a responsibility as old as humankind and his eyes hiding the secret of our seemingly peaceful village.

His words I now pass on to you.

"What happens when the clock tower needs to be fed?"

# The Optimal Mode

## Television Animation in America, 1948–2010

### By David Perlmutter

The relationship between television and animation in America has been one that has been more conflicted and contradictory than it would appear on the surface. Though it has produced a number of great programs that are considered to be classics among TV shows as a whole (and, arguably, ones that will likely achieve this status in the future), the genre has frequently been viewed negatively by critics as an economic project bereft of academic merit, a genre fit only to entertain children, and a medium of inculcation of "negative" values in that same audience. Most of these assessments were arguments that the producers had no control over, since they were reflective of larger social and economic trends at the time of their original production and exhibition, and, in fact, had little relevance or reference to the texts of the programs and the ideas within.

In recent years, television animation[1] has been taken more seriously, though this tends to favor the more visible and recognizable programs at the expense of the more obscure ones. What is needed in the future is a more balanced approach to study, one that is able to treat television animation programs on a fair and individual basis to understand their specific contributions to the genre, while at the same time keeping a unified sense of the genre intact. Through this method, it will become more possible to view television animation as Marshall McLuhan spoke of it in the 1960s, as the "optimal mode"[2] of television through which it accomplishes television's objective of presenting enlightening and challenging material for consumption by its audience.

### The Beginnings: 1948–1965

An offshoot of the established theatrical animation community, television animation began in commercial terms along with television itself in America in 1948. The first major series, *Crusader Rabbit* (Syndicated, 1948; 1957) began in this

---

[1] Television animation in this context refers to animated films originally produced for exhibition on television, as opposed to theatrical animation, which was produced originally for exhibition in motion picture theatres.

[2] Marshall McLuhan (Eric McLuhan and Frank Zingrone, eds.), *Essential McLuhan* (Concord, ON: House of Anansi, 1995), 135.

year, produced by Jay Ward and Alex Anderson in Los Angeles. As most series of this kind would be in the following years, the series was abbreviated in length, airing only in segments of six to seven minutes, the average length of a theatrical animation film. Because of this abbreviated length, caused by the technical limitations of the genre at that time, television animation existed marginally for the first nine years of television's existence. Whether original films or repackaged older theatrical material, it was seen chiefly during this period only as segments of local children's programming or in the odd television commercial as a gimmick of sorts.[3]

Television animation producers, however, were eager to have their art exposed to a wider audience, and, as the 1950s progressed, the potential for the genre to be viewed on its own terms increased. This was chiefly due to the intervention of two men who entered the field out of economic desperation and made the genre their domain for an extended period.

William Hanna and Joseph Barbera were a veteran team of theatrical animation directors who were dismissed by their longtime employer, MGM, in 1955 as a consequence of the increasing contraction of the theatrical animation industry.[4] They brought to the field not only considerable creative and financial acumen, but also an innovative new manner of producing animation. "Limited animation," as it was known, involved a more circumscribed manner of animation production, with an eye toward eliminating the more time-consuming aspects of the animation process to allow it to be produced on a more cost efficient basis. Purists of theatrical animation cried foul, claiming the art of animation was mutilated by the process, but Hanna and Barbera knew full well that animation could not be produced in the theatrical fashion within the time constraints television demanded and thus did not attempt it. Nevertheless, their work was often seen negatively by purists of animation, due both to its limited production process and its enormous commercial success.

Hanna and Barbera started the same way as the other

3    For an understanding of the artistic and political evolutions of animation in this transitional period, see Amid Amidi, *Cartoon Modern: Style and Design in Fifties Animation* (San Francisco: Chronicle Books, 2006).

4    The lives and careers of Hanna and Barbera have been well documented. Writings on the men and the studio include Ted Sennett, *The Art of Hanna-Barbera* (New York: Viking, 1987); Michael Mallory, *Hanna-Barbera Cartoons* (New York: Hugh Lauter Levin Associates, 1998), and Jerry Beck, *The Hanna-Barbera Treasury* (San Rafael, CA: Insight Editions, 2007). Equally valuable and illuminating are the two men's autobiographies: William Hanna and Tom Ito, *A Cast of Friends* (New York: Da Capo, 2000), and Joseph Barbera, *My Life in 'Toons* (Atlanta: Turner Publishing, 1994).

animation producers of the time. After securing an alliance with Columbia Pictures and its Screen Gems television subsidiary, their first series, *Ruff and Reddy,* a segmented adventure serial, aired on NBC in 1957 as part of a national children's program. Increasingly, though, they sought and gained a wider vehicle for their work. Through the guidance of Screen Gems executive John Mitchell, and the enterprising salesmanship of Joseph Barbera, they quickly sold a successful syndicated series, *The Huckleberry Hound Show* (Syndicated, 1958), which consisted entirely of three entirely new television animation films, a revolutionary format for the time. The series was an enormous success, winning an Emmy Award for Outstanding Children's Programming, the first television animation series to receive this honor. Two other series with a similar format, *Quick Draw McGraw* (Syndicated, 1959) and *The Yogi Bear Show* (Syndicated, 1961), firmly established Hanna-Barbera as the dominant voice of American television animation during this period.

These series were successful in attracting a mixed audience of both children and adults, and, with the encouragement of John Mitchell, Hanna and Barbera sought to produce material that would attract the latter group more specifically. Though the very idea of a television animation series airing in prime time for adult consumption was seen as an audacious gamble, they persisted and gained the support they needed. *The Flintstones* (ABC 1960–66) was the result. An animated sitcom set in a uniquely devised prehistoric universe, the series originally was designed with an adult audience in mind but, as it progressed, it shifted toward escapist fantasy directed at children, indicating the direction the genre was now taking. Hanna and Barbera's innovations continued with three other groundbreaking series: *Top Cat* (ABC 1961–62), about a feline con man and his gang of associates; *The Jetsons* (ABC 1962–63; Syndicated, 1985–87), a science fiction sitcom; and *Jonny Quest* (ABC 1964–65), an over-the-top action-adventure series that featured the studio's most elaborate and realistic animation to date.

Other studios began entering the picture following Hanna-Barbera's success. The most aggressive challenger to their dominance was Jay Ward,[5] who had begun producing in the late 1940s and now returned to the field after a long absence. Ward approached animation production and promotion in a far different way than did Hanna-Barbera. Rather than limited animation, he used "runaway" production methods, where his films were animated in Mexico after being planned and recorded in California. More revolutionary, he developed a satirical form of comedy that openly ridiculed everything within its grasp. Working closely with actor/writer/producer Bill Scott, Ward created, in *Rocky and His Friends* (ABC 1959–61) and its

---

[5]     For a biographical study of Ward, see Keith Scott, *The Moose That Roared: The Story of Jay Ward, Bill Scott, a Flying Squirrel and a Talking Moose* (New York: Thomas Dunne Books/St. Martin's Griffin, 2000).

KONG KONG
PHOOEY

Josie
AND THE
PUSSY
CATS

QUEST

successor, *The Bullwinkle Show* (NBC 1962–65),[6] a remarkably frank and insurrectionist style of animation for its day and time, which would prove to be enormously influential on the genre in its later, more mature period. Despite his success, Ward burned many bridges in the television industry, particularly through his extravagant self-promotion, and he thus failed to build his company into a substantial business à la Hanna-Barbera. After one final series, *George of the Jungle* (ABC 1967–70), the producer was relegated to the sidelines as a television commercial producer until he abandoned production in the mid-1980s. But his influence would continue to endure, especially in the years following his death in 1989.

Two other studios that emerged in this period also deserve recognition. Total Television Productions, the creation of former advertising executives Buck Biggers and Chet Stover in collaboration with animator Treadwell Covington, produced a handful of successful programs in the early 1960s, most notably *Underdog* (NBC 1964–66). Biggers and Stover's approach was halfway between Hanna-Barbera and Jay Ward, largely meshing the latter's formats and production methods with the former's unthreatening blandness. The fact that both they and Jay Ward used the facilities of the Val-Mar/Gamma studios of Mexico led to their works being confused by some historians due to the similarity of their production methods. Biggers and Stover were, however, never as controversial or threatening in their approach as Ward was even when their narratives presented opportunities for this. Total ceased production in 1969 when their longtime corporate sponsor, General Mills, withdrew its support. A more enduring business prospect was developed around the same time by two other ex-ad men, Arthur Rankin, Jr. and Jules Bass, who made their mark with both traditional cel animation and an innovative stop-motion figurine process they dubbed "Animagic." Their hugely successful specials, including *Rudolph the Red Nosed Reindeer* (1964), *Frosty the Snowman* (1969), and *Santa Claus Is Coming to Town* (1970), mined new territory for television animation as a producer of friendly, engaging holiday-themed entertainment. Rankin and Bass built on this success to turn their eponymous company into a major power broker in theatrical and television animation in the 1970s and 1980s.

## *The Rise of Saturday Morning: 1965–1969*

With the shifting of television animation's audience toward children as opposed to adults, the programming was scheduled less often on weekday afternoons and evenings as had been done before

---

6      For Total Television's history, see Buck Biggers and Chet Stover, *How Underdog Was Born* (Boalsberg, PA: Bear Manor Media, 2005). For studies of Rankin and Bass's work, see Rick Goldschmidt, *The Enchanted World of Rankin-Bass* (Issaquah, WA: Tiger Mountain Press, 1998) and *Rudolph the Red Nosed Reindeer: The Making of the Rankin-Bass Holiday Classic* (Bridgeview, IL: Miser Brothers Press, 2001).

and in a specific cluster of time designed to maximize profit on the economic potential of the perceived audience. Led chiefly by Fred Silverman, the head of daytime programming at CBS in the late 1960s, the networks developed programming on Saturday morning as the specific target area for the children of America at the expense of other audiences. In this early period, traditional formats fell by the wayside as the major studios concentrated on producing series that would attract wide audiences during the time periods involved. Superhero narratives were the dominant voice in this period to the exclusion of others, which posed problems for the established studios such as Hanna-Barbera which had heretofore specialized in comedy. However, this gave important boosts to the profiles of newer studios, specifically Filmation, headed by Lou Scheimer and Norm Prescott, and DePatie-Freleng, an alliance between veteran theatrical animation director Isadore "Friz" Freleng and former film studio executive David DePatie. These two studios, along with the previously mentioned Rankin-Bass, would compete with Hanna-Barbera for dominance in this domain in the following two decades. Superhero narratives shown during this time included both established stars from comic books (*The New Adventures of Superman* [CBS, 1966–67]; *Spider-Man* [ABC, 1967–69]; *The Fantastic Four* [ABC, 1967–69]) and heroes newly created for television animation (*Space Ghost and Dino Boy* [CBS, 1966–68]; *Birdman and the Galaxy Trio* [NBC, 1967–68]).

As fruitful as this period was for the networks and studios, it was curtailed by forces beyond their control. The blossoming of these action-oriented programs coincided with a period of social turmoil in American life, culminating in the assassinations of Martin Luther King, Jr. and Robert F. Kennedy in 1968, and television animation was erroneously incriminated for "contributing" to this problem in ways its critics failed to justify. The networks feared a backlash from these critics, in particular Action for Children's Television (ACT) headed by Peggy Charren, even though that group's criticisms of Saturday morning had more to do with the potential for commercial exploitation of the audience rather than anything involved in the actual program narratives. The response of the network executives, which reflected their ignorance of television animation as an artistic product as much as it did its potential as a commercial vehicle, nearly ended up destroying it as an artistic force.

## *Changing with the Times: 1970–1990*

The increasing isolation of television animation to Saturday morning in the early 1970s, coupled with the backlash against their supposed use of "violence" as a narrative strategy, made it far easier for the genre to be censored in a negative way. Listening and seemingly catering more to the limited gripes of the genre's critics than to its actual producers, network censorship departments drew up and enforced content restrictions on television animation, arguably more than on any other programming genre in television before or since. These restrictions limited the traditional narrative strategies that had been employed by the studios, from action narrative staples such as punching and kicking, to long-standing slapstick comedy staples, to even absurd propositions such as dunking a cat in a bowl of spaghetti, all on the limited justification that children were supposedly "vulnerable" to being influenced by anything remotely "negative" presented by the medium. It was suggested that, as the genre that children most interacted with, television animation had to set the standards for the rest of the medium to follow. However, similar standards were not enforced on other forms of programming seen by children, especially ones directed as adults, which rendered this censorious action both unjust and incredibly hypocritical.

Not surprisingly, conflict regularly existed between the network censors and the animators they were supposed to regulate. Both sides portrayed themselves as the victims of each other's manipulations, saying that the other was unwilling to cooperate with them. But this was expected among two groups of people who had no prior understanding of the way the other operated and, in fact, detested the other as a meddler in the smooth operation of their processes. Unchecked, the conflict was allowed to endure across two decades, though it only rarely affected the production and broadcast process.

Conflict existed less often, however, between the networks and studios willing to play by the rules. Filmation, under the guidance of Lou Scheimer, became television animation's dominant studio in this era precisely for this reason. Scheimer, unlike other producers, was aware of the fact that children were television animation's primary audience, and he was willing and able to tailor his product to meet

the demands of both the networks and the wider audience. At the same time, he was able to create subtle politicizations that allowed it to advance in social progressive terms. Chief among these programs was *Fat Albert and the Cosby Kids* (CBS/Syndicated, 1972–84), based on the stand-up comedy routines of Bill Cosby, who served as the series' executive producer (making him the first African-American to hold this position on a television animation program). A groundbreaking program that effectively combined educational lessons, social realism, and slapstick comedy, *Fat Albert* pointed to a new direction for television animation. It no longer had to be a genre full of seemingly "empty" and "violent" entertainment; it could be an effective conveyor of social, educational, and even political messages as well.

Yet *Fat Albert*, and other similar Filmation shows that followed in its wake, were more the exceptions than the rules. More often than not, producers tended to follow the model of Hanna-Barbera's long-running *Scooby Doo* series (CBS/ABC, 1969–86): wooden characters, simplistic plotting, and the mere suggestion of "comedy" and "action" that was neither funny nor exciting but simply purported to be. Even more negatively affected than this were superhero narratives, typified by another long-running Hanna-Barbera series, *Super Friends* (ABC, 1973–86). As with comedy, this subgenre was purged of anything seen to be challenging to a young child's mentality, with the superheroic lead characters more often seen lecturing the other characters on moral issues rather than actually being superheroes. Even more problematic was the use of a quartet of "ethnic" superheroes— Black Vulcan, Apache Chief, El Dorado, and Samurai—designed to broaden the traditional Caucasian-centric ranks of superheroes, but who instead came off as monumentally ill-conceived and even racist.

The 1980s brought other trends that further compromised the artistic integrity of television animation. First and most prominent was the economic deregulation of the Reagan era, which permitted and even encouraged certain television animation programs to effectively function as program-length commercials, creating exactly the fusion between program and sponsor that Peggy Charren and ACT had foreseen during the late 1960s. Even when the programs themselves were well-produced and enjoyable, as some of these series were, the taint of commercialism ran rampant and provoked a new wave of backlash and criticism against television animation. This was, however, negative stereotyping that not all the series of this kind deserved. One had to consider the studios producing them, after all. *He-Man and the Masters of the Universe* (Syndicated, 1983) and its spin-off, *She-Ra: Princess of Power* (Syndicated, 1985), were produced by Filmation and applied the education-plus-entertainment format the studio developed in the 1970s to the action-adventure genre without skimping on the thrills the latter was known for. At the other end of the spectrum were *The Transformers* (Syndicated, 1984) and *G.I.*

*Joe* (Syndicated, 1985), which served simply as vehicles for the title toy products, nothing more, nothing less. At the same time, the new format of syndication—presenting programming as a daily block on stations independent of the networks—was used as something of a declaration of independence from the draconian network censorship of the 1970s, with the result that the series had more free range artistically than their predecessors. In the case of a new studio, DIC, headed by Hanna-Barbera veteran Andy Heyward, it launched their career—along with resuscitating free-wheeling slapstick to television animation—with *Inspector Gadget* (Syndicated, 1983).

The other major development of the 1980s was an increasing tendency, through a tenuously defined concept called "pro-social values," for these programs to give at least a surface appearance of providing educational values for and encouraging social activism in their viewers. Taking their cue from yet another long-running Hanna-Barbera hit, *The Smurfs* (NBC, 1981–89), there was a tendency in these narratives to stress two long-standing but conflicting concepts of American nationhood—the importance of individual action and thought, and the equal if not greater importance of group unity and confidence—in a manner that mirrored the social conservatism of the era's politics. *The Smurfs*, as the creation of Belgian cartoonist Peyo Culliford, also typified the final major trend of the decade: the adaptation of popular characters from comic strips, comic books, and other media to television animation, the idea being that a "built-in" audience would provide a level of success greater than that of truly original characters. While exceptions to this rule did exist, most notably *Muppet Babies* (CBS, 1984–92), *Garfield and Friends* (CBS, 1988–95), and *The Flintstone Kids* (ABC, 1986–88), the majority of these series were haphazardly produced and had terribly lackluster content. Truly innovative productions were rare and ended up being punished for this innovation by the misunderstanding of censors within and outside of the networks. *Mighty Mouse: The New Adventures* (CBS, 1987–89) typified this attitude: it was canceled chiefly because Donald Wildmon, a prominent conservative media critic, vastly misinterpreted a single action in one episode and objected vehemently. The nadir of both the "built-in" and "pro-social" trends was the 1990 special *Cartoon All Stars to the Rescue,* in which the major stars of the genre at that time teamed up to confront drug abuse in the same manner in which their predecessors in theatrical animation had eagerly embraced the pro-war, pro-America nationalism of the early 1940s. The presence of Bugs Bunny in both contexts simply reinforced this idea.

Had the networks continued to schedule programming in this manner on Saturday morning, there is no telling what might have become of animation on television. But, by 1990, they were no longer the only game in town.

## Resurrection: 1990–2001

In many respects, 1990 marked the end of one era in television animation and the beginning of another. The era that ended was that of Saturday morning and the syndicated action serials, brought to heel by the 1990 Children's Television Act passed by Congress, which drastically limited the amount of programming that could be produced for purely commercial, non-educational reasons. This, coinciding with a demographic shift that drastically reduced the size of Saturday morning audiences, ultimately led to the three major networks abandoning the once profitable forum and genre, typified by NBC's decision to schedule a weekend edition of its profitable news and lifestyle franchise *Today* in the spot once occupied by animation in the early 1990s. The other networks tried to hold on, especially after the Walt Disney Company in the mid-1990s purchased ABC and its Saturday morning schedule became a centralized vehicle for the parent company's animation products. Yet, gradually, they reduced their presence as animation providers in favor of newer, more liberal vehicles—the outlaw "fourth network," FOX, and the cable channels Nickelodeon and Cartoon Network, who became the new power brokers in television animation as the new century dawned.

The beginning of the other, more positive, era fired its opening and most enduring shot with the premiere of *The Simpsons* (FOX, 1990–present). The creation of underground cartoonist Matt Groening, *The Simpsons* almost immediately reshaped the form, attitude, and context of television animation, in the same manner as The Beatles had reshaped rock music in the late 1960s. Embracing a host of socially liberal and progressive causes, creating and developing

dozens of Dickensian characters, and mercilessly deconstructing the culture of both past and present America, the series made it possible for television animation to be something considerably more than mere escapism, much as *Fat Albert and the Cosby Kids* had created the promise of such an existence in the 1970s. Once its impact was felt across the television and animation communities, a gauntlet had been dropped socially and creatively. There would be no going back to the inoffensiveness of the prior decades; instead, future television animation programs would be forced to define themselves within the context of, and using the same narrative and satirical strategies as, this monumental achievement.

Suddenly liberated from the traditional constraints of censorship, and encouraged by the freedoms offered by the new programming forums available to them, a huge number of talented writers, animators, producers, and directors began the creation of a new canon of television animation programs, programs that were far richer and deeper than their predecessors in their use of parody and satire as dramatic devices, capable of stunning, multi-faceted character studies and bold political statements, while at the same time both respecting and facetiously mocking the animation traditions of the past. There is not enough space to adequately discuss all of them here, but a few noteworthy examples do exist. *Beavis and Butt-head* (MTV, 1993–97) and *Ren and Stimpy* (Nickelodeon, 1991–98; Spike, 2003) took the traditional slapstick comedy aesthetic of television animation to shockingly sado-masochistic ends; both generated considerable controversy precisely for this reason. The same could be said for *South Park* (Comedy Central, 1997–present), which took a more gross-out, Rabelaisian approach to the small-town American terrain already mined by *The Simpsons*. While these series marked an extreme approach to the use of television animation for satirical purposes, other programs chose to attack by subtler means. *The Powerpuff Girls* (Cartoon Network, 1998–2004) typifies this approach. A brilliantly conceived and executed program that combined jaw-dropping animation and special effects never before seen in the genre with a richly nuanced blend of social justice, feminism, and criticism of established power structures in its narratives, *The Powerpuff Girls* represented what the genre could achieve at its best when allowed to develop and grow on its own terms. Much as *The Simpsons* rewrote the book on television animation as a whole, the heroines of this show led the fight against the archaic stereotypes of the superhero subgenre and forced it to change radically almost overnight. The same could be said of other series which took the formats of other television staples and used them as a context for satirical re-examinations. One of the most notable of these was the underappreciated *Secret Files of the Spydogs* (FOX, 1998–99); as its name applied, it ridiculed the espionage subgenre while providing unexpected empowerment for its leads. Yet it was the sitcom format, because of its adaptability and flexibility, that proved to be the dominant structure, as reflected by such diverse examples as *Rocko's Modern Life* (Nickelodeon, 1993–97), which blended Bob Newhart/Billy Wilder styled ensemble comedy with the surreal, off the wall slapstick of Tex Avery, and *The Weekenders* (ABC, 2000–01; Toon Disney, 2003), which, in a format incredibly witty and intelligent by television animation standards, applied postmodern and audience-engaging narrative approaches to the "average" lives of four supposedly "normal" middle school kids. The new legitimacy of television animation was best confirmed by the fact that so august a figure as famed film director Steven Spielberg was now producing it. Teaming up with the reactivated animation division of Warner Brothers, Spielberg produced a trio of funny, highly acclaimed programs — *Tiny Toon Adventures* (Syndicated/FOX, 1990–95), *Animaniacs* (FOX/WB, 1993–98), and *Pinky and the Brain* (WB, 1995–99) — that updated the approach of the studio's classic "Looney Tunes" and "Merrie Melodies" for a new generation without making any sacrifices or compromises along the way.

But the boldest step taken by the new animators was the reintroduction of television animation as a prime-time network attraction a quarter-entury after it had been eliminated from this venue. FOX launched this with *The Simpsons,* and other programmers countered with other attempts that met with failure in response by overtly or covertly imitating them. In truth, it was FOX itself that proved best able to give animation this forum and allow it to diversify there. Its success in this field led ultimately to television animation controlling the network's entire Sunday night lineup by the following decade. Their chief successes apart from *The Simpsons* in this regard were *King of the Hill* (FOX, 1995–2009), a neo-realistic depiction of a stoic, socially conservative propane salesman and his family and friends; *Futurama* (FOX, 1999–2003), a hilarious but controversial science fiction farce from *Simpsons* creator Matt Groening; and *Family Guy* (FOX, 1999–2003; 2006–present), a breakneck sitcom with a whirlwind pace that either intoxicated or intimidated viewers depending on their patience. It would be this series — revived from cancellation on at least two occasions — and the mindset of its creator/ star, Seth Macfarlane, that would replace *The Simpsons* at the head of the artistically audacious group of television animators in the following decade.

### *Maturity (?) 2001–2010*

Whereas in earlier decades it was hard to find and restricted to specific timeslots and occasions, by the twenty-first century it became impossible to escape television animation. The traditional venues continued their support of the genre, while at the same time new avenues opened up in unexpected places. They came in all sizes, shapes, and flavors—edgy, irreverent, saccharine, educational, badly done, and well done—at any imaginable spot and timeslot on the dial. Television animation in this new century was not only ever present, it was increasingly a force to be reckoned with, an attitude its creators increasingly began internalizing as they further pushed the genre's boundaries.

If the early post-9/11 period suggested a cautious, restrictive backlash against the liberalism of the previous decade, this was not suggested by the diversified, pluralized approaches taken by television animation. Indeed, its maturity as a purveyor of socially relevant, satirical narratives seemed increasingly apparent, even if its characters were not legally or mentally "mature" by any means. This duality was most obviously apparent in one of the last great network Saturday morning programs, *Fillmore* (ABC, 2002–04). A soberly minded and produced series that eschewed traditional animation slapstick and "acting" in favor of satirizing the prime-time police drama through the vehicle of a middle school safety patrol, *Fillmore* provided another example of how increasingly multi-faceted television animation was becoming. The program's variegated characters, multi-layered plots, and probing psychological underpinnings brought a much-needed seriousness to an age group—and, indeed, a genre—that had been far too often written off as unworthy of such consideration and treatment. It criticized the emerging socially conservative, tough-on-crime political stance of George W. Bush in a way that was considerably subtler and more effective than a more blatant "comic" approach would have been.

With the networks having largely abandoned Saturday morning television by this time, the onus for keeping the traditions alive came to be concentrated in the FOX network and the Nickelodeon, Cartoon Network, and Disney cable channels, which began engaging in something of an animated arms race as they fought for the attention of both children and adult consumers. Nickelodeon concentrated its efforts on a balance between broad comedy, as typified by *The Fairly Oddparents* (2001–06), and programs that balanced this approach by combing it with other structures, such as the superhero genre. *My Life as a Teenage Robot* (2003–06) was the most successful of these, continuing the tradition of feminine empowerment begun by *The Powerpuff Girls*, while at the same time adding the insecurities and fears of teenage femininity, along with an atavistic embrace of science fiction and animation clichés from the distant past, to the mix. *Danny Phantom* (2004–07) and *El Tigre* (2007–08) took this approach to superherodom in new directions, while *The X's* (2006–07) applied it less successfully to a fusion of the family sitcom and spy genres. At Cartoon Network, the emphasis became more focused on slapstick, although a satirical edge was quite evident at times. *My Gym Partner's a Monkey* (2005–09) and *Camp Lazlo* (2005–08) used the structure of the sitcom and the mechanics of the middle school and summer camp respectively as vehicles for hilarious, kid-friendly sociopolitical satire, while *Chowder* (2006–08) brought a touch of Edward Lear/Lewis Carroll-esque nonsense to television animation, typified by the ravenously hungry but incredibly naïve and stupid title character. Much in the same vein was *Foster's Home for Imaginary Friends* (2004–06), which, in the form of the deceptive but likable Blooregard Q. Kazoo, featured a style of con artistry not truly seen in television animation since the 1960s. Disney typified an approach that was halfway between the other two, seeing as, by the end of the decade, veterans of the other two studios now began dominating their approach. *The Replacements* (2006–08) was a modern-day Arabian Nights fantasy with a touch of Tom Sawyer, allowing its lead characters—and their viewers—to experience vicariously a wide variety of empowerment fantasies. This was also apparent in *Phineas and Ferb* (2007–present), though it was balanced by the title characters' sister, whose obsessive need to "bust" them for their activities provided much fuel for the fire. Also providing this were the adventures of their pet platypus, Perry, who was effectively given a show-within-a-show as he perennially foiled the evil but incredibly incompetent mad scientist Heinz Doofenshmirtz without saying so much as a single word. At FOX, meanwhile, Seth Macfarlane was increasingly becoming the genre's Norman Lear, as he added two more programs to the Sunday night lineup in addition to *Family Guy*. *American Dad* (2005–present) was a wickedly ruthless and scathing satire directed originally at the social conservative elite, typified by the title character, a resourceful, ultra-

conservative CIA agent who does his job all too well and repeatedly alienates himself from his family as a result. In more recent years, especially with the end of the Bush presidency, the show's comedic approach has broadened considerably, but, as with many other series of this time, right-wing isolation, conservatism, and ignorance remain the butt of many of the jokes. A more recent addition is *The Cleveland Show* (2009–present), which created a vehicle for *Family Guy*'s least visible supporting character to become a more fully dimensional lead character, while at the same time continuing the parent show's tradition of satirizing American culture and society with a vicious cut-to-the-bone approach that endears it to many fans.

## *Conclusion*

Television animation has been many things over the course of its existence, many contradictory in nature. It has been both bland and exciting, evasive and confrontational, stoically willing to endure and passionately resistant. Consequently, the true nature of the genre and that of its many programs remains frustratingly elusive no matter how many of them you may watch. As with other literature and film texts, however, a close reading of these programs provides a stunning understanding of how far this genre—and the country in which it was created—have changed over the course of sixty-two years. A better understanding of these programs and their influence on American society and culture will make scholars and viewers better prepared for what television animation as a whole and in parts may provide for us in the future.

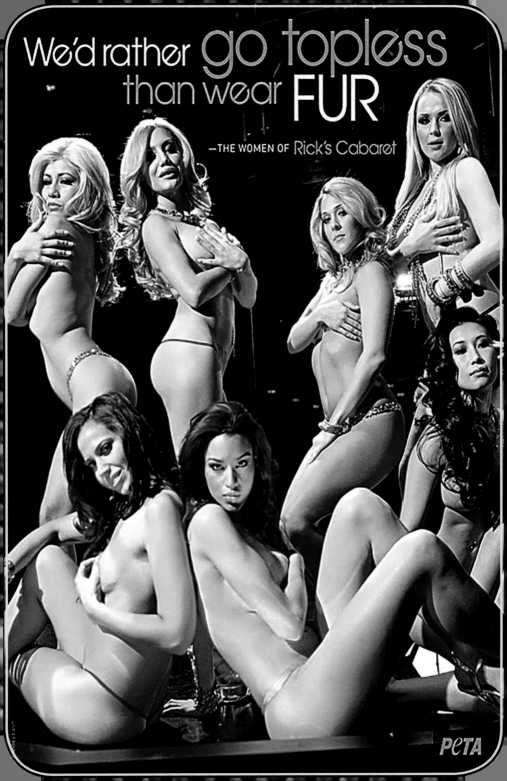

# By Ellen Denton

Liana looked out at the bland expanse of rock and sand stretching as far as the eye could see. The wind spoke in a murmuring chorus of tongues as it flooded through holes and clefts in the rock. It lifted her hair and made her clothes billow out like sails, but instead of cooling her, it intensified the suffocating heat and made her sweaty skin gritty with blown sand. It was sometimes hard for her to believe that in the past people did not live in places like this, or were not housed in cramped, stifling quarters with no climate controls. The ancient writings told of those times. There were so many power cells back then that people had machines that heated and cooled the air, moving machines that carried them up and down through sky-high buildings, machines that transported them across the ground or through the air at great speeds, and did all kinds of other wondrous things. Now, the few permanent power cells that remained after the Blood Storm were connected to and used only to power the computers, as it was upon these that all past wisdom was stored, and with them resided the hope of restoring Earth to what it had once been.

It was time for her designated shift. She gave a final, pensive look to the vista of shifting sand, then returned to the work hut where fifteen watchers, all sticky with sweat as she was, hunched over glowing consoles. Liana didn't know for sure if the computers were in some way living entities. There was much discussion and speculation about this among the people like herself who tended to them. Because of her uncertainty about this, she had always been a little afraid of them and treated them with great respect. She now slipped into the chair in front of her own workstation and started again diligently scanning the streams of strange symbols rolling in columns down her screen. Had someone been watching her closely, they would have seen her usual monotone expression and, in the dimness of the windowless hut, the dark, scrolling figures on the white screen reflected in her eyes. They would have then seen her pupils suddenly widen, as she lurched forward to stare in shock at what had just appeared on the screen.

By the time Liana was born, almost three hundred years had already passed since the Blood Storm of 2050 had killed most of the people on the planet, destroyed the machines, and laid to waste just about everything else. According to stories handed down from generation to generation, the computers and their power cells survived because they were deep underground when the cataclysm happened. There were many myths about how they came to be found and eventually brought to the surface, but the facts on how this really did occur had long since been buried in the past.

There were two bodies of information on the computers. One was a vast storehouse of data contained in millions of files. They spoke of many things great and small that had existed or transpired on the planet at one time or another. There were writings, photographs, and moving pictures of all kinds. Some years ago, someone figured out how to access these, and projects to classify and codify the information in these files were begun. There were a limited number of computers available to view and study these, however, so even with extensive hours of work put into it, it was a long process that would continue for many years.

Initially, it was considered that everything found in them was true and factual, just because it was there and spoken of or shown, but in the winnowing of information over the years it became obvious that some things were true, while others were only creatively written but fictional stories about science.

One of the last entries that had been made in one of the files told how the Blood Storm was brought about by terrible weapons of mass destruction in the form of great and powerful bombs, which were hurled every which way in a full global war. Information like that, though, was clearly not true, as no people in their right minds would create such things, let alone throw them at each other. Fictional things of that sort were relegated to the interesting, entertaining, but "not useful" category.

There were many factual scientific items, however, that would ultimately be of great value once enough information was recovered about how exactly they worked, and even though it would likely be hundreds of years before the resources could even be developed to build such things again, the current generation of people knew that it was their responsibility, and would be the responsibility of those who followed them, to work ceaselessly and bit by bit to unearth the data and organize it into useful form.

One item of strongly focused research had to do with devices pre-cataclysm called time machines. The earliest mention of time travel found so far was by a man named H. G. Wells, who wrote about the existence of one such machine as far back as 1895. There were many later mentions of these as well. If the full information about how these devices worked could be recovered so that they could be built again, it could change the fate of mankind. Unfortunately, despite the numerous writings about time machines that had been found, the data on how to actually build one remained sketchy at best.

Other items of great interest were the different types of intelligent but non-human life forms that had once inhabited Earth at the same time as man. It was known that these really did exist because there were not just drawings or writings about them, but actual moving pictures. There was, for instance, a race of creatures called vampires. They were similar to men and women in appearance, but were able to turn into little, leathery winged, flying animals at will, and they also sometimes lived for centuries. The implications of this for future generations of man were staggering, but any really useful information on how they did this had not yet been coaxed out of the computer files.

Even more fascinating was an entire race of entities from what appeared to be some sort of odd-looking parallel universe to Earth. These beings often had strange physical shapes and incredible abilities never seen in humans. Over the years of siphoning information from the files, certain representatives of this parallel universe had appeared repeatedly in the moving pictures of them, so it was assumed they had some special importance or standing. One was called Mickey Mouse, one was called Mighty Mouse, one was called Bullwinkle, and there were others as well. Like the vampires, though, the information on how these people or creatures could do what they could do continued to elude the researchers.

Liana's job involved not the millions of computer files, but the other body of information that appeared on the computers called the Symbol Stream. It was because of this that there was unending speculation and argument about whether or not the computers were living entities in some way.

A computer screen remained blank until someone typed certain things on a keyboard, then tapped on other things, which brought up one of the data files. Nothing ever appeared on a screen without a person summoning it forth through these procedures. The exception to this was the Symbol Stream. Sometimes, when a computer was turned on, or even as one of the files sat open on the screen, columns of some kind of code would suddenly appear and start to scroll down the screen. This flow of symbols might last for minutes, hours, or days, and once begun, it could not be stopped through any means employed by the user, except to turn off the computer. When the computer was

turned back on, if the stream had not already finished running of its own accord, it would still be there. No one knew what this was, why it was, or where it came from.

It was believed by some that the computers were living entities and that the symbol stream was their means of communication with one another, but the majority believed it was sent from a location not on Earth and that it was an attempt to communicate with people here. Analyzers had been attempting to decode the symbol stream for many years, because a civilization that could send a message over such a great distance would have greatly advanced technology and thus held out much hope for the future of Earth. Up to this time, the meaning of the symbols in the four scrolling columns of code had never been deciphered.

Liana was not a decoder. Her job was to watch a stream when it occurred and record any changes or new symbols that appeared, as often the streams were identical, just repeating the same thing over and over. She had been watching this one for two days now, when something amazing happened. The stream briefly stopped, and when it resumed, one of the four columns now appeared in ordinary English. The other three had changed into languages she had seen in files about other countries. Whether these communications were from the mind of some living, sentient computer or from living beings in places unimaginable distances from Earth, one thing was clear: whoever it was had finally found a way to get through to man.

Liana stood up and screamed for her supervisor to come over. Startled by the outburst, everyone in the hut stopped what they were doing to look at her, then looked around and at one another with puzzlement or fear. She hadn't screamed just to get her supervisor's attention, but because of what she had seen in those first few moments of reading the slowly scrolling English.

As it turned out, the Symbol Stream wasn't coming from a sentient computer that was alive and well on Liana's desk; it was coming from actual people, but they weren't a million light years away. They were in fact just a mere five and a half miles southeast of the work hut.

Years ago, when the flood of the Blood Storm was reaching high tide, the possible had finally become the inevitable: the great global war had taken things past the point of no return; humankind would not survive. Those not killed outright would eventually succumb to the aftermath of sickness, clinging fang and claw to the dying envelope of atmosphere encircling the globe.

In an effort to prevent the ultimate and complete extinction of the race, a network of large, underground enclaves was constructed. By 2050, the technology had already been developed to enable sustained air, food, and water supplies to be used in these; they would last for centuries, if needed, and keep those few survivors going until they could come up to the surface once again. The hope was that they would begin repopulating the world.

There had been five such underground groups in the desert area that was Liana's home. Three of them had long since succumbed to underground oxygen system malfunctions, outbreaks of contagious illnesses, and other unplanned for mishaps.

Liana's group had survived. How and when exactly the transition from underground to the surface had occurred, nobody alive today knew for sure. Five and a half miles away, the other group was alive, but permanently entombed within their underground structure. A series of freakish sandstorms whirled over fifty tons of sand on top of the two poorly situated surface hatches, making it virtually impossible to open them again from inside. The Symbol Stream was a repeated call for help to anyone anywhere who might ever see it. If nothing else, its presence would let people know there were others still somewhere alive.

It had taken years for an electronics genius named Miles Eldridge to figure out a way to use his own computers to override, and then have the Stream appear, on computers in other locations, and many more years to finally figure out a way to have the messages appear as something other than a stream of meaningless digits and symbols.

A team of thirty people from Liana's enclave made the five-mile journey in the devastating heat to dig out and free the underground Eldridge enclave. It was a day of great rejoicing for all, as more humans now walked upon the earth. For everyone in Liana's group who had been working so diligently for years with the computer files, it was also a chance for the two groups to merge their knowledge about Earth's past technologies and to redouble their efforts to make them a reality once again.

It would be quite a while though before any of the Eldritch group would want to talk of such things. For now, all they wanted to do was look at the wide, blue sky, feel the sun, walk for miles in the sand, and breathe the seemingly endless ocean of fresh air.

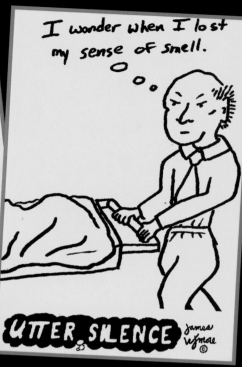

# King of the Dead

## Legendary Filmmaker George A. Romero on Politics, Film, and the Future

### Interview by Jason V Brock

**Jason V Brock:** Greetings, Mr. Romero, thanks for chatting with us.

**George A. Romero:** My pleasure.

**Brock:** Excellent. I'd like to begin by discussing some things that don't get much play in most film-related interviews, such as your feelings and thoughts on events happening in the US political scene. I ask because your films usually have an undercurrent of sociopolitical focus—dealing with racism, voyeurism, sexism, that kind of thing. So what *do* you feel right now about the current political situation in the United States?

**Romero:** I think it's frightening! It's scarier than my movies, I'll tell you that.

**Brock:** Yes, I'm inclined to agree; now we have angry ideas about stepping on people's heads at Ron Paul conventions! So, you know, it's pretty insane. You have to forgive me—I'm a liberal.

**Romero:** Oh hey, come on!

Left: *Romero directing on the set of* Day of the Dead *(1985).*
Right: *The director at a recent convention appearance.*

**Brock:** Liberal is like a dirty word now; it's been morphed into "progressive." I mean, what the hell does that mean? I don't even know what a progressive is! I'm a liberal like John Kennedy—I want the greater good, and all that, for everyone. It's not all about the bottom line for everything. Money is just a means to an end, you know?

**Romero:** Yeah, I know. Just a way to get things done.

**Brock:** So what bothers you the most about the current political climate?

**Romero:** Well, I think that people are just reacting. It's a deep—it's a knee-jerk reaction . . . it's the old "throw the bums out syndrome." There hasn't been enough time for anything to really develop. I'm hoping that, some of this, some of these radical conservative ideas will all blow over.

**Brock:** I agree with you. I think Barack's done a pretty good job, actually. He's had some formidable obstacles to overcome, the resistance and so on, but you know, what can you do? You can't win everybody over. . . .

**Romero:** Right, I mean there's no telling. I do think he's a bit timid.

**Brock:** I agree with that. Has been, at least.

**Romero:** You know, if he would just open his mouth sometimes and just . . . pop off once in a while! I think then he might do a lot better.

**Left:** *Romero (assisted by Streiner) directs Judith O'Dea in the apocalyptic classic* **Night of the Living Dead** *(1968).*

**Right (Clockwise from Top):** **Night of the Living Dead** *cast photo - Judith Ridley (with a can of chocolate syrup, used as blood), Karl Hardman, Kyra Schon, Marilyn Eastman, and George Romero.*

**Brock:** I understand what you mean. I think the whole world would be better off if he did that, to be honest!

**Romero:** Yeah. [laughs]

**Brock:** So getting to your work. I have a question I've been curious about: I read in a couple of places that *Night of the Living Dead* was influenced by Matheson's novel *I Am Legend*. Is that true?

**Romero:** Oh, yeah, completely. I mean, I basically was inspired by that book. I guess that's a loose way of saying that I ripped it off! [laughs] But definitely that was the inspiration. I wrote a short story that explored my take on those ideas. I knew I couldn't use vampires because Matheson had, so I thought that I'd invent a new sort of monster. . . . I never called them "zombies." I never thought of them as zombies because to me, zombies were, you know, those guys in the Caribbean: the voodoo zombies; my guys were the *neighbors*. People you knew, people you cared about. Essentially the rules had somehow changed and they weren't staying dead. So I thought I'd come up with something new, but everybody then writing about *Night of the Living Dead* called them zombies and you know, that's the way it is. So now they're "zombies," even though I don't think that they should necessarily be *called* zombies, because zombies are not dead. My guys are dead, certainly!

**Brock:** It's interesting that you bring that up because that was one of my other questions. Actually, two of those things were! One: That short story that you wrote—has it ever been printed?

**Romero:** Nope.

**Brock:** No? I'm surprised. . . .

**Romero:** No, it hasn't. I mean it was a short story that I wrote and never actually tried to get published. We turned one part of it into the first film [*NOTLD*] . . . a friend of mine and I, Jack Russo, wrote the script together.

**Brock:** I know you've written other short fiction. Do you write novels proper?

**Romero:** I am in the process right now of writing a novel, but I've never had anything published. You know, I'm still working, I'm still making movies, so it's hard to find the time to sit down and concentrate on writing a book. So I fiddle at it whenever I have a couple of weeks, but I've never really had the time to pursue it with any energy.

**Brock:** That's too bad because I've admired your cinematic writing. . . .

**Romero:** Well, thank you, but it's . . . I guess . . . you know, you have to make a choice.

**Brock:** Right.

**Romero:** And, to me, movies are too much fun! I mean I grew up wanting to make movies all my life and lucky enough to still be able to make them, so you know, I'll always choose that until the day comes when nobody wants me to make a movie again. Then maybe I'll be able to sit down and concentrate seriously on a book.

Above: *John Amplas as a modern vampire in 1976's* Martin.

Facing Page: (Top) *Romero in a promotional still from* Day of the Dead.

(Bottom) GAR (L) *Showing an extra how to be a 'zombie' on the set of 1978's* Dawn of the Dead; *filmmaker Dario Argento looks on. (Photographer unknown.)*

**Brock:** Interesting. You mentioned you were careful not to use or overuse the word zombie, which I've always noticed about your oeuvre. What I think is interesting about that is you always have a "human side" to the dead people in the films, even making major characters out of them, such as Bub in *Day of the Dead*. Where does that fit with your personal belief about spirituality regarding the mythos of zombies?

Are you trying to bring that personal aspect that in there? That they're still human in a way?

**Romero:** I don't think that it has anything to do with, in my mind anyway, spirituality. It is purely that I sympathize with these . . . "creatures." I mean they're *us*; they're us after we're dead. And I think that some people have made too much of a connection between, you know, an afterlife, or some sort of spiritual connection with the phenomenon as I describe it. And I just . . . I don't think of it that way. To me it's a natural disaster. I feel sorry for these guys, like I feel sorry for animals in the wild that have to cope with things, and maybe aren't prepared to; I'm not trying to, you know, send any sort of message about afterlife or anything like that.

**Brock:** Fascinating.

**Romero:** My stories are essentially about people; they're about the humans and how they react stupidly to situations, or mishandle situations. And the "zombies" are a disaster. It could be anything, it could be a hurricane, it could be a tsunami. It's just a huge sort of game-changing thing that's going on out there and people refuse to accept it. They keep on with their own agendas and they keep trying to think of life as it always was. And I think unfortunately that's what happens to us in the real world. I mean, we want everything to be the way it always was. We want a job, we think that we deserve a certain amount of money, you know, and that's the way we want things to be. We get angry if it's *not* that way. And we don't recognize that there are huge things happening, huge changes in the world that might affect life as we know it, and that we have to pull together and try to work things out—just the way we always have, except we don't seem to be doing it anymore.

We have to try to pull together and defeat our obstacles. I mean, if we want a good life, we have to build it for ourselves, not just assume that it's in some way owed to us.

**Brock:** That's well put, and I agree. So how do you feel about the violence in the films themselves? Do you feel that it's just necessary to underscore the point that we are still just humans trying to do the best we can against what's going on out there in the cosmos?

**Romero:** Well, that's the way *I* view it. I know that a lot of people don't! A lot of people feel that the violence in my films is gratuitous, but I have to say that my films to some extent are comic books; I mean, the violence is sort of like the same sort of violence that's in a cartoon. Coyote and the Road Runner—it's *that* kind of violence. I know that a lot of people *don't* like it, but that's my prerogative as a filmmaker.

**Brock:** Right.

**Romero:** So, you know, you either like it or you don't. And if you don't, don't bother to go see it.

**Brock:** I agree. I don't think it's gratuitous; I think it's very necessary the way you've put it together. *Especially* in a film like *Dawn of the Dead*, which pushed a lot of boundaries. And I think, well, even *Night of the Living Dead*, they all did it in their own ways, but *Dawn of the Dead* in particular resonates with me, I don't know why. I put it right up there with some of the grand American cinema of the 1970s, you know: *Taxi Driver*, *Network*, things like that.

**Romero:** Wow! [laughs]

**Brock:** I personally think *Dawn* is one of the best films ever made in American cinema.

**Romero:** Wow! Wow! That's a great vote of confidence and I thank you.

**Brock:** [laughs] No need to thank me! But . . . because it also has that European flair, you know, courtesy probably of the environment that you wrote it in. . . . I think I read you wrote it in Rome with Dario Argento, correct?

**Romero:** Yeah.

**Brock:** Also, the outstanding music from Goblin added to the entire ambiance. I think it has a European sensibility but an American anxiety, if that makes sense.

**Romero:** Well, that's a great way of putting it, I think. . . . It does, at least the *American* version does.

**Brock:** Yes.

**Romero:** I think that Dario's cut—there was a cut that he did—is a bit more, I don't know . . . it was a hammer to the head. I mean, he cut all the *humor* out of it. [pauses] He and I are great friends and we've talked about this together often. I just think he cut too much of the humor out of it, and I think that maybe what you're talking about in the American side of it is the humor. I mean, that ability to laugh at things that are senseless.

**Brock:** Well, I think it's an absurdist situation.

**Romero:** Yeah.

**Brock:** The characters find themselves in this strange predicament. I think that the humor is definitely needed to add emotional ballast to the intense . . . *trauma* of the circumstances.

**Romero:** Well, I'm glad to hear you say that; and it *is* absurdist. I mean, you know, it's not *meant* to be taken literally. I don't know. . . A lot of people now are writing about, "Well, the eventual zombie apocalypse, and what if it happens?" And I'm here to tell you that it *ain't* gonna happen, so forget about it! I mean, don't take it so seriously, it's ridiculous.

**Brock:** I think it feeds into that *fin de siècle* kind of zeitgeist that people have lately; you know, about the looming apocalypse, that type of thing. The whole absurdist idea is interesting to consider; I like Ionesco and Beckett, playwrights like that, and writers such as J. G. Ballard and William S. Burroughs; there was lot of farcicality going on in that stuff. They don't mean it to be taken seriously.

**Romero:** No, exactly: That's the point. You have to exaggerate and be a bit ridiculous in order to make your point stand out sometimes.

**Brock:** Right. Incidentally, I appreciate your candor about all this.

**Romero:** Sure.

**Brock:** So I want to ask you about a few general things. As I said, I think that the American version of *Dawn*, your version, is the better of the two major cuts of the film, although I enjoy them both in different ways—

**Romero:** I do too. I do too. I enjoy the other version and I understand the . . . sort of visceral *dynamic* that it has. But it . . . I don't know, it's just not *my* film, you know? It's not exactly my vision. I prefer not to take things so earnestly; I would rather lighten it up a little bit.

**Brock:** So did you actually film the ending for *Dawn of the Dead*? Where Fran committed suicide?

**Romero:** Well, we didn't need to film much of it because . . . The short answer is yes! [laughs] We did film the shot of Peter with the gun to his head and that was going to be the last shot. We were going to cut on the sound of a gunshot. So we shot that, but then we shot more, where we decided *not* to do it. So yes, we shot that too. And we shot the scene of Fran coming out of the helicopter and standing up high... theoretically to stick her head into the helicopter blades. And again, all we did was cut it short. So in that sense we did shoot both of those scenes, but during the shooting of the film it's funny, man; I mean, when we were making the film I said, I had this like little elf—or goblin—on my shoulder saying, "You know, this *is* the sequel to *Night of the Living Dead*, even though it's ten years later." And I wasn't thinking of it entirely that way. So there was some goblin saying to me, "But it *is* a sequel, and so it has to be just as tragic . . . everybody has to die, *ba-boom*," all of that. And it was during the making of the film that I said "wait a minute, it's still dark." In other words, if it's a contagion and the world is still in trouble, that's still a dark ending. . . . However, if I like these couple of people,

I can save them, particularly if we don't know what's going to happen and the future looks bleak; I can certainly save them for the moment. So some of it came to me during the making of the film; of course, that's the way I decided to do it in the end.

**Brock:** Fascinating. I like the disjointed kind of super-narrative you have, with the original three films, in particular—all the films, actually, in that they aren't linked by *character*, they are linked by *circumstance*. I think that's a novel postmodern idea—that you can take a set of understanding and comprehension on the part of the audience and extend that into a universe.

**Romero:** Well, that's funny. I think that happened accidentally because the second film came so long after the first film. I think that general audiences didn't remember or care about or want to be bothered with the first film, and I think that happened almost accidentally. In other words, I was saying, OK, this is the same phenomenon but we're going to pick it up a little later and we will, you know . . . just a little bit of back story, enough for you to understand what's going on even if you haven't seen or know about the first film. And so, OK, that worked. Then, the third time, I said, "Well, do the same damn thing." I'll take it a little further and do enough backstory in it that you're not lost if you're a newcomer. I really think that was accidental, but then it became a shtick. I said, "Wow! This is cool." And then, when I made *Land of the Dead*, which was, like, *way* later, I did the same thing again; it seemed to work so . . . And then, it was only with *Diary* . . . because I had the concept for *Diary* involved . . . I wanted to do something about film in the journalism and emerging media, and I said, "Well, this can work here." My idea was to have students as they're out shooting a student film the first night that the zombies began to walk. I said, "OK, I have to go back to the first night." And so that drove me . . .

It's exciting the observations that you make, because I'm most proud of that—that you can actually make a *series* of films. It's not completely unique, granted. I mean, James Bond has been in movies since the '50s, right? And he doesn't get older. They have to use different actors but it's the same James Bond. So it's not a completely unique thing. But I really liked the idea that you could tell a story over the years without referring to the same characters, or even to the same *decade:* the cars are different, everything has advanced and yet, somehow . . . it has a narrative progression.

**Brock:** Yes; I would call it a "prismatic narrative," because it's like a prism—it takes a whole idea and explodes it. That's really a thought-provoking, realistic approach.

**Romero:** Thanks, I try to keep things interesting!

**Brock:** That makes me think a little bit of *Martin.* Now that's a pretty serious film as far as the way you treated the folklore of the vampire. How do you feel that holds up in retrospect? Do you feel that it succeeds?

**Romero:** [pauses] I do. *Martin* is my favorite film of mine. I do think that I was successful; I think probably for the first time as a filmmaker was trying to translate something from the written page into film. And I like it. It's the most serious film I've made, and a lot of people say it's the most personal film I've made; I'm not sure I agree with that. I think maybe a film called *Knightriders,* which I think might actually be more of a personal statement of mine.

**Brock:** That's a very good film.

**Romero:** I'm glad you like it. *Martin,* to me is, just . . . I felt that I was successful as a screenwriter and a filmmaker and it remains my *favorite* film. And we made it with a bunch of young people that were, I mean, cast and crew numbered, you know, twelve or fourteen people on most days! Everybody was really collaborative, and did a terrific job in it. John Amplas was wonderful.

**Brock:** Yeah, he's very good, and Tom Savini. Wasn't that one of the first times you got to really work with him on screen? I read he was to be involved with *Night of the Living Dead* before he had to go to Vietnam. Is that true?

**Romero:** No, it's not true. He was going to be involved in an earlier film that we were going to make which had nothing to do with *Night of the Living Dead*; he was a young guy who I liked as an actor. I met him when we were trying to cast another little film, sort of a coming-of-age, teenage movie. So I went around to high schools and looked at high school plays that people were putting on. And I saw Tom and I thought he was *terrific*. He was in one of these high school plays and I wanted him to play the role in this film that we were going to do. Well, it all blew away; we never got the money to make the film. I lost track of Tom. When he came back [from Vietnam], it was right when we were getting ready to shoot *Martin*. He re-introduced himself, and he had done a couple of small films. That was when we really first got to work together was *Martin*; not only did he do the effects, but he was an actor in it.

**Brock:** Yes, he was. He's underrated. He was very good.

**Romero:** He's really good. I think that's what he would like to be in life, so yeah, I think he'd like to drop the rest of it. Since he has that school now in Pennsylvania, the production and makeup effects school, he's sort of tied to that. But he's done a lot of acting and he's a really good actor.

**Brock:** He is; he's a nice guy, too. I only met him once, but he was very nice to me. I've e-mailed him a couple of times.

**Romero:** He's a great guy. I mean he's just the kind of guy you need to have around. I don't say this about a lot of people, but he's inspirational. I mean he just keeps the ball rolling and he's terrific; just a bundle of energy, and *very* talented.

**Brock:** One more thing I wanted to comment on about *Dawn of the Dead* is that it's a fantastically edited film, referring specifically to your version. I think for most people, editing is the invisible art—

**Romero:** It is.

**Brock:** How do you feel about the tendency now toward remaking a lot of these films? You know, like *Dawn of the Dead*? How do you feel about that? I mean, is that a good trend, do you think?

**Romero:** [pauses] You know what? It's hard to have an opinion about it because I don't always think it's wrong, I just think that it's often

done for the wrong *reasons*. Like they remade a film of mine called *The Crazies* . . .

**Brock:** Yes.

**Romero:** . . . and they had *no* eye at all for the politics in that film. Somebody said, "Well, here's an old movie we can acquire inexpensively and remake it." Basically all they wanted to do was, I think, turn the crazy people into zombies and make another, sort of, *28 Days Later* out of it! I think Breck Eisner did a good job with that film, I just think it was . . . misguided.

There are times when I think that you could do it and possibly be successful. I'm not sure what that is. There's an old film of mine called *Season of the Witch*, that I would love to remake because I just don't think I did a good enough job with it, and I didn't have enough money and I'd love to remake that. I actually . . . there was this thing going around a while ago that I was going to remake *Deep Red*, called *Dario Argento's Deep Red*, which . . . That turned out to be a misunderstanding because it was Dario's brother Claudio doing this. He called me and said, "Would you like to remake *Deep Red*? I happen to think you can remake it and take some of the opera out of it and make it a sort of straight Hitchcock-type thriller." So I said, sure, I'd be interested in talking about it. But at the time I thought Dario was involved: he wasn't. The moment that I found out Dario was not involved, I said, "No, forget about it."

**Brock:** Wow.

**Romero:** And I've been talking to some people who want to remake *Children Shouldn't Play with Dead Things*. I'm interested in that too, but I don't know if it's ever going to happen. I mean, I've had this weird career! I say no to a lot of things. If I'm intrigued by something right off the bat I'll say OK and investigate it and try to find out whether it's real and whether there's any sort of creative process that I can have some degree of control over. I mean, that's always the stuff that bothers me. I don't take "jobs," if you know what I mean. I don't want to just sort of "take a job." Like "Here's the gig—come make this movie." I've never done it, and I don't think I ever will. I hope I won't; at this point in my life I probably wouldn't.

So, on the one hand, I don't think you can *automatically* say that remakes are terrible. Most of them are, but I think it's usually because the *motive* to remake them is terrible. Nobody seriously approaches the idea for a remake in terms of trying to "improve it," or because we can "do it better now because we have computer effects," or whatever.

That's *never* the approach. It's usually just, "Here's a great old title like *Halloween*. We can make a lot of money on this again." And that's usually what it's about—making a *lot* of dough. That's disturbing, but I don't think you can therefore automatically say that remakes are bad as a result.

**Brock:** I concur with that to a degree; I suppose it's all in the intention, as you're saying. I admit I'm still a bit conflicted over the "remake-itis" and "sequel-itis" afflicting Hollywood, though! [laughs] So, after *Martin,* what are your favorite films that you've done that didn't quite meet your personal goals? You mentioned a couple; what I mean is, what do you think *you* could have done better? What are you most disappointed by?

**Romero:** Well, with regard to my biggest personal disappointments, there are two films—*There's Always Vanilla,* which had a million titles, and *Season of the Witch;* they were the two films that we made right after *Night of the Living Dead.* We didn't have enough money; we were sort of spunky filmmakers trying to do the best we could with limited resources, and we should probably *not* have attempted films that were . . . [pauses] I don't want to say *heavy,* but that were so serious. I don't know how to phrase it exactly. . . .

**Brock:** Ambitious? Kind of ambitious in their scope?

**Romero:** Yes. Yes, good word. And so those two are the most disappointing. And behind my favorite film *Martin* comes *Knightriders,* and then a little film that I made called *Bruiser,* which I just really love and nobody ever saw. Those are my favorites, and they're not among the zombie films! Among the zombie films, I think *Day of the Dead* is probably . . . it remains my favorite. I don't know if it's the *best,* but it remains my favorite.

**Brock:** *Day of the Dead* is fantastic. Now I have to say I saw *Day of the Dead* when it came out—*in the theater!* It was me and one other black guy in the entire auditorium, and that's too bad. It got, I don't know. . . just not enough people saw it. I thought it was great; Joe Pilato was excellent. All the acting was quite good.

**Romero:** It's very arch; the performances are really sort of broadly stroked and all that, but that's what it was meant to be. It's meant to be a comic book, so you have to sort of forgive it for that. But you know what happened to that film, all of a sudden, I mean, there was a guy that wrote the most *scathing* review of that film that I've ever read; the most scathing review of *any* of my films that I've ever read. And he wound up three years later doing jacket notes for it on the DVD release and apologizing for the review!

I find that my stuff . . . I don't know, I don't want to make the *same* movie over and over. The fans want the same movie over again, it seems—I don't know, it's this TV mentality. People tune in to *CSI: Miami* every week, to see *exactly* the same show! I'm always trying to do something different; some of the fans out there want it to be the same as the last one. When they first see one of my films like, *Survival of the Dead*, they don't get it. But then I meet fans at conventions and they say, "We thought it was great!" It's going to take a while, but I predict that eventually *Survival of the Dead* is going to be the one of the favorites among the fans. It takes a while for my stuff to catch up; I don't know *when*, I don't know *why*, and I don't exactly know *what* that's about except that I know that if I have an idea to do something and do it a little differently, that's what I do and I'm not sure that sits well with a lot of the fans.

**Brock:** I think that kind of phenomenon happened to Carpenter with *The Thing*.

**Romero:** Oh yeah.

**Brock:** You know, that movie bombed, sadly, but it's really one of his best films, I think. Or perhaps his best *realized* film.

**Romero:** I think it is, completely. But you know, it wasn't *entirely* the fault of the fans in that case. It was a Universal film; they didn't like it *in the least*. They didn't support it and thought it was terrible. That's actually how I met John; after I saw *The Thing* in the theater. So I wrote him a letter, and I'd read a couple of really *terrible* reviews. I wrote to John through his agent and I said, "John, you know, keep going, man, because it's just really great." And it's how John and I got to meet and, you know, we're still friends. I didn't see his last film, *The Ward*, but I'm just pulling for the guy.

**Brock:** Interesting. Along the Carpenter lines, I wanted to ask you something about one other film. How did you feel about *Return of the Living Dead*, and that treatment by Dan O'Bannon?

**Romero:** Hated it.

**Brock:** What was it you didn't . . .

**Romero:** You want me to put it simply?

**Brock:** [startled] Yeah—don't hold back! What was it that you didn't care for?

**Romero:** Oh man! [laughs] I mean, I just thought it was . . . I thought it was ridiculous! Too comedic. You know, my zombies don't *talk*: they *can't*. They're too *weak* to dig their way up out of graves. And I have a whole different reason for using these creatures. Anyway, I hated that usage. And this is not to say that I don't like anybody spoofing the genre, because I love *Shaun of the Dead*. I mean, I thought *Shaun* was really almost *too* referential. So that wasn't my complaint. I just thought *Return* was capitalizing on the trend at the time. They bought the title from my partner, Jack Russo, who had written a novel called *Return of the Living Dead*. They bought it promising to involve him; they promised that they were going to do his script. In the end, all they wanted was to buy the title, and that's all they did, and I thought they thrashed it.

**Brock:** OK! [pauses] That's too bad. Do you still work with Russo?

**Romero:** Oh, we see each other all the time. We haven't worked together for years, but we see each other a lot. There's a project on the table that we're talking about doing together. But . . . Listen, Jack is one of my oldest and best friends, but that's not why I'm saying this about *Return*.

**Brock:** I understand; you're certainly entitled to how you feel, and that's perfectly fine. Regarding this venture with Russo though, do you think that'll ever get off the ground?

**Romero:** I don't know. I don't know, man. It depends on . . . you know, all of a sudden, zombies are *hot*. [laughs]

**Brock:** Right . . . right.

**Romero:** We were just together, and we'd say, "Hey, maybe we should make a buck out of this somehow!" But, you know, again, I'm just being honest about it. I can't tell you whether anything's going to happen. I don't know. It all depends, unfortunately, because you're only good as your last movie and how successful that was. And I've been really lucky with *Diary of the Dead* and now *Survival*. It looks like it's going

to wind up making a lot of bucks on video. I don't feel "left out in the cold." But, of course, they're not *huge*, like *Zombieland*, or whatever. And, you know, every once in a while you say, "Wait a minute, how come everyone else is getting rich on this and we're not?"

**Brock:** I completely understand. Did you like *Zombieland*?

**Romero:** I thought it was . . . [pauses] I thought there was some really great dialogue in it. I can't say that I *liked* it. Again, I have a peculiar take on this stuff. I mean, in my mind zombies are—or, *my* zombies—are something horrific that has happened to the world. And, as I said, *my* stories are more about humans and their reactions to this phenomenon. And so I have a completely different view from these other guys. I don't get. I have a lot of fun dreaming up ways to kill zombies. And I can do things that are more clever now that I can use computer graphics. I have really a lot of fun with that! But that's not the point of my films. Seems to me that was the point of that film.

**Brock:** I'll be honest with you, since you were honest with me—I hated *Zombieland*. Ugh! [laughter from both] That was a *dreadful* movie. I mean, I like Woody Harrelson; I think he's a good actor. But I was like, "This is just not working for me." I don't know . . . And it was such a big hit, too! That's what shocked me—

**Romero:** Well, you know what? That's the amazing thing. It's the *only* zombie film that has really blown the roof off, as far as box office. It's the only one. Which is why I say that it's been video games much more than films that have made these zombies so popular. I mean, I think it's why there are these zombie conventions and stuff. I think it's video games more than movies; that's actually a little disturbing to me, because zombies have become anything you want them to be anymore. That's not *my* zombies, you know. My guys will still be slugging along, moving slow as death until . . . until I'm done, anyway! [laughs] Then, maybe I will come back and make one final film!

**Brock:** Do you feel you have accomplished everything you set out to when you were younger? I mean, your career has taken some unexpected turns, a lot of them for the good, but is this what you . . . maybe not what you thought was *going* to happen, but are you pleased and do you feel that your career is right where you wanted it to be?

**Romero:** It's a difficult question that you're asking here, man!

**Brock:** [laughs]

**Romero:** I mean . . . I can't answer that with subtlety. Pleased? I am *extremely* pleased. I've been blessed. I've had a hell of a lot of luck. I've had terrific things happen to me. I'm seventy-odd years old, I'm still making movies, and I'm still making money and, you know, how can you be displeased with that?

Now, the other side of that coin is that when you come up wanting to make movies, you don't say to yourself, "I want to make horror movies." You say to yourself, "I want to make *movies*." And I know that I have movies in me that I will *never* get hired to make, that I would love to make. And of course, there's a certain disappointment that comes with that. So, I can't tell you that I'm . . . You know, people will say, "What is this guy complaining about?" It's like Stephen King wrote a couple of novels about the disappointment of a successful novelist, and everybody got all over his ass saying, "What the hell . . . What the hell does Steve King have to complain about?" And so I'm sure that people will say the same thing about me, and I'm not complaining. Like I said right up front, I've had a *wonderful* life, and I'm still doing it. Of course, there are things that I would like to do that I haven't been able to do, and I think partly because of being sort of locked in this niche, I probably will never be able to do them.

So maybe when I've finally put down the camera and tried to seriously write a novel or two . . . You know, maybe some of that stuff can come out. The point is that I have a lot of hope that it's still possible and I guess maybe that's the whole secret of longevity or whatever. You know, it's like John Huston was directing his last film in a wheelchair with a breathing mechanism. I'll probably do the same damn thing!

# Horror Science Fiction Fantas

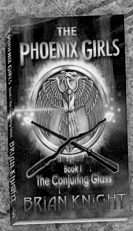

**THE PHOENIX GIRLS**
Book I
The Conjuring Glass
BRIAN KNIGHT

978-1-936564-72-9  $14.95

**LIMBUS, INC.**
Benjamin Kane Ethridge
Jonathan Maberry
Joseph Nassise
Brett J. Talley
Anne C. Petty

978-1-936564-52-1  $17.95

**FOREVER MAN**
Brian W Matthews

978-1-936564-65-1  $13.95

J. G. Faherty

978-1-936564-63-7
$13.95

TEROVOLAS
Edward M. Erdelac

978-1-936564-54-5
$15.95

Twice Shy
Patrick Freivald

978-1-936564-50-7
$16.95

THE DEVIL OF ECHO LAKE
Douglas Wynne

978-1-936564-53-8
$16.95

THE DONORS
Jeffrey Wilson

978-1-936564-46-0
$16.95

Dead Reflections
CAROL WEEKES

978-1-936564-70-5
$13.95

JOKERS CLUB
Gregory Bastianelli

978-1-936564-30-9
$11.95

THAT WHICH SHOULD NOT BE

978-1-936564-14-9
$12.95

THE VOID

978-1-936564-43-9
$16.95

THE DEMON
Renaissance Drive
Elizabeth Reuter

978-1-936564-25-5
$11.95

Cemetery Club

978-1-936564-23-1
$16.95

ANNE C. PETTY
THE CORNERSTONE

978-1-936564-67-5
$13.95

The Pentacle Pendant

978-1-936564-27-9
$12.95

90 Minutes to Live

978-1-936564-33-0
$12.95

**JOURNALSTONE**
YOUR LINK TO ARTISTIC TALENT

WWW.JOURNALSTONE.COM

Women SCORNED
Angela Meadon

978-1-936564-38-5
$11.95

Pazuzu's Girl

978-1-936564-36-1
$13.95

# It Was Raining the Day the Children Decided to Kill Their Grandmother

## By Earl Hamner

It was raining the day the kids decided to kill their grandmother. They had been shut up in the house all day and were bored. Granny wouldn't let them turn on the TV because she said it let electricity into the house. So there was nothing fun to do. Mom and Dad had left early for the court hearing, and the minute they were out the door Granny started sucking on her cough syrup bottle.

First thing happened was Teeny thought Granny had dozed off and went in Granny's purse, the black one with the broken zipper, and stole a couple of goobers that were left over from when the bag broke and they spilled every which-a-way. Romey said he wanted a goober too. When Tenny when back to get him one Granny was just pretending to be asleep and grabbed her hand and held it in the fire so Teeny would know what it was going to be like when she died and went to hell for stealing.

"I wish she would die," said Vardelle after Granny finished her cough syrup and dozed off with spit dribbling out of the corner of her mouth.

"She's so mean maybe somebody will kill her," said Tenny hopefully. Her hand had gotten all red and puffy from her lesson.

"We could do it," said Perk. He was the youngest but smart all the same.

"How?" Asked Teeny.

"Stick a butcher knife in her heart," said Perk.

"Naw," said Vardelle. "It would get blood all over everything and Mom and Dad would wonder about it."

"Push her off a cliff?" Suggested Romey.

"Nearest cliff's at Goshen Pass," said Vardelle. "Be easier to smother her."

"Why don't you all do it?" suggested Tenny.

Vardelle thought for a minute and then she nodded and told

each kid what to do, and they followed her directions to the T. Romey held one of her scrawny old blue-veined hands. Tenny held the other one and Vardelle took Tenny's dirty old comfy pillow she dragged all over the place and held it over Granny's face until she stopped breathing. The mean old thing hardly fought back at all, she was so shit-faced from the cough syrup.

They dragged her out to the old pasture and pushed her down the well that nobody used anymore and put the top back on. Then they went back home and played the TV real loud and made chocolate fudge with walnuts and took out the dirty book Dad had hidden under his mattress about how to do it and all and called up the zoo and asked if Mr. Lion was there and every single one of them took a good sip of the Jack Daniel's Old Time Tennessee Sipping Whiskey from behind the bar and when Teeny said she was going to tell what all they had done Vardelle slapped her black and blue until she promised not to tell.

When Mom and Dad came home from the court hearing they asked the kids what they'd been doing all day and they said, "Nothing."

# The Devil and Sir Francis Drake

### by Adam Bolivar

*The Moon's my constant Mistresse*
*& the lowelie owle my morrowe;*
*Yᵉ flaming Drake and yᵉ Nightcrowe make*
*Mee musick to my sorrow.*

—Tom O'Bedlam

## I.

Genealogy has always been a passion of mine. Little could I have imagined how close it would lead me to the very brink of madness. My grandmother had always maintained that we were descended from Sir Francis Drake, the legendary Elizabethan privateer. I have heard others make similar claims, that their families were related to royalty, or this or that famous person, but these assertions were never substantiated with factual proof, only rumor and family legend. Still, I imagine if anyone were to shake his family tree hard enough, a few notable apples would inevitably fall from the upper branches. Consider: every person has two parents, four grandparents, eight great-grandparents and sixteen great-great-grandparents. Determined genealogists who comb the ever-propagating branches of their ancestries can doubtlessly connect themselves obliquely with almost any historical figure they fancy. It has been said that every person is at least the fiftieth cousin of every other human being on earth. But at this level, relation becomes remote to the point of absurdity. There must be a standard by which inheritance is determined, a means to establish lineage.

Obviously, a direct descendant would be favored over an indirect one. One is more apt to bequeath one's fortune to one's own child than to a nephew or a cousin. However, this standard can become impractical over time, for what if one begets more than a single child? The fortune must be divided amongst them, and then amongst all their children, until at last the legacy is spread so thinly that it amounts to nothing.

And what if there is a title, some singular honor that can only belong to one person at one time? Which of one's children will inherit it? A rule, however arbitrary, must be adopted in order to determine who will be pronounced heir.

The two factors that present themselves as standards for inheritance are precedence of birth and sex. There are some traditions, such as the Iroquois and the Pictish, that reckon bloodlines matrilineally, and others that reckon them patrilineally. Each method is as arbitrary as a coin toss, yet each is equally useful. The English tradition is patrilineal—that is to say, one's heir is one's oldest and nearest male descendant.

Of course, it thrilled me to no end to believe that I was a descendant of Sir Francis Drake, and I devoured any account of his life I could lay my hands on. I eagerly read of Drake's exploits—his treasure-raids in the Caribbean, his heroic circumnavigation of the globe, and of course his triumphant clash with the Spanish Armada in 1588. The man had supernatural reserves of luck and cunning, and, with astonishing ease, he rose from his humble origins as a vicar's son in Devon to become vice-admiral of the Royal Navy and one of the richest men in England.

The first proof of my relation to Sir Francis Drake came after my grandmother's funeral, for death is always an event that shakes a family tree, and strange fruit can fall. I had always felt an ineffable connection with my grandmother, such as I felt for no other family member. We were of the same ilk, she and I—bookish, gentle and shy.

My mother telephoned to inform me of my grandmother's closeness to death, and I immediately took the first train from Boston to Richmond to be at her side. The illness was very far advanced, and my grandmother was in the throes of shedding her mortal coil. She could not speak and passed in and out of semi-consciousness. I think she was aware of my presence, but there was a haunted look to her earthy brown eyes. She did not want to go; leaving us behind would not be easy for her.

My mother, my great-aunt, and I did our best to make her comfortable. It was on the morning of All Hallow's Eve when she left. We were summoned to the hospital at the dawn of a clear,

cloudless morning, though there was little warmth in the sun that day. I was not a witness to the moment of her passing, though I heard Azraël's wings beating in the distance. I felt her still-warm hand, but it was not a human hand. Her body was a husk now, and my grandmother no longer inhabited it. My great-aunt was cognizant of this fact and, without any ceremony, yanked the diamond wedding ring from her sister's finger and gave it to my mother.

"I reckon this belongs to you now," she said.

At the time, I had thought this action to be somewhat callous, but my great-aunt explained it to me. "You have to take the wedding ring off right away after someone dies. If you don't, the finger will swell up, and it becomes much more difficult." She was over eighty years old and had a considerable storehouse of experience with death to draw from. I filed this little piece of wisdom away in the vault of my memory for future use.

Now there was only the funeral to attend to, and a strange business it was indeed. Fortunately, my grandmother's minister was able to guide us through the unpleasant necessities that accompany preparing and laying to rest a loved one's earthly remains. There was a subdued service in her beloved Episcopal Church, accompanied by the somber attire and lack of weeping which is the custom amongst Anglo-Saxons. No wailing and beating on the breast for us. Only the occasional tear out of the corner of the eye, which was quickly disposed of with a clean white handkerchief. I watched as the coffin was solemnly borne out to the churchyard by four square-shouldered pallbearers and laid to final rest in an already-dug hole next to my grandfather's grave. The minister sprinkled a handful of earth on top of the box and recited the time-hallowed words: "Ashes to ashes. Dust to dust."

She was gone. It was over. My grandmother was no more. I could not help but stare into the hole that had swallowed her up, wishing I could snatch her back into life again. But in the end, I had to turn away.

At this church it was the custom after a service for the congregants to assemble in a small annex for tea, and this funeral was no exception to that rule. This gathering was more subdued than others I had been to, though it was interesting to see so many relatives assembled in one place. It was like a family tree brought to life. My great-aunt was speaking in hushed tones to a distant cousin of mine, whom I had heard tell of but never met. And neither did I meet him that day. At one point in their conversation, he glanced at me with a knowing expression and then turned to resume speaking to my great-aunt.

That night my mother and I slept in the empty house where my grandparents had lived, and finding that I could not fall to sleep, I stole out of my room to take a last survey of the house. My grandparents' house was not a large one by any means. There was a master bedroom, in which my mother lay slumbering. There was a guest bedroom, in which moments ago I had lain restlessly beneath crisp white sheets. Now I was hunting, a lone wolf in the dark.

My instinct told me to go through the door to the attic, for any family secrets would be hidden in the attic. I was immediately greeted by a familiar musty smell, which brought back memories of childhood. The stairs creaked reassuringly beneath my feet. I climbed the stairs and into my grandmother's attic.

It was dark but for the light of the moon, which shone in through the bare, uncurtained window, and cast a silver glow into the darkened chamber. It would be an ideal location to perform necromantic rituals. Why should such an idea enter into my mind? It was only the beginning of such thoughts, as I would discover over the course of the next month.

The moon was shining in through the eastern window, and a shimmering finger of silver light (was it Lilith's finger?) pointed at an old wooden wardrobe that sat in the middle of the attic and towered over the hobby horses and other forgotten relics of youth. I was drawn ineffably to the wardrobe, as though some invisible force were pulling me forward. My hand reached out of its own accord and my fingers closed on the cold silver knob cast in the shape of an acorn. It was the acorn of a mighty oak, whose roots reached down deeply into the soft warm earth of time.

Inside the wardrobe were mementos of my grandparents' life together: a white wedding gown wrapped in pink tissue paper and a suit of men's formal wear. It was undoubtedly the attire my grandparents had worn on their wedding day. Sequestered out of sight in the back of the wardrobe was a cedar chest. I dragged the chest to the front, and opening it I found a stack of letters neatly tied together with a red ribbon. The letters were postmarked 1857 . . . 1858 . . . 1859 . . .

Eagerly undoing the ribbon, I opened up one of the letters and strained my eyes to read the crabbed handwriting by moonlight.

*Powhatan Sanatorium*
*December 21st, 1859*

*My dear sister,*

*Would that I had never opened the cover of that accursed book! I shall always rue the day that I read those pages. Oh, I pray that you are never witness to the horrors I have seen. If you have an iota of sanity left, you will burn it until it is thoroughly reduced to ashes. If only I had the courage to do so myself. But I have learned the secrets that should never be known to Man, and now I am in their thrall. They will come for me soon, the strange winged things that*

*flutter through my nightmares. Our only hope is with you now, sister. Burn the book! Leave no trace. Let our family's terrible legacy die, as it should have perished centuries ago.*

—J. D.

Beneath the letters at the bottom of the trunk was a large bundle of black wool, which had the pronounced musty smell of something that had been kept in an attic for a very long time. All my instincts told me to leave it undisturbed where I had found it, close the wardrobe, and go back to my bed. But alas, the Fates had not chosen such a tranquil path for me to follow. Perhaps it was the moon, the will of Lilith, or invisible puppet strings that impelled my helpless limbs. Slowly I unwound the swath of black wool, which had swaddled its contents for the better part of a century.

It was a book—I knew that it would be—a large black book, like a family Bible. The cover of the book was embossed with a coat of arms that I knew from my researches had belonged to Sir Francis Drake: two silver stars on a field of black, divided by a silver fess, waver. Queen Elizabeth had granted him these arms after his famed circumnavigation of the globe—the first Englishman to do so. Previously, Sir Francis Drake had attempted to use the traditional arms of the noble Drakes of Ashe. But the head of that family, Sir Bertrand Drake, rebuffed Sir Francis's claim, for he could not prove his relation to them. He was, after all, of common birth, whatever his achievement in life.

But was Sir Francis Drake's claim genuine after all? Was his family . . . our family . . . a branch of a far older line of Drake . . . the Dragon . . . whose roots stretched back to the days of the early Saxons . . . and further . . . to the very forest primeval where elves glowered and flashed their silver swords in a moonlit bower? Dare I open the book?

Of course I must. I had come this far. What kind of Drake would I be to shrink from this discovery and run cowering back to my bed? I opened the cover of the book, and a folded document came fluttering down to the floor like an autumn leaf. Eagerly, greedily, I snatched up the paper and unfolded it. It was a pedigree, carefully drafted with an artistic flourish, that traced my family line from Sir Francis Drake's brother Thomas to my great-grandfather, John Drake. With jubilant glee, I reveled in the confirmation of my descent from Sir Francis Drake—an elusive fancy that I had nurtured from earliest childhood. But as I examined the chart more closely, I ascertained that there was another line, issuing from the oldest son of my great-great-great-grandfather, James Drake. This line was of a higher precedence than my own and threatened my claim to being the heir to the Drakes.

This chart had been drawn a century ago, and there was every possibility that this other line was now extinct. But how could I know for sure?

Crestfallen, I closed the book and carefully wrapped it up again in the swath of black wool in which I had found it. At least the book was mine. I was not a Drake by name, but I was one by blood. The book had belonged to my great-grandfather, and I was its rightful owner. The moon had retreated beneath the clouds now, and it was in darkness that I had to stumble across the creaking attic floor. Carefully climbing down the narrow stairs, I clutched my inheritance to my breast and retreated to a cold sleep disturbed by fitful dreams.

The dispersal of my grandmother's estate happened efficiently, for there are hidden, toothy mechanisms in place to dismember a person's life as soon as it ends. For my part, I received a check for five hundred dollars, and another five hundred was allotted to the Episcopal Church. The house and whatever else remained of the estate were ceded to my mother. She has no siblings, and neither do I. The closets full of clothes my grandparents had accumulated over a lifetime were consigned to the care of the Salvation Army. And then our business there was concluded. The shuttered house was locked for the last time until it could be sold, and I hastened to take the first train to Boston, my strange inheritance stowed beneath the clothes in my suitcase.

Once back at my small apartment in Allston, I settled into my old routine and did not look at the book again, still bundled in musty black wool inside my unopened suitcase, which I had shoved to the back of a closet upon my return from Richmond. The peak of the colorful foliage had passed, and the streets became filled with piles of dead leaves as autumn wore on. I worked as a glassblower's assistant then, and after trudging through miles of chilly wind wrapped in an overcoat and scarf, it was a relief to stoop before the hot furnace, heating bars of colored glass so that they drooped on the end of a puntil like melting honey. Then the day came to an end, and I made my weary way back to my apartment building in the darkness of premature night. It was not until weeks later that I received the letter.

It was a night like any other November night in New England: cold, star-speckled, and with a light sprinkling of snow of the ground. I came home from my job with sore limbs and an empty belly. The letter presented itself to me the moment I opened the mailbox. The pale blue envelope stood apart from the usual dreary concoction of bills and circular advertisements. Ignoring everything else, I snatched this prize from the box at once and beheld it with wonder. My name and address were writ large on the front in black ink with a curving, archaic hand.

There was no return address, and the postmark was smudged, though I could make out the letters N.C., no doubt the state from which this missive had originated. From whom could it be? I knew no one in North Carolina, though the place struck a chord with me, for I had run across this locality more than once in my genealogical research. I galloped up the stairs to my apartment and, bolting the door behind me, zealously tore open the envelope.

*My dear cousin,*

*First, let me express my heartfelt condolences at the death of your grandmother. I do not take the passing of any family member lightly. There are precious few of us left. I feel it is time for me to introduce myself. My name is Albritton Drake. We share an ancestor in common, and I think we may have other things in common as well. I would be honored if you would consent to be a guest at my house. There is much we should discuss. Take the first train to Fiddle Creak, North Carolina, tomorrow and I will have my driver meet you at the station. Bring the book.*

*Yrs most sincerely,*
*Albritton*

I read the brief letter again and again, entranced by the sloping calligraphy, the texture of the cream-colored paper, the way the pitch-black ink was absorbed by the fibers of the dry, thirsty parchment. It was a letter from a living, breathing Drake! My disappointment at learning that I was not Sir Francis's heir was mitigated by this invitation to meet a bona fide Drake in the flesh.

But my mind was filled with questions. How did my cousin know where I lived? Why had I never heard about him before? And most mysterious, how did he know about the book I had found in my grandmother's attic? The book. It still lay in my unopened suitcase at the back of the closet. It was waiting for me, calling me. I knew that it was time for me to open it again, that I could dally no longer. There was an urgent quality to my cousin's letter. I drew back my curtains to look at the moon rising over the gambrel roof of the house across the street. It was nearly full, as it had been the night when I had found the book in my grandmother's attic.

My cat Phaedra nuzzled my legs and meowed expectantly. Reflexively, I stooped down to scratch her chin and stroke her long gray fur. I set the letter down on my writing desk and crossed over into the kitchen to fetch a tin of tuna fish from the pantry, open it, and dole out its contents into Phaedra's bowl. Yes, first things first, I thought. I did not know how long my visit would last, and I had to provide for Phaedra's welfare while I was away. Leaving the cat to savor her long-awaited supper, I took the spare key off of its peg, stepped out the door, and climbed the stairs to the apartment above mine.

Hesitating, I rapped three times in quick succession, followed by two more knocks—our secret code so that she would know it was I. I heard her familiar voice, made husky from smoking too many cigarettes.

"Just a minute."

I waited, and a few moments later the door opened and there was Samantha, wearing her usual paint-spattered smock. Samantha was a graduate student at the Museum School, and over her shoulder I saw one of her pieces, an unfinished portrait of me seated on a wooden throne. A giant's hand reached down into the perspective of the painting. The hand was poised to pick me up, throne and all, like a chess piece.

"Hi, Hens," she said, calling me by her own personal diminutive of my name. "Do you want to come in? I was just making tea." There was a familiar awkward pause.

"I'm sorry; I can't," I found myself saying, though some part of me yearned not to, the part that clung to life and love and hope. With a tremendous effort, I quashed that part of myself and shoved it back into the innermost recesses of my heart. "I have to pack for a trip. A cousin of mine has invited me to visit him at his house in North Carolina. I'm leaving tomorrow morning."

It was an absurd thing to say. Why couldn't I come in for tea? Would I need to pack all night? But I said it nonetheless. An ironic smile played across Samantha's lips. She held out her palm to accept the key she knew I was about to place there.

"I suppose you want me to look after Phaedra while you're gone?" she said.

"If you wouldn't mind," I answered, not meeting her gaze. I took the spare key out of my pocket and dropped it into her outstretched palm. Her hand closed around it.

"You know I love that kitty."

"Thank you," I said softly, almost in a whisper. "Well, I guess I'd better go." There was a pause.

"Of course," she said. I turned to head back to my apartment. There was another pause, and this one seemed to stretch on for an eternity, though it could only have been a few seconds. I thought Samantha was going to say something, and the part of me locked in my innermost heart desperately hoped that she would. But she did not.

"Have a safe journey," was all she said, and the door closed with a click. I shambled back downstairs to my apartment where Phaedra was waiting, curled up in a chair and purring contentedly now that her hunger was sated. It was time to open the book.

I bolted the door and turned off the lamps. Drawing back the curtains to allow the moonlight to stream into the room, I found a book of matches in my desk drawer and lit a half burned-down candle set in a dusty brass candlestick. I cannot say what drove me to such a ritual, only that I felt uncanny primordial urges, just as I had in my grandmother's attic a month before. Lilith had begun her dance.

Opening the closet door, I dragged out the suitcase. I undid the latches and opened the suitcase's lid. The musty smell of a million attics engulfed the apartment, and Phaedra rose from her slumber. The cat stretched her back and eyed my movements curiously. In the moonlight, her eyes shone an eerie emerald green.

The bundle of black wool lay at the bottom of the suitcase, and I placed it upon my writing desk. Phaedra arched her back and flattened her ears. Something about the bundle of wool tensed the cat, but she trusted me and did not hiss or run away. Though not properly full, the moon exerted a considerable influence over the night. Lilith was dancing faster now. I unwound the black wool until the book was revealed, black and leathern, and I placed it lovingly upon my writing desk. The book. It was time.

Lifting the heavy binding of the book, I removed the genealogical chart that was tucked inside and unfolded it once again. I traced my finger down the lines of descent from Sir Francis's brother Thomas — down the generations, across the Atlantic into the colonial wilds of Virginia, and then North Carolina. Albritton Drake. He was the true heir. There were no dates associated with his name, but judging by his place on the chart in relation to the other names, he should have been a contemporary of those who lived and died in the eighteenth century. Surely not, I thought. The original Albritton Drake must have had heirs who were also named Albritton. It was a common enough practice in old families. I would have to ask my cousin more about his particular branch of the family when I met him.

I carefully refolded the chart, obeying the creases that had been imprinted onto the paper generations ago, and set it aside. Steeling the last remnants of my nerve, I peeled aside the flyleaf and beheld the frontispiece, which portrayed the profile of a wyvern — the ancient arms of the Drakes. The wyvern was depicted in loving detail, each individual talon on its feet sharply delineated, each scale on its knotted, barb-ended tail etched with miniscule perfection. No, the wyvern's inky pupil did

not just dilate. Its eye was not watching me with sardonic interest, threatening to swallow my very soul into its infinite abyss.

I forced my eyes away from the wyvern and moved them down the page to read the pompous black-letter printing, stamped by a press that long ago must have become worm-rotted timber in some Jacobean knacker's yard.

Yᵉ *BOOKE OF MOONES*

Printed by John Dee at yᵉ
behestt of Sir Frauncis Drake
London
1583

My mind reeled at the implications of this new knowledge. I had heard of John Dee, the magus and sometime court astrologer to Queen Elizabeth. Once revealed, the connection was obvious. Sir Francis Drake was a favorite of the Queen and a prominent figure amongst the glittering array of personages that had made up her court. The two men had surely crossed paths. And if Drake had been interested in magic, whom else would he consult?

I thought again of the legends that hinted at Sir Francis Drake's dealings with the devil, and with a shudder quickly banished such notions from my mind. These were the gossipy tales of the ignorant peasantry of Devon, who also spoke of piskies and the headless hounds that haunted the trackless wastes of Dartmoor. I would give these dim murmurings no weight. And yet it was with hackles raised, with a freezing, unknowable fear that I turned the page and read on.

At that moment there was a gust of wind outside and the flimsy latch on my window gave way, causing the window to spring open and admit a frenetic burst of cold air, which billowed my curtains, extinguished my candle, and caused the pages of the book to flap madly like the wings of bats. I hurried to fasten the window again, inserting a flat strip of wood beneath the latch to secure it, cursing myself for not thinking to do it before. I did not need to relight the candle, however, for the moon's brilliant glow was more than adequate for me to read what was printed on the page. Did the wind open the book to this page by chance, or was something more than chance involved? Was this somehow a part of the dance of Lilith?

In the midst of a swirling sea of Latin, Greek, and Hebrew letters, I came upon a solid body of English, archaic in style, but easily understood. My lips began to move of their own accord. I read the words aloud—in a whisper at first, then louder and louder, until my

ravings became as a wolf howling at the moon:

*"Blacke Shepheard! Blacke Shepheard of yᵉ Wood! Heare mee, thy humble servant, crawlynge vpon yᵉ duste to know but a tayste of thy Infinite Pow'r. I ynvoke thee, Father of Darkeness, to fill what cannot be fill'd, to revoke yᵉ yrrevocable, to brynge Life where once was Death. I have caste yᵉ sigills and scatter'd yᵉ powder'd bones. I have consecrated yᵉ Vessell of Kyndred Blood. I svmmon yᵉ departed back across yᵉ Yawninge Gulph Beyonde yᵉ Gate where yᵉ Sentinell stands. I command hym who holds yᵉ Key to openne the Gate. In yᵉ Name of yᵉ Shepheard, openne yᵉ Gate! Blacke Shepheard! Blacke Shepheard of yᵉ Wood!"*

## II.

I departed before dawn. The day broke brisk and bright over Boston as I dragged my battered old suitcase behind me and made my way to Union Square through a flurry of snow. The events of the night before swirled around my head like some half-remembered dream, and yet I knew they were real. *Blacke Shepheard! Blacke Shepheard of yᵉ Wood!* The name was seared into my consciousness like a brand on the hide of a glassy-eyed cow.

The invocation to which the pages of *Yᵉ Booke of Moones* had inevitably opened, and which I was impelled against my will to read aloud, served some malevolent purpose. Yet that purpose was obscure to me. The only thing that registered clearly in my memory was the sound of the scurrying of the rats in my walls after I had read the incantation aloud.

I boarded a streetcar amidst a trickle of bleary-eyed passengers. The ride passed in a blur—Harvard Street to Beacon Street to Massachusetts Avenue to Boylston Street. I disembarked at Park Square and stumbled the rest of the way on foot with my burdensome suitcase in tow, until I arrived at my destination, South Station.

The usually bustling train station was nearly deserted at this hour, and I approached the ticket counter without having to negotiate the usual queue of impatient travelers. At first the clerk was thwarted when he consulted his accustomed station guide for my destination. It was only after resorting to a little-used blue directory that he was able to determine that there was such a place as Fiddle Creak, North Carolina. Muttering ungraciously, he issued me a ticket for a train due to depart in less than five minutes. I ran to the appropriate berth and managed to scramble onto the train seconds before it pulled out of the station. Bells clanged and whistles blared. I flopped into an empty seat and watched as Boston flashed before my eyes and gave way to the sparser suburbs to the south. Fortunately, the uniformed train conductor arrived promptly to punch my ticket, so I could drift off into a deep slumber, troubled by dreams of a moor. . . .

The moor stretched on endlessly, both in space and time, and at its heart was a circle of standing stones. Somehow I knew that I was in Britain, though I had never been there before. Was this an ancestral memory of Devon, or Cornwall perhaps? As I walked toward the stone circle, I passed by a herd of sheep grazing as sheep had grazed there for thousands of years, and would graze here for thousands of years to come. One of the sheep was unlike the others. It was a black sheep, a ram with a crumpled horn, and he gazed at me with ebon eyes, a gaze that pierced me to the soul. We were brethren, he and I; the black sheep and I recognized each other. No, it was not it a sheep. It was a barefooted shepherd, clutching a curling crosier, his face shrouded beneath the cowl of a monk's habit. I passed by him hurriedly and stumbled toward the stones.

There were two men waiting for me. One I had seen before in portraits. He was garbed in a tight-fitting black velvet doublet, hose, and a ruffled collar as wide as a platter, in the style of the Elizabethans. It was none other than my famous ancestor, Sir Francis Drake. He gazed at me with avuncular kindness and, it seemed, a hint of sadness, as one might feel for a sacrificial goat. The other was wearing the garments of the eighteenth century: brown frockcoat, tricorne hat, breeches, and buckled shoes. He held a formidable black tome under his arm. I recognized it to be $Y^e$ Booke of Moones. He exchanged glances with Sir Francis, who nodded, and said with a sonorous voice like rolling thunder . . .

"Fiddle Creeeeek!"

I was jerked awake from my slumber. After traveling by train for a day and a half, I continued to have the same dream every time I closed my eyes. I peered out my window upon a lush landscape of well-plowed pastures and green-leafed trees, so unlike the snowy cityscape I had started from. I could almost imagine that it was spring again as I disembarked from the train, giddy with the scent of magnolia blossoms. I stood entranced at the sight of the Spanish moss swaying from the branches of ancient oak trees until my torpor was broken by the sound of a honking horn. A young moppet of a man with straw-colored hair hopped out of a brand-new Model A and hoisted my suitcase with enviable ease.

"Howdy do," he said in a lazy Southern drawl. "Jack's the name. Mr. Drake sent me to pick you up."

I extended my hand, which Jack took into his and shook vigourously. He deposited my suitcase and its coveted contents into he boot of the still-idling Model A. Then he opened the passenger door for me like a chauffeur. Nodding my thanks, I placed my foot onto the running board and wearily hoisted myself into the leather-padded seat, which conformed itself comfortably to the contours of my body. Jack closed the door and hurried around to the driver's side to take his place behind the wheel.

"Hold tight now," he said, and winked at me as he put the automobile in gear. Despite its rumbling and groaning, the roadster navigated the bumpy dirt road with surprising smoothness. I inspected my driver with a curious eye. Jack wore a battered felt hat with a feather tucked jauntily into the ribbon. Tattered blue overalls covered a threadbare collarless shirt from which most of the buttons were missing. The only thing new about Jack's outfit was a pair of shiny black oxfords, one of which was busily operating the Model A's clutch. Jack caught me admiring his footwear out of the corner of his eye and laughed. I averted my gaze guiltily.

"Nice shoes for a country boy, huh? Mr. Drake gave 'em to me in boot for some odd jobs I do for him. I reckon they come out of his own closet. Fit me like a glove, though. Now don't that beat all?"

I could only dumbly nod my agreement, too fatigued to muster the energy to make small talk. Instead I looked out the window and admired the scenery. There was something fairytale-like about this countryside into which I was entering deeper and deeper, leaving behind sanity and the world I knew. The words from the book echoed in my head, as I drifted off into haunted slumbers once again. *Blacke Shepheard! Blacke Shepheard of y$^e$ Wood!* I was awoken from my nap by Jack's cheerful drawl.

"Here we are. Buckland Manor."

I opened my eyes and found that we were parked in front of a sprawling mansion of red brick walls and steep white gables, a relic of the vanished glories of the Southern planters. Judging from the grandeur of this estate, the scions of my cousin's branch of the family were obviously folk of wealth and prominence. They were aware of their descent from Sir Francis Drake, for the house had been named after the admiral's own manor house in Devon, Buckland Abbey. I wondered why these Drakes were not mentioned in the official histories of Sir Francis Drake's family. Jack came around to open the door for me, and I stepped out onto the gravel, which crunched beneath my feet.

There was a man standing in the doorway of the house. This could be none other than my cousin, Albritton Drake. He regarded me with a strange smile and gave a little formal wave, which I awkwardly returned. My cousin was wearing a tailored tweed suit of contemporary cut. But although his attire was not as archaic as it had been in my dream, he was unmistakably the same man I had seen standing in the circle of stones with Sir Francis Drake. Jack hauled my suitcase out of the boot of the Model A.

"I'll jes' take this on up to the guest room for ye," he said. "Then I'd best get on home. Ma'll be expectin' me to do a couple of chores afore supper." Before I could thank him, the genial young man carried my suitcase across the lawn and, tipping his hat to his employer, disappeared into the front door of the house. Albritton Drake extended his right hand, a gesture I returned, and our hands clasped in a firm embrace.

"Welcome, cousin," he said, in a grave, masculine voice appropriate to his age, which I judged to be about fifty. "You must be tired after your long journey. Why don't you go up to your room and refresh yourself? Dinner will be served in an hour and we can talk then. I've no doubt you have many questions you want to ask me."

"Thanks," I managed to reply. "That sounds swell."

My words were not eloquent, but they were all my overtaxed brain could come up with. Entering the front door, I was overwhelmed by the opulence of my cousin's house. A crystal chandelier hung from the ceiling, and as I climbed the marble staircase I passed by a row of portraits of nobleman dressed in the garments of the seventeenth and eighteenth centuries. These must be members of the Drake family, I ascertained. They peered out from the oil with piercing, haughty eyes as a dull and disheveled offshoot of their line shuffled past their vanished splendor. I was the poor relation.

The door to my room was open. I shut it and, fully clothed, flopped wearily on top of the neatly made bed. I longed to have a proper night's sleep before meeting with my cousin. But I could only drowse for half an hour before necessity forced me to rise and attend to the trivialities of my toilet, which were performed with the aid of a pitcher of water and a washbasin. I donned the same black suit I had worn to my grandmother's funeral and descended the staircase to dine with my cousin. The suit was somewhat wrinkled now from lying in a suitcase for a month, but it was my best.

Albritton met me in the foyer and escorted me to the dining room, which was already set with a variety of regional delicacies: roast pork, sweet potatoes, black-eyed peas, and collard greens. My cousin seemed intent on putting on a show of Southern hospitality. He was obviously proud of the land his branch of the family had adopted as its home. We were attended to by a sad, rat-faced footman

wearing tails and white tie, though my cousin was still sporting the same tweed suit he had worn earlier, probably in deference to my own lack of evening wear. His graciousness was impeccable. Once we were seated and glasses of Burgundy wine were in hand, my cousin started to make conversation.

"Let me offer you my sincerest condolences on the passing of your grandmother," he said. "The loss of any member of our family is of course a great tragedy to me. I regret I was not able to attend her funeral, though I was given news of it by our mutual cousin Whitlock. His family is only related to the Drakes by marriage, of course. But our houses have been allied for many generations."

"I'm very interested in the history of our family," I said. "There are some gaps in my research. I was hoping you might be able to fill them in. From what I understand you are the closest successor to Sir Francis Drake himself."

Albritton arched an eyebrow, perhaps surprised that I had come to the point so quickly.

"Indeed," he replied. "Sir Francis Drake's nephew, also named Francis Drake, inherited the estate, for the admiral had no children himself. In recognition of the wealth and prestige that come of being the heir to such a famous man, James I created Sir Francis's nephew the Baronet of Buckland Monachorum, an hereditary title. He was the first baronet, and he had a line of successors until the fifth baronet died in 1794. It was assumed in England that the fifth baronet was the last of the line, and the title considered extinct. However, there was another line not accounted for. The youngest son of the first baronet had a grandson who emigrated from England to America before the Revolutionary War. He was our mutual ancestor. When the last English baronet died, the title rightly passed to me, for I am the oldest of the direct male line. I am the sixth Baronet of Buckland Monachroum."

I paused in mid-chew of a mouthful of greens and was forced to wash it down with a swallow of Burgundy. I noticed that my host had not touched his own food.

"The *sixth* baronet? You mean your ancestor was the sixth baronet, don't you? I thought you said the fifth baronet died in 1794."

My cousin fixed me with his disconcertingly pale blue eyes, and I shivered. There was something very old in those eyes, something cruel and not of this world.

"There are many things you should know—the first of which is that you are not in fact my cousin. You are my nephew. My great-great-great-nephew."

My fork clattered to my plate. I at once lost all appetite for eating, delectable as the meal was. Somehow sensing this fact, the black-and-white-garbed footman removed my plate. I seized the glass of Burgundy and took a healthy gulp.

"But that would make you . . ."

"One hundred and seventy-five years old, yes. I am not accustomed to being so forthcoming with such information, but the circumstances force me to accelerate my disclosure. The blood moon is tonight. I trust you have brought $Y^e$ *Booke of Moones*?"

Dumbly, I nodded an affirmation. My cousin's—no, not my cousin—my great-great-great-uncle's manner became brisk and businesslike.

"It is well. I think we are finished with the formalities of dinner. Would you be so kind as to fetch it for me? I will meet you in the library and we will continue our discussion there."

The library of Buckland Manor was every bit as impressive as I would have imagined. I felt like an initiate to some society of Gnostic mysteries as I crept into the sepulchral chamber, the echoes of my footsteps disturbing the silence of the hushed cloister. Stacks of books ascended to the vaulted ceiling. Some of the books were so old and arcane they looked as if they would crumble to dust at the slightest touch. Albritton was waiting for me there, looking impatient and feral as his eyes fixed greedily on the bundle of black wool, which I clasped to my chest. My relative appeared older than he had before, gaunter and paler. It was as if his human appearance were only a glamor, an illusion that was rapidly fading as its usefulness became outlived.

"The book," he rasped, in a much higher-pitched voice than the one he had been using earlier. "Is that the book?"

"Yes," I answered nervously, becoming more aware now that surrendering the book to his possession may not be the wisest of courses. "I have it."

"My younger brother Benjamin uncovered our family's secret work—what we have been plotting for so many generations and unable to accomplish. He stole $Y^e$ *Booke of Moones* from out of the library and claimed to have burned it. I would have killed him with my own hands, brother or no. But Father loved him better than me and would not punish him. Father was a fool! For a century, I have

kept myself alive by sorcery, feeding on the life-blood of animals, and the occasional infant when need be, and traveled the world in search of certain grimoires, trying to retrieve the knowledge that was lost to us. I found fragments, tantalizing scraps in *Olde Solomon's Booke* and *The Secret of Secrets*. But the key was missing—the invocation of the Black Shepherd. Then I discovered that my dear brother had lied! He had not burned the book at all. He had only hidden it. The book had been passed down through the generations of his descendants, and now it has come to you, dear nephew. But the book does not belong to your branch of the family, which does not even bear the ancient name. It is mine. You will return it to me. Now."

Against my will, my feet propelled me toward my mad uncle. Though I resisted with every atom of effort I could summon, Albritton's wizardry was too powerful. He snatched the bundle from my grasp and cackled with delight. The last vestige of humanity had deserted him now, and I beheld Albritton Drake for what he was—a gibbering, one-hundred-and-seventy-five-year-old ghoul.

"Now Benjamin," he crowed in a high-pitched whine, a voice that was more demon than human, "your descendant will pay the price for your trespass against our family's work. The admiral will walk the earth again in this new vessel of flesh that I have procured for him, for only one of our own blood is worthy enough for his spirit to inhabit. The Drakes will be mighty, as we were in the old times. *Silvae Pastor Atratus!*"

There was a click, and one of the bookshelves swung open to reveal a secret passageway behind it. Whatever mechanism operated the assembly had been triggered by the phrase he had just spoken. My body was still not under my own control, and I followed helplessly in Albritton's wake into the unutterable darkness, which swallowed me like a hungry maw.

We descended a flight of stairs that led to a mazy catacomb beneath the house. A musk of death lingered in the catacomb, a whiff of slavery and cruel secrets, of a family tree gnawed at the roots by its evil doings as Nidhogg gnaws at the roots of Yggdrassil. The darkness was nearly total, but Albritton traversed the catacomb with the eyes of a ghoul and the surety of seventeen decades of familiarity. I followed a few feet behind him, my every movement aping his, for my body was in his thrall.

After what seemed an eternity, the catacomb came to an end. We had walked what I estimated to be a half a mile when we came to a flight of steps carved from living rock, ascending to an aperture into the night air. I found myself in a clearing in the forest, surrounded on all sides by poplar trees. At the sky's zenith, where there should have been a full moon was only a dull red orb. The blood moon. The only light came from the stars, which shone as pinpricks in the cold, late November sky. After so long in the darkness of the catacomb, my eyesight was acute, and I was astounded to see a circle of standing stones arranged in the center of the clearing—the same stones I had seen in my dream. I saw Albritton as well, and his appearance was more ghoulish now than ever. His eyes were sunken into their sockets, and his flesh was stretched tightly over his bones. My relative resembled nothing more than an animated corpse. And yet, he was full of energy, hopping from foot to foot like an imp.

"I removed these stones from Cornwall and smuggled them to North Carolina for the ritual. According to the admiral's letters, Dr. Dee had insisted that these stones must be used and no others."

I wanted to cry out for him to stop, but I could not even command my own vocal cords. Not that Albritton would have paid any heed. He was far too absorbed in his work. Unwinding the black wool from around the book, he placed the terrible heirloom atop the flat stone in the center of the circle. The altar. Albritton—if it truly were Albritton Drake, not merely the vehicle for some alien entity—slowly, reverently began to open the book's cover. At that moment, a voice rang out in the darkness.

"Howdy do!"

Albritton's concentration was abruptly shattered by this unexpected exclamation, and his spell over me was broken. I was able to wrest free from his mental clutches at last and turned my head to see a straw-haired man wearing a battered felt hat standing on the edge of the clearing. It was Jack. He waved at us and flapped his elbows like a chicken's wings.

"Cock-a-doodle-do!"

Albritton Drake emitted a shrill piercing shriek, and then ran toward Jack with what could only have been the intention of rending him limb from limb with his bare hands. But the maddened ghoul never reached his grinning tormentor. The ground collapsed beneath Albritton's feet, and he fell into a deep pit, which had been concealed by sticks and grass. It took me a moment to realize that Jack must have dug the pit earlier as a trap. And that was not the only preparation he had made. Hefting a sizable pickaxe, which until then had been hidden in the scrub, Jack nimbly leapt across to the lip of the pit before the spry ghoul could scramble out.

"Tantivy!" cried Jack as he brought the tip of the pickaxe crashing down onto the ghoul's head. Albritton Drake was no more. $Y^e$ *Booke of Moones* lay open on the altar stone, its pages flapping wildly in the breeze, as if the book itself were angry at having its intentions

thwarted. With all my strength, I forced the cover of the book shut and rewrapped it in the swath of black wool. Jack clapped me on the back.

"I reckon you're Mr. Drake now," he said. I paused a moment to consider. Of course he was right. Now that Albritton was dead at last, I was the heir to the Drakes. I knelt down at the edge of the hole and examined the twisted remains of the ghoul who had been my great-great-great-uncle. The façade of flesh was withering like old leaves and in a matter of seconds; there was nothing left but a skeleton wearing a tweed suit. On the finger of the skeleton's hand was a gold ring. I slipped the ring off the skeleton's finger and held it in my palm. It was a signet ring, engraved with the coat of arms of the Drakes—my birthright. Was this the talisman that had given Albritton the power to manipulate my actions? Given him life when there should only have been death? I dropped the ring into the hole with Albritton's bones.

"We should bury him," I said. "And then we should set fire to the book. I think it's for the best."

"I reckon so," Jack smiled. "I reckon so."

The next morning Jack drove me back to the train station in the Model A, which I had given to him for his services. Buckland Manor was mine now, and I would have to think long and hard as to what I should do with my haunted legacy. As we drove away, I cast my eyes back at the horrible manse, with its centuries of secrets tucked away beneath the steeply sloping gables. I had not been able to find a trace of the rat-faced servant who had served me dinner the night before. I wondered if he had been but a phantom, or a ghoul like his master. I must admit I had not tried very hard to look for him.

The book proved impossible to burn until we unwrapped the black wool in which it was swaddled, and then flickering red flames shot up from the leather binding like the very fires of Hell itself. I thought I could hear Sir Francis Drake's shade roaring with rage as the pages crackled, a wolf howling across the Yawning Gulph Beyond the Gate, and then all was silent. Only ashes remained. Jack asked me if he could keep the wool. He thought it would make a fine shawl for his mother. I gave it to him as a trophy. After all, he had killed the tiger. It was only right that he should have its skin. Jack waved to me from his shiny new roadster as I boarded the train.

"Y'all come back now, here? You're welcome in Fiddle Creak anytime. I'll drive you anywhere you've a mind to go!"

I may return to Fiddle Creak one day. But for now, I settled back in my seat as the train pulled out of the station and rocked me gently to sleep. No more did I dream of stone circles and ancient gods. This time I dreamt of Samantha.

*Mr. Stephen Grendon in his Twenties*
*(Image by Steve Sorrentino)*

*What was famous Wisconsin author August Derleth up to when he breathed life beyond the printed page into one of his most famous literary characters? Was he harboring secret motives, or did he mean it only as a hoax? Indeed, a mystery there is, one that might never be solved, but here at last for the first time are the facts comprising . . .*

# The Weird Literary Life and Times of Stephen Grendon

## By John D. Haefele

In the novels *Evening in Spring* and *The Shield of the Valiant* and four volumes of short stories, August Derleth conveys to readers the "life" of Stephen Grendon:

> In *Place of Hawks* [1935] Steve is a small child, and readers share his memories and associations and observations as he travels around with his grandfather; in *Country Growth* [1940] Steve is an older child, growing into adolescence and further learning the region in which he lives; in *Sac Prairie People* [1948] and in *Wisconsin in Their Bones* [1961] Steve struggles through further love experiences from high school days into adulthood. (Schroth 35)

All these comprise the semi-autobiographical components of Derleth's encompassing Sac Prairie Saga, in which Grendon is the well-known literary *alter ego* of Derleth himself. What is little known is that Derleth documented other events unrelated to the Saga about Grendon's "life," in Arkham House publishing ephemerae, in blurbs accompanying anthology appearances bylined "Grendon," in the collection *Mr. George and Other Odd Persons,* and in two elusive *Capital Times* (Madison, WI) book reviews. These add up to a clever deception that would have confused, but also "connected" across different genres, Derleth's many readers involving a fictional character who not only serves to communicate real events, but for a while "exists" in the real world, as author, editor, and critic of weird fiction and science fiction.

Derleth's earliest versions of the vignettes that make up *Evening in Spring* include references to popular and pulp fiction writers he appreciated as a young man—for example, to his mentor H. P. Lovecraft asides to "Hastur" and "Randolph Carter" (*Essential Solitude* 259 & 337). But these were discarded from the settled version we have today, which Derleth maintained "sprang full-bodied from heart and head, having

been written in twenty days early in 1941, the same year of its initial publication by Scribner's" (viii). Indeed, there remained only these hints: "While I [Stephen Grendon] was [. . .] trying to decide between *Sherlock Holmes* and *Tom Sawyer,* I heard the front doorbell ring. I put *Sherlock Holmes* into my pocket and tiptoed downstairs, meaning to get out of the house unseen if it were some one for me" (56); "In the morning Grandfather Adams came over to where I was sitting in the summer kitchen arranging my funny papers by date and paper, putting all those Aunt Bertha had sent down from Minneapolis on an especial pile, since they had Dwig's *Tom Sawyer* in them in addition to *The Katzenjammer Kids* and *Hawkshaw the Detective"* (254).

Grendon returns as a character in *The Shield of the Valiant,* which Derleth completed during 1943 and 1944. The year after its publication, in a new foreword for a reissue of *Evening in Spring,* Derleth explained: "If I indict a brief for *The Shield of the Valiant,* it is perhaps because this novel is actually in a very real sense a continuation of *Evening in Spring"* ([vii]). At the same time, Derleth begins to address Stephen Grendon *outside* the pages of the Saga, as if to a real person separate from himself; it was a charade he would perpetuate for almost two decades. Not until recounting the origins of the stories purportedly written by Grendon and later collected in *Mr. George and Other Odd Persons* (Arkham House, 1963) does he admit the hoax. There he says:

> The tales in this book were written all in one month twenty years ago specifically to swell the log of *Weird Tales.*[1] Since that estimable and lamented magazine already had enough stories by August Derleth in its files, the byline of Stephen Grendon was used—which was not really a foolproof disguise for there were among the readers of *Weird Tales* some few who were familiar with my autobiographical novel, *Evening in Spring,* first published in 1941, and recognized the name of the narrator in that novel as the author of the stories by Stephen Grendon. (vii)

If we accept the admonition that begins *The Shield of the Valiant*— "Though certain events and characters in this book may suggest facts

---

1        If Derleth is referring to the year 1943, at least one story ("A Gentleman from Prague") in the collection was not written until the following year: "On each of the last 5 nights I have done something I haven't done since I was a student at U. of Wisconsin 15 years ago—that is, written a new short weird tale every night. / I don't know when or where they'll appear, but their titles for your future reference, are as follows [. . .] 'A Gentleman from Prague' (Derleth to Rah Hoffman, 8 Feb. 1944). But "The Ghost Walk," also bylined Grendon (*Weird Tales,* Nov. 1947) is not in the collection, so perhaps these two stories offset in Derleth's mind. Grendon's "Open, Sesame!" and "The Song of the Pewee," having science fiction themes (and for that reason they are not in the *Mr. George* collection), were most likely written when they first appeared in the *Arkham Sampler* (1948–49).

and persons of recent history, the author has not portrayed here any person who now lives or has lived. / The characters and incidents of this narrative, as here presented, are fictitious" (facing [1]) — we are forced to admit that Derleth walked a perilously thin line. Consider, for example, Grendon's relationship with a certain "H.P.L.":

> Steve kept up a large correspondence with people all over the United States and in England; among them was a recluse in Providence, Rhode Island, who wrote weird and *outré* fiction, and who had for a decade written a letter a week to Steve, filled with all kinds of fascinating lore and information, a semi-invalid whose vast store of knowledge had helped to shape Steve's own writing. Like Steve, he too kept up a wide correspondence, and, though many of his correspondents had never met him, "H.P.L.," as he signed himself, had a singular reality. (64–65)

Who would not recognize this as a description of Derleth's actual relationship with Lovecraft? Further, it seems possible Derleth might have put it down this way for more than one reason. Far-fetched it may be, but by using "H.P.L." — initials only — Derleth would bring to mind among readers (in ensuing years) his 1945 biographical sketch of Lovecraft: *H.P.L.: A Memoir*. More importantly, Derleth may have been providing a foundation for Grendon's association with the weird tale tradition, the beginnings of establishing his quasi-reality, for reasons still fuzzy even to him.

And just as it happened in real life, we learn that Grendon's "reclusive H.P.L." "died quite suddenly and unexpectedly in his middle forties" (257–58). Grendon's reaction portrayed by Derleth is likewise autobiographical:

> On this May night he was engaged in the melancholy task of examining the great number of letters H.P.L. had written to him, all in his fine, spidery script, and he paused from time to time to turn over phrases here and there. [. . .] Tonight, weighed down by the unalterable fact of H.P.L.'s death, he sought refuge in nature and the night" (257–58)

In the middle 1940s, Derleth was writing and selling fiction "by Derleth" to *Weird Tales* and by establishing a pseudonym he could sell even more. And yet it is difficult to accept 'too many by Derleth in the offices of *Weird Tales*' as the *only* reason for Grendon stories, and there remains unanswered the question of why Derleth recycled the Grendon name. When the opportunity presented itself, perhaps Derleth was weighing the advantages of establishing a new *authority* for the field of fantasy

(though not a separate *identity*, since Derleth would have Grendon perform similar duty in the real world). Or perhaps he recognized a different aspect of the situation—the opportunity to pull a literary hoax. At any rate, not only does the non-existent Stephen Grendon enter the real world without disclosure that he is only the pseudonym of a writer, but Derleth includes a Grendon story in the celebrated *Sleep No More* anthology he is assembling in 1944, wherein a careful introduction is made:

> **Stephen Grendon** (1909–) is a comparatively new name in writing. He made his first appearance in print in 1941, and *A Gentleman from Prague* represents his initial publication in *Weird Tales*. The owner of one of the finest libraries of macabre fiction in the Midwest, Mr. Grendon is the author of two forthcoming novels—*The Lock and the Key,* and *The Saint and the Devil*. ([327])

Derleth knew exactly how readers would interpret these words, how they would misconstrue these literal truths. It is *fact* that "Grendon" was a new *name* in fiction; it was not a Grendon *story* as one might think, but Grendon *himself* who made a first appearance in 1941, in the aforementioned *Evening in Spring*; the story in *Weird Tales* was not Grendon's *initial* appearance there, but his first *anywhere*. The one clue Derleth does provide about Grendon's true identity is similarly spot-on, for Derleth himself was born in 1909. A telling remark showing how determined Derleth was at this time to establish the Grendon identity turns up in private correspondence:

> I myself am just now finishing *The Shield of the Valiant,* which will come to about 225,000 words in this final draft. I hope I won't have to rework it, though at that, it won't be too much of a job, just time-taking, for I have yet to finish *The Lock and the Key* later this month and in May. (Derleth to Rah Hoffman, 11 Apr. 1944)

With this we know not only that Derleth planned to write at least one of the Grendon-novels mentioned in *Sleep No More,* but that it was underway ("I have yet to *finish*. . . ").[2] And still, in *Who Knocks?* (1945), Derleth is compelled to drop fresh clues about Grendon's identity:

> **Stephen Grendon** (1909–), who first appeared in print

---

2     Derleth first proposed writing *The Lock and the Key* to E. P. Dutton & Co. in 1941, probably to help pay down the new mortgage he held on Place of Hawks, the home he had built. Using a *non de plume* would be necessary so as not to break existing contracts, but it does not explain why he chose and continued to use "Stephen Grendon" in the manner he did. A perusal of certain unpublished or incomplete literary works discovered posthumously at Derleth's residence may yet turn up one or both of these novels.

five years ago, will have his first book, *Mr. George and Other Odd People,* published soon by Arkham House. An anthology edited by him, *The Sleeping and the Dead: Thirty Uncanny Tales,* will appear late in 1946, and a novel, *The Lock and the Key,* will follow soon thereafter. Mr. Grendon lives in Wisconsin and looks on his writing very largely as an avocation. A naturalist and countryman, he is interested in Boy Scout activities and juvenile-delinquency control. His work in the genre of the supernatural has so far appeared only in the pages of *Weird Tales,* and sparingly, since he is not a prolific writer. ([55])

Anybody who knew anything about August Derleth should easily have identified the "countryman" and "naturalist" who regards literary work an "avocation." But Derleth complicates things with a bit of misdirection, saying Grendon (so unlike himself) is "not prolific." At this perceived stage of Grendon's career, Derleth's assessment could only have seemed truthful. Derleth expands Grendon's résumé, identifying him as the editor of a new anthology.

The next year Derleth adds another credential to Grendon's legacy, a lengthy review he ghost-writes for the *Capital Times* (10 Feb. 1946), portions of which address *The Best of Science Fiction,* issued by rival publisher Crown in 1946. Not surprisingly, Grendon's "The 'Scientific' Escape" opinions correlate closely with Derleth's own:[3]

The atomic age, with its thermonuclear bomb and the contacting of the moon by radar, came most opportunely for the vociferous proponents of a development of fantasy known as "science-fiction," which, says John W. Campbell, is not to be known as "pseudo-science." Not very long ago Donald Wollheim put out *Portable Novels of Science*—and a very good collection it was, too—and now two more books of science fiction and one of fantasy are available to those who like this particular kind of escape reading. [. . .] Mr. Conklin's 785-page anthology is the first such anthology of short science-fiction. It has a preface by John W. Campbell, Jr., editor of Astounding Science-Fiction, perhaps the best magazine of its type now appearing on the stands; the preface is restrained and, on the whole, intelligent. As much cannot, unfortunately, be said for Groff Conklin's introduction, which is neither restrained nor intelligent. Indeed, a careful reading of it indicates that Mr. Conklin's qualifications for the editorship of this or any other anthology are far from apparent. He can refer to

---

3    Derleth often reviewed science fiction books in his regular column, having established at the time of this review definite criteria regarding quality.

supernatural fiction, for instance, as a "less savory branch of fantasy," and write pompously about science-fiction on the level of an avid adolescent fan, without realizing that for every science-fiction writer who has written a distinguished work, there are a hundred in the field of the supernatural story. He is apparently unable to realize that for every "great name," as he puts it, in science-fiction, there are something like two hundred in the field of the supernatural, and that more than half his great names are also known—in many cases, far better known—for their work in the domain of the supernatural. [. . .] It would be a mistake, however, to turn to this collection of science-fiction stories and expect to find, as in a collection of supernatural fiction, distinguished writing. Distinguished writing in the average science-fiction story is purely an accident of parentage; most of the writers represented in this collection, apart from the well-known names, simply have no concept of a good writing style.

The reading public may expect more compilations like Mr. Conklin's, perhaps more intelligently introduced and edited. Mr. Conklin's introduction is primarily a defensive defiance, as any scientifically-minded reader could have told him; he might better have admitted at the outset that the stories in this book were not being presented as literary masterpieces, but purely as examples of today's "scientific" escape writing, and let it go as that. [30?]

The crew at *Weird Tales* knew what was up, but they committed a *faux pas* that did require Derleth to say something, only he responded carefully enough not to reveal the whole truth: "The new WT commits a grotesque error, as perhaps you noticed, announcing 'Mr. George' as by me, and inside by Grendon," wrote Derleth to Malcolm Ferguson (2 Jan. 194[7]).[4] Lacking the pertinent facts, Derleth knows Ferguson will leap to the seemingly obvious—but wrong—conclusion. Indeed, the charade may have been close to ending. Derleth begins his retreat in the *Arkham House / 1946 / Bulletin*: "The rise in production costs made it necessary for Rinehart & Company to ask that seven out of the projected thirty stories for *The Night Side: Masterpieces of the Strange and Terrible*, be deleted [. . .] Mr. August Derleth has taken over from Mr. Grendon the anthology, *The Sleeping and the Dead*. / This, too, had to be shortened, though it still contains thirty fine stories" (3–4). But later that year, in *The Night Side* (third in the Derleth trilogy), there is a new potted biography in which Grendon's career seems alive and well:

---

4    Or did Malcolm know? A year earlier Derleth had mentioned a Grendon "yarn" in a letter to Ferguson (1 Jan. 1946), but then on the 10th he is explaining, "Grendon looks a lot like me, but he's younger, of course; he'd have to be."

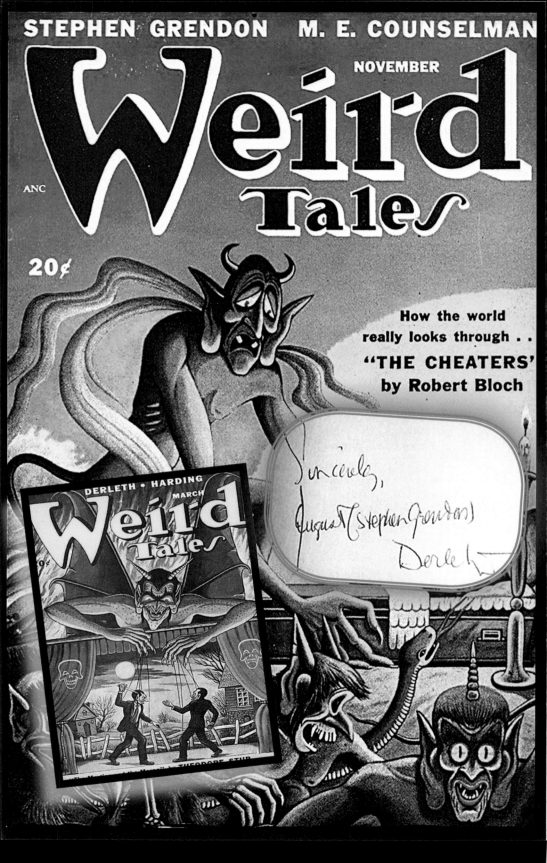

**Stephen Grendon** (1909–) has completed a first collection of his own fine stories, *Mr. George and Other Odd People,* which Arkham House will publish early next year. An anthology co-edited by him, *The Sleeping and the Dead: Thirty Uncanny Tales,* will appear this year. Mr. Grendon is a native of Wisconsin and it is in that State that he now lives and writes, though he considers writing primarily an avocation, and is not prolific, having appeared only in *Weird Tales, Crime Doctor Mystery Magazine,* and a few less-known magazines. His stories have a singular variety, and among new writers, while his work is traditional, he ranks high.

Mr. Grendon writes ghost stories for very much the same reason given by H. R. Wakefield, because he believes in psychic phenomena "not as manifestations of the supernatural, but as something which has a natural explanation science has so far not given us."

And apparently it was, for Stephen Grendon soon adds a new venue, selling a story to *Avon Fantasy Reader* for the June 1947 issue:

Unlike the other titles in this book, this marks the first appearance of 'Bishop's Gambit' anywhere. You would be right in thinking this an innovation; it is. We shall, from time to time, purchase first-run tales if they seem to fit with the pattern of the collection. It seemed to us that Stephen Grendon's ghost story rounded out the field for this number. Grendon, a protégé of August Derleth, has sold a number of stories in this genre the past few years, and a whole collection of his spooky fiction has been accepted for publication by Arkham House next year. (95)

But introducing *The Sleeping and the Dead: Thirty Uncanny Tales* (which also appeared in 1947), Derleth repeats: "Mr. Stephen Grendon began the selection of stories for this anthology, and I took over after the initial pieces were chosen. / To Mr. Grendon, therefore, must go some of the credit for the compilation of this anthology" (3). And in *Books from Arkham House 1947–48* we find: "Begun by Stephen Grendon [*The Sleeping and the Dead*] has been taken over by August Derleth and completed for publication October 27, 1947, by Pellegrini & Cudahy" (14).

Certainly Grendon's "arrangement" with Arkham House was assured. In the same stock list (referring to a slightly retitled *Mr. George and Other Odd Persons*) Derleth exclaims: "Among newer contributors to *Weird Tales* and similar magazines, Stephen Grendon has shown a marked variety in his work. / That variety is clearly demonstrated

in stories in this first collection" (13–14). Then, in the *Arkham House /
Bulletin / January / 1947* he adds: "Following the books already definitely
scheduled for publication, as soon as possible, Arkham House and/or
Mycroft & Moran will publish [. . .] *The Death Fetch and Other Gothic Tales,*
edited by Stephen Grendon." Nothing in Derleth's advertising material
intimates Grendon is anything but a real person. Nor is there so much
as a mention of Grendon in the "Work in Progress" or "To be Published"
sections of *August Derleth: Twenty-five Years of Writing 1926–1951,* his
auto-bibliographical booklet. But, masquerading as "John Haley,"
Derleth does mention anthologies and Grendon in the *Arkham Sampler*
(Winter 1948):

> *The Night Side* and *The Sleeping and the Dead* [. . .] offer a
> highly diverting variety, ranging from such a delightful
> whimsy as Kantor's 'The Moon-Caller' to the memorable
> horror of Stephen Grendon's 'The Extra Passenger.'
> Mr. Derleth himself is represented not only by brief
> introductions to the two books, but by a short story,
> "Glory Hand." (88–89)

For the *Sampler* as well, Derleth writes two new Grendon-stories,
shifting their emphasis from the weird tale to early science fiction. In
1948's autumn issue we learn the following: "For our fifth issue, that
is Volume II, Number 1, coming in January, 1949, we are presenting a
special science-fiction number. / This issue will contain new science-
fiction stories by A. E. Van Vogt, Ray Bradbury, and Stephen Grendon"
([94]). And Derleth enlarges upon his latest promotional angle for
Grendon, which is to emphasize his versatility as a writer—projecting
the anticipated list Arkham House titles in *Books from Arkham House 1949
and Later* [Mar. 1949], Derleth writes: "Of the younger authors addicted
to the creation of weird fiction, there are not many with the ability to do
such a variety of tales as Stephen Grendon. / Arkham House is proud to
be able to publish his first collection of uncanny fiction, which includes
the long title story, one of the most popular novelettes ever published
in *Weird Tales*" (18). Grendon's second—*The Death Fetch and Other Gothic
Tales*—is also described:

> In all the available literature of the weird, there is no good
> anthology of Gothic fiction, out of which the fantasy of our
> own time so largely grew. Stephen Grendon has prepared
> the first such collection and Arkham House is to publish
> it. This fine anthology contains the following stories: "The
> Death Fetch," "The Two Sisters of Cologne," "A Ghost of
> a Hand," "The Spectre Hand," "The Tregethans' Curse,"
> all Anonymously written; "Discovery Concerning
> Ghosts," by George Cruikshank; *The Castle of Otranto,*

a novel by Horace Walpole; "Leixlip Castle," by Charles Robert Maturin; "The Vampire," by John William Polidori; "The Haunted House of Paddington," by Charles Ollier; "Chantry Manor-House," by Mrs. Hartley; "The Phantom Coach," by Amelia B. Edwards; "The Signal-Man," by Charles Dickens; "Jerry Jarvis's Wig," by Richard Harris Barham; and "The Dream Woman," by Wilkie Collins. (26)

And, in private correspondence, Derleth continues being cagey, choosing words carefully in answering pointed questions: "Stephen Grendon is a separate entity, but admittedly strongly influenced by my own work" (Derleth to Dr. Marvin B. Wolfe, 9 Sept. 1948).

Grendon's next sale was to Donald A. Wollheim in 1949, for *The Girl with the Hungry Eyes* (Avon), one of the earliest "paperback" anthologies to feature original stories. Presumably Wollheim himself added inside-the-cover copy for "Mrs. Manifold," calling out Stephen Grendon alongside Fritz Leiber, Jr. and William Tenn and delivering the hook: "The devil could bridge the gap between her Singapore saloon and her London boarding house." Around this time Grendon did a pithy analysis of Algernon Blackwood's "The Willows" for *Masque*, demonstrating how this story is "distinguished by a universality which comparatively few stories in the field of fantasy ever achieve."

In the meantime, Derleth kept the pot boiling in that year's autumn *Sampler*: "Stephen Grendon's first collection of stories, *Mr. George and Other Odd Persons*, will appear sometime in the future from Arkham House." Bracing personal opinion about science fiction, he adds that Grendon's "The Song of the Pewee," one of his two SF stories, is "outgrowth of his amazement at the pother often raised by so-called science-fiction fans" (122). Derleth reprinted both SF stories in *Far Boundaries* (Pellegrini & Cudahy, 1951), where he describes "The Song of the Pewee" as "satirizing the regimentation of man in time to come" (x).

A year later Derleth added Grendon's "Mr. George" (described on the jacket as a "terrifying novelette about a little girl, her spectral friend and three designing murderers") to *Night's Yawning Peal* (Arkham House). A decade later, still by Grendon, "Mr. George" would be filmed in Hollywood, a first-season episode of *Thriller*, and broadcast on 9 May 1961. In 1963, Grendon's "The Tsanta in the Parlour" was reprinted in *When Evil Wakes*, edited by Derleth for London's Souvenir Press; inside, the first new Grendon-blurb in years was essentially the last clue Derleth provided for Grendon's real identity:

**Stephen Grendon** (1909–) is the pen name of a well-known American writer, whose work in the domain of the macabre has been sparingly published and widely viewed on the television screen. His first collection, *Mr. George and Other Odd Persons*, is forthcoming.

The last ever was composed in 1962, for Arkham's *Dark Mind, Dark Heart*:

**Stephen Grendon** (1909–) is the author of many macabre tales, most of which appeared in *Weird Tales,* and in such anthologies as *The Night Side, Who Knocks?, Sleep No More, Far Boundaries, Night's Yawning Peal, The Supernatural Reader,* etc. He is author of two forthcoming books—*The Lock and the Key,* a novel, and *Mr. George and Other Odd Persons,* a collection of his best supernatural stories. ([63])

Derleth was determined to see *Mr. George and Other Odd Persons* published, promising again c. 1962 in the advertising brochure *New Books from Arkham House:* "Also in the offing are collections by Robert E. Howard, *Stephen Grendon* [my emphasis], Howard Wandrei, M. P. Shiel, Donald Wandrei, Carl Jacobi, Manly Wade Wellman, J. Sheridan LeFanu, E. Hoffmann Price, and Clark Ashton Smith" (2); he meant with this book to let the proverbial cat out from its bag. In "Books of the Times: Macabre Tales" (*Capital Times,* 17 Oct. 1963: 18+) he admits, "The collection seems to me one of my strongest in the macabre vein and is the only one to appear under the Stephen Grendon byline"; and in "Now Ready" of the *1964 Books from Arkham House* brochure: "All the stories written under the by-line of Stephen Grendon for *Weird Tales, The Arkham Sampler,* and *Avon Fantasy Reader* are collected into this handsome volume with its eye-catching jacket by Robert Hubbell" ([1]). The 2546 copies *Mr. George and Other Odd Persons* were duly stamped, making the last Arkham for 1963: "The identity of Stephen Grendon was certainly no well-kept secret. / Those readers who were familiar with August Derleth's novels in the Sac Prairie Saga [. . .] had met 'Steve Grendon' in those books, and knew that it was too outrageous a coincidence to accept as a separate identity the Stephen Grendon who wrote stories, many of which were not unlike August Derleth's in *Weird Tales* and elsewhere" (jacket).

Not *The Death Fletch and Other Gothic Tales* (which would have been an important book in the classic Arkham era), nor either of the novels (unless one or the other exists under a different title) were ever completed. Additional adventures springing from the early "life" of Stephen Grendon were recounted by Derleth in the post-1963 "Steve and Sim" series, but the literary career of Stephen Grendon—weird tale and science fiction author, friend of Lovecraft who sent stories from Sac Prairie out into the real world, editor, and book reviewer—had come to its end.

## Works Cited

Derleth, August. *Evening in Spring*. Sauk City, WI: Stanton & Lee, 1945.
— — —. *Mr. George and Other Odd Persons*. As by Stephen Grendon. Sauk City, WI: Stanton & Lee, 1963.
— — —. *The Shield of the Valiant*. New York: Scribner's, 1945.
Lovecraft, H. P., and August Derleth. *Essential Solitude: The Letters of H. P. Lovecraft and August Derleth*. Ed. David E. Schultz and S. T. Joshi. New York: Hippocampus Press, 2008. 2 vols.
Schroth, Evelyn M. *The Derleth Saga*. Appleton, WI: Quintain, 1979.

*In addition, especial thanks to Walden Derleth and the late April Derleth for allowing me to quote from the August Derleth Papers, and to Rah Hoffman (and Donald Sidney-Fryer) for access to correspondence in Rah's private collection.*

## Chronological Listing of First Appearances by Stephen Grendon

"A Gentleman from Prague." *Weird Tales* (Nov. 1944)
"Alannah." *Weird Tales* (Mar. 1945)
"Dead Man's Shoes." *Weird Tales* (Mar. 1946)
"The Extra Passenger." *Weird Tales* (Jan. 1947)
"Mr. George." *Weird Tales* (Mar. 1947)
"Parrington's Pool." *Weird Tales* (July 1947)
"Bishop's Gambit." *Avon Fantasy Reader* No. 3 (1947)
"The Ghost Walk." *Weird Tales* (Nov. 1947)
"Mara." *Arkham Sampler* (Winter 1948)
"The Night Train to Lost Valley." *Weird Tales* (Jan. 1948)
"The Wind in the Lilacs." *Arkham Sampler* (Spring 1948)
"The Tsanta in the Parlor." *Weird Tales* (July 1948)
"Blessed Are the Meek." *Weird Tales* (Nov. 1948)
"Open, Sesame!" *Arkham Sampler* (Spring 1949)
"Balu." *Weird Tales* (Jan. 1949)
"Mrs. Manifold." *The Girl with the Hungry Eyes*. NY: Avon, 1949.
"The Blue Spectacles." *Weird Tales* (July 1949)
"The Song of the Pewee: An Episode of Twenty-Fifth Century History." *Arkham Sampler* (Autumn 1949)
"I Wish I Had Written That: 'The Willows.'" *Masque* 2.2 (1950).
"The Man on B-17." *Weird Tales* (May 1950)
"Miss Esperson." *Dark Mind, Dark Heart*. Sauk City, WI: Arkham House, 1962.

# + + *[NameL3ss]* Classic Interview + +

# *Rod Serling*

### By William F. Nolan

**Prefatory Note:**

I had the chance to interview Rod Serling at his California home in Pacific Palisades in February of 1963 for the debut issue of *Gamma* magazine (I was the managing editor at the time). It was printed just once (*Gamma* only had a run of five issues), and without any byline, and appears here for the first time under my name. It has not been edited or updated.

So . . . step into my time machine and travel back half-a-century for a visit with a very busy Mr. Serling in this early portrait of an icon.

*— WFN*

*You'll find out all about **Rodman Edward Serling** in this pithy, revealing interview with the gifted creator of TV's* The Twilight Zone. *Let us preface our visit with Mr. Serling by pointing out that his three paperback collections of* Stories from the Twilight Zone *are all runaway best sellers (with the first of the series now in its eighth printing). Rod lives the Good Life, in a lush house overlooking the ocean in Pacific Palisades, dictating his work in a spacious poolside studio containing his "golden girls" (the Emmys he has won for such television milestones as* Patterns *and* Requiem for a Heavyweight*), bound copies of his many scripts and an attractive secretary who keeps busy transcribing his award-winning words. Outspoken as always, Rod says what he believes—which has made him one of the industry's most controversial personalities. Here, without further ado, is uncensored Serling.*

**William F. Nolan:** As one of the "pioneers" of TV, you seem to have survived its many changes, while most of the old guard (Chayefsky, Mosel, Foote) have more or less deserted the fort. Can you explain this?

**Rod Serling:** I'm still in television—though I'm doing other things now

too, such as screenplays—because I was lucky enough to sell a series to CBS, *The Twilight Zone*, in which I could continue to function creatively. The live dramatic shows that developed and supported the Chayefskys and Mosels just don't exist anymore, and so they got out of TV, headed for Broadway or took up screenwriting. I was fed up myself when *Zone* sold, and if it hadn't I probably wouldn't be in the game today. In fact, I've only written two or three other teleplays since *Zone* got rolling.

**Nolan:** How many of the *Twilight Zone* scripts have you written?

**Serling:** Well, we went on the air in the autumn of '59, and now our fourth season is underway. . . . Counting the new hour-long scripts I did for it the total is over half a hundred. Under my contract I had to write 80% of the first two season's shows. Now the pressure is off, which is a helluva big help. The grind was more than I'd bargained for. As exec producer as well as writer I had to sweat out all kinds of stuff—ratings, set costs, casting, locations, budgets. . . . Time was a luxury. If I dropped a pencil and stooped to pick it up I was two weeks behind schedule.

**Nolan:** When *Twilight Zone* was dropped by the sponsors after its first season, didn't a lot of fans write in to complain of this?

**Serling:** Not exactly. We *knew* we had a strong show, so we sent out appeals to the viewers, asking them to write us if they wanted *Zone* to continue. We got over 2500 cards and letters in response, all of them urging us to stay on TV. This sold the sponsors, and we were able to continue.

**Nolan:** What awards has *Zone* garnered?

**Serling:** Quite a few. In January of 1960, it won a double award—as Best New Program (edging out *The Untouchables* by a single vote) and as Best Filmed Series. We also won the Screen Producers Guild Award as Best Produced TV Series of the year. Then there are the Emmys I got for writing *Zone*. And we've also won the "Hugo" awards, of course, from the science fiction conventions. And the Golden Globe Award this year. All very gratifying.

**Nolan:** Wasn't *Zone* originally planned as an hour series?

**Serling:** Actually, yes. I did a pilot at the hour length, *Time Element*, about a man who re-lives Pearl Harbor, and this appeared on the Desilu Playhouse in November of 1958. Then we decided to go for the half-hour format. This season we shifted over to the hour length. For next season, looks like we'll return to the half-hour format. It suits the show at that length.

**Nolan:** Up to *Zone*, you'd written no fantasy or science fiction. Why did you plan a show of this type for your first series?

**Serling:** For two reasons. Because I loved this area of imaginative storytelling—and because there had never been a TV series like it. The strength of *Twilight Zone* is that through parable, through placing a social problem or controversial theme against a fantasy background you can make a point which, if more blatantly stated in a realistic frame, wouldn't be acceptable. Because of this, from time to time, we've been able to make some pertinent social comments on conformity, on prejudice, on political ideologies, without sponsor interference. It offered a whole new outlet, a new approach. I know I've been knocked by some veteran science fiction writers who've spent the better part of their lives in this creative area—I've been called an opportunist who's taken this story form that these guys have sweated out for years and used my reasonably affluent name to just step all over them to get *my* show on the air. Well, all I can say to these people is, I'm sorry they feel this way. *Zone* was an honest effort on my part. I tried not to step on any toes, but with a show such as this, you're almost bound to.

**Nolan:** Come to think of it, you *did* write a science fiction script for MGM, didn't you?

**Serling:** It was never produced but I did a full screenplay on *No Blade of Grass*. This was a beautiful science fiction yarn, and I'm sorry it never got off the ground. Maybe it will be made some day.

**Nolan:** How much of *Twilight Zone* do you own?

**Serling:** 50%—plus the fact that I own the negatives of the show. Eventually, we hope to send it all over the world.

**Nolan:** As the host on *Zone* you've been called "a thin Hitchcock." How do you like stepping in front of the TV cameras?

**Serling:** There was no running character we could use as host, so CBS picked me. I had done some promotional films for them and they looked at these and decided on giving me a try. Actually, I photograph better than I look. Now people see me on the street and they say "Gee, we thought you were six foot one," and I know they're thinking "God, this kid is only five feet five and he's got a broken nose!" But I think I've improved a lot since the first season, and the ham in me is pleased with this.

**Nolan:** What about your highly publicized troubles with censorship? Has the situation improved since the days when you battled the sponsors over *Noon on Doomsday* and *A Town Has Turned to Dust*?

*Below: Rod Serling in the 1950s and early '60s . . .*

*(Top) Publicity images of Serling at work.*

*(Bottom) Serling enjoying time at home with his family. (Photographer unknown.)*

*Facing Page: Keenan Wynn, Jack Palance, and Ed Wynn in Serling's 1956 CBS* Playhouse 90 *masterpiece,* Requiem for a Heavyweight.

**Serling:** In the overall field of TV, there's been no real improvement. If anything, it's worse. Sponsor interference is a stultifying, often destructive and inexcusable by-product of our mass-media system. Ideally, a sponsor should have no more interference rights than an advertiser in a magazine. At one time the networks could have demanded and received creative prerogatives. They could have demanded some kind of cleavage between the commercial and the artistic aspects of a program. But they gave this prerogative away.

**Nolan:** Do you miss the tooth-and-nail sponsor battles characteristic of your *Playhouse 90* days?

**Serling:** I never liked it. For years the newspapers portrayed me as the two-fisted kid who fought for every show I got on the air, a petulant little bastard who battled with everybody. In contrast to some guys who never spoke out maybe I was controversial. I went on record but many other writers did too who didn't happen to get the publicity. Chayefsky, for

example, was as tough and honest a guy in his reaction to pressures as anyone I know. Same with Reggie Rose. We all spoke out to keep certain ideas and themes intact—and as often as we lost we sometimes won. But, if you stay in the game long enough you begin to pre-censor yourself.

**Nolan:** How would you rate your present *Twilight Zone* efforts with your earlier work for shows such as *Playhouse 90*?

**Serling:** This is like comparing a short story to a novel. I've written *Zones* in a day—I averaged one a week for a while—and I used to spend months polishing a *90*. The scripts are often written and produced much too fast. We aim for quality but we don't always achieve it.

**Nolan:** You don't seem fully satisfied with your present output. Have you thought of doing a Broadway play?

**Serling:** Many times. I've tried to write for Broadway, but my attempts have not pleased me. I tried like the devil to turn *Requiem for a Heavyweight* into a legitimate play, did six rewrites, then gave it up when David Susskind agreed to produce it as a film. I did the screenplay, which seemed to turn out pretty well. I'd say my principal goal is to write a good novel, which is the toughest of all to bring off. I sweated blood on those Bantam short story collections, so I know how far away I am from the craftsmanship required of a novel.

**Nolan:** We've heard you don't use a typewriter. Why?

**Serling:** In the beginning, back in the early '50s, I used to bang out the stuff myself, in a kind of one-handed, punching style, which was tough on the keys. Then I began to use a Dictaphone, to save time, and found I liked it. Now, with my dialogue, I get a chance to "sound it out." I really play the ham, too. With the big, emotional scenes I shout and roar and play all the parts. It helps to "live it up" as much as possible.

**Nolan:** Let's examine your early years. How did you get into professional writing?

**Serling:** I grew up in Binghamton, New York, and edited the school newspaper. My father was a wholesale butcher, and a good one, but he didn't want me and my brother Bob (**Ed.:** Robert J. Serling, author of *The President's Plane Is Missing*) stuck behind a meat counter. Wanted us to go to college. War came along, and I joined the Army paratroopers in '43, took up boxing in the service, won seventeen of eighteen bouts, then broke my nose in two places and quit. Spent three years in the Pacific then went on to Antioch College in Ohio under the G.I. Bill. I really didn't know what I wanted to do with my life, but I felt a need to write, a kind of compulsion to get some of my thoughts down, so I began doing radio scripts, working part-time as an announcer at WINR. In 1950, when I was a senior, a script of mine took second place in a *Dr. Christian* contest, and my wife Carol and I got a free trip to New York out of it. By then I was hooked.

**Nolan:** Did you start selling right away?

**Serling:** Well, I sold a TV script for $100 shortly thereafter, then got forty rejections in a row! Television was in its primitive stage then, and radio was dying. In order to eat, I became a staff writer in Cincinnati. The grind was murderous—everything from soap commercials to public-service announcements to half-hour documentaries. I learned discipline, absorbed a time sense and a technique, but I was desperate to break away. They had me doing "folksy" bits for which you only needed two elements: A hayseed M.C. who strummed a guitar and

said "Shucks, friends," and a girl yodeler whose falsetto could break a beer mug at twenty paces. I also had the chore of composing prayer messages for an ex-tent revivalist, a fat-faced slob I cordially detested on sight. So, when I sold three radio scripts in the winter of '51, I walked out for good. I earned around $5,000 in my first year of freelancing.

**Nolan:** Wasn't *Patterns*, in January of 1955, your first real success?

**Serling:** That's right. I'd written seventy-one other scripts up to that time, but it took *Patterns* to put me over, and it was an instant hit. One minute after that show went off the air my phone started to ring; it's been ringing ever since! Because of *Patterns*, within two weeks, I got twenty-three bids to write teleplays, several screenplay offers, fourteen requests for interviews, two luncheon invitations from Broadway producers and bids from a book publisher. I suddenly found that I could sell practically everything I had in the trunk, and I had twenty of my scripts telecast that season, earning $80,000. I still blush when I think of some of the bombs I unloaded that year, but I was the hungry kid left all alone in the candy store. Man, I just *grabbed!* My first screen job was at Fox on a war flick called *Between Heaven and Hell*. I turned in a script that would have run for nine hours on the screen. As I recall, it was over 500 pages. I didn't know what the hell I was doing. They just said "Here's fifteen hundred bucks a week—write!" So I wrote. They eventually took the thing away from me and handed it over to six other writers, but I lay claim to the fact that my version had some wonderful moments in it. In nine hours of script, by God, there *has* to be couple of wonderful moments!

**Nolan:** You got your first Emmy out of *Patterns*. How many do you have by now?

**Serling:** Got one for *Requiem*, one for *The Comedian*, and couple for *Twilight Zone*. I've been damned lucky.

**Nolan:** How did success affect you when you jumped from $5,000 a year to $80,000?

**Serling:** You can't throw overnight success down your gut and expect ready digestion. Life took on a glittering, unreal quality. I wandered through a crazy, whipped-cream world where everything was suddenly mink and mobile dollar signs. In '59, for *Playhouse 90*, I did a fictionalized version of the problems you encounter which I called *The Velvet Alley*. The externals of the play were definitely autobiographical—

the pressures, the assault on values, the blandishments that run in competition to a man's creativity. I left strips of flesh all over the studio with that one. Success can be rugged. The major fear is once you've got it, will you lose it? You become accustomed to a gardener, and a big house and a pool, and a Lincoln in the driveway. As creative artist, if acquisition becomes more important than the work you put out, then you're in deep trouble. That's what happened to the protagonist in my teleplay.

**Nolan:** Can you continue to expand in TV?

**Serling:** I doubt it. Part of this has to do with the age we live in. There's a general tendency toward escapism, because everyday reality is awfully tough to swallow. We're living on the doorstep of the Hydrogen Bomb and we don't know, between Monday and Friday, just what the hell is going to happen to us. In drama, this means the public can't accept strong meat; they want to forget their troubles with cowpokes and private eyes. So a serious writer, with something to say beyond "Howdy, pard," has to turn to other fields. Television tries to please everybody. To achieve what the sponsor thinks of as "the mass level" you end up with blank verse written on a marshmallow! And after a

while, when you're told things like troops can't *ford* a river if Chevy is the sponsor, you just don't give a damn.

**Nolan:** How do you escape the TV grind?

**Serling:** We still manage to get away once a year for two months up on Lake Cayuga in New York. We've got a cabin up there built by my wife's great-great-grandfather. We take the kids, Nan and Jody, and head for the lake each summer. I do a lot of boating and water skiing and fishing up there. Helps keep me in shape. Fact is, I'd go nuts without those two months.

**Nolan:** Of all your 200 or more produced teleplays, can you pick a favorite?

**Serling:** I'd have to give the nod to *Requiem*. It brought me the most satisfaction, and I think it is my best job of writing. Its basic premise is that every man can and *must* search for his own personal dignity. My ex-prize fighter did just that, and I think there was particular poignance in having a discarded, battered hulk of a man move out into the world that had cheered him and was now alien to him.

**Nolan:** Coming back to the present state of TV, don't you think that pay television might be the answer to better programming?

**Serling:** I wish I could see it that way, but I don't. The guys behind it will want to milk as many quarters or half-dollars as possible out of people, so meaty, controversial themes, appealing to a more limited audience won't be welcome. TV is diseased, and a dab of Mercurochrome isn't the answer when it's obvious that the total organism needs major surgery.

**Nolan:** Then you don't link your future with TV?

**Serling:** I don't know *what's* in my future. But I'd like to do more screenplays, work for the legitimate stage, maybe even try my hand at direction—just once, to see how it feels from that end—and then tackle the novel. I just hope to God I can take the time off to do that novel. I'm a security-hungry guy, and I work best under pressure. And you can't do a good novel under pressure. So, I can't plan too far ahead. As Jonathan Winters says, "It's tough enough getting through Saturday."

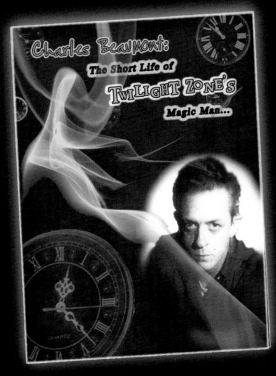

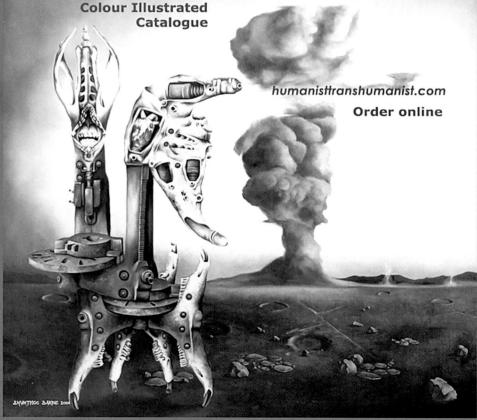

# humanist transhumanist

## Symbolism*Surrealism*Fantastic Art
### VAKRAS          RAYMOND

**Colour Illustrated
Catalogue**

humanisttranshumanist.com

**Order online**

'boy-kouros' - oil on canvas 2004

# COLLECTIONS

## By JC Hemphill

Oscar's cell phone rang, disturbing his nap. It never rang. The last person he gave his number to was his art broker and ex-lover, Susie, but even she hadn't called in months. Which explained the finished work filling his studio apartment—tons of output, but no buyers. He imagined his paintings as mass-produced junk meant for tourists in beachside towns. A machine pumped them out, each the same as the last, and a conveyor belt transported them to a plastic bin that hadn't been emptied in a long time and now the paintings were spilling onto the floor. Soon, the assembly line would back up and jam, and when that day came, Oscar vowed he would give up painting for good.

Because really, if success hadn't happened by then, it wasn't going to.

So even though he cursed the phone for waking him, hope coaxed him into stirring. Maybe Susie finally decided to line up a new exhibit.

"Hel—" He stopped and cleared the phlegm from his throat. "Hello?"

A pleasant male voice spoke, "Good afternoon, sir, would Mr. Nuñez be available?"

The man's clear and courteous tone—like names being read at a graduation—marked him as a telemarketer.

"Nope, wrong number."

"Oh, well . . . a shame. Our records indicate that this number belongs to Oscar Nuñez. We'll just have to visit his residence. My apologies for disturbing y—"

"Slow up a sec. Did you say you were going to go to his, uh, home? Not that it matters to me, but why would you do that? Is he in some sorta trouble?"

The man on the other end went silent, and an odd tension hung over the dead calm. This guy was official, no doubt about that. He's on somebody's payroll, somewhere, and whoever was signing his checks wanted to find Oscar badly enough to make house calls. That in itself held Oscar's attention.

"I'm afraid I'm only at liberty to discuss that with Mr. Nuñez."

"All right, suppose I could find this . . . *Mr. Nuñez*, was it?"

"Then I would be more than happy to speak with him. And we wouldn't need to send a liaison to his home," the man said, and Oscar

heard the subtle condescension he knew so well from the many authoritarians who failed to discipline him throughout grade school. It was that exact tone that made him want to rebel. Principals and teachers were just uninspired dictators on their own little power trips, and the better he understood that, the more he yearned to skip class or break a window or TP some random house.

And just like that, Oscar's curiosity waned and he became annoyed.

"You know what, dude, I'm tired. You woke me from my midday beauty sleep, so I'm about to hit you with some honesty. *I'm* Oscar Nuñez, but I ain't buying nothin'. I'm happy with my car, life, and health insurance. I can't buy myself food, so I sure as hell can't donate to charity, even if it's for starving children with starving puppies. I don't have television or Internet service and I'm cool with my nineteen-bucks-a-month payment on this phone. If you got something important to say, we can talk. Otherwise, I gotta get back to bed."

Despite the verbal lashing, the voice continued with an audible smile. "Hello, Mr. Nuñez. My name is Andy and I'm calling from Waterhouse Collections. How are you doing today?"

He would have hung up at the word collections if the guy's unrelenting charm hadn't been so disarming. It was as if he pushed the reset button on their conversation.

"Peachy." Oscar spit the word out like a bad taste.

"Splendid. I'm calling today to inform you of a great way to save money. Could I *squeeze* just a minute of your time, Mr. Nuñez?"

"Sure, let's see where this goes." He shrugged and scanned his cluttered apartment. "I guess I got time."

"Great. First of all, let me take this opportunity to inform you that your overdue balance of thirty-six hundred dollars and six cents from Credit National, N.A. has been transferred to Waterhouse Collections for handling. As such, we are willing to negotiate a lowered lump-payment as settlement or a payment plan with a lower interest rate. Which option sounds satisfactory to your needs?"

Oscar smirked. This guy was smooth, his speech strategic. He drew his prey in with sweet words, slapped them in the face with cold facts, and then sneaked the question of immediate repayment in while his victim was stunned. And the way he asked, it almost sounded noncommittal. Oscar would bet this guy closed a large number of accounts this way. Most people were probably so off-kilter by the time he asked "Which option sounds satisfactory?" that they chose one instead of hanging up as they normally would.

"I'll take option three," he said and pressed end.

Something about Andy lingered afterwards. He could still hear that melodic yet forceful voice. "Could I *squeeze* just a minute of your time, Mr. Nuñez?" Creepy.

Oscar couldn't go back to sleep, so he painted. Working in a frenzy, he painted freeform, using bold, dusty colors and broad, wide strokes. He went for hours, almost falling into catatonia. When he finished, he dropped his brush in a Mason Jar full of water, stepped back, and admired the portrait of a bald stranger. His creation was unlike anything he had ever painted. It was clean, yet raw. Clear, yet abstract, and somehow haunting in its beauty. It hinted of Lucien Freud, but was fully his own.

But deep down, beneath the exhilaration of a finished work, lay a panicked fear and questions he wasn't ready for stirred.

Oscar rolled out of bed the next day in time for lunch. He grabbed a box of Frosted Flakes from the top of the fridge and discovered all the bowls were dirty. Scattered around the apartment, no doubt. He settled for a glass mixing bowl. He didn't mind. Being able to see the cereal from all sides was kinda cool. Inspiring, even.

A fully painted canvas appeared in his mind. He pictured a glass bowl filled with Berry Captain Crunch—the colorful puffs would draw the eye better than Frosted Flakes—as an old hag handed it to a Dutch maiden, like Snow White. No. Better yet, it was Snow White and dwarfs climbed over one another in the distance to warn her, but she wasn't listening. Not at all. She wanted that cereal and they weren't going to stop her in time.

"Powerful," he said and began eating.

After he placed the mixing bowl at the bottom of an already leaning stack of dishes, he moved to the corner of the apartment that he referred to as the office. He was all set to start the piece. Even had the title in mind: Grimm Desires. But when he confronted the painting from last night, he paused. The man in the portrait looking back made his heart skip. Whether from surprise or revulsion, he wasn't sure. The bald man he had painted sat in a straight-back pose and wore a black suit. The sharp angles of his face conspired with deep shadows to form a gaunt, almost fragile-looking man. But something behind his well-manicured grin screamed confidence, power, and a seething malice toward all who viewed it.

He took the painting down and stuffed it behind a row of other half-finished abortions and the rejected children he never wanted but couldn't let go of.

With a fresh canvas on the easel, he squeezed out a bump of

canary and white paint for Snow White's dress, but when he went to apply the first stroke, he couldn't. Not physically, but mentally. The image of the bald man stayed with him like a bad dream, faded but no less disturbing.

He washed his brush out and flopped down on the futon. Without a TV, the futon faced the three windows of his apartment and the corner of the building next to his. On good days, when the neighbors across the way left their blinds open, he got direct sunlight.

Today wasn't a good day.

He was about to turn the stereo on for motivation when his cell phone rang. He groaned, walked over to the milk crate that acted as a nightstand, and answered. "Yo."

"Good afternoon, sir, would Mr. Nuñez be available?" a familiar voice asked.

"You again?"

"Is this Mr. Nuñez?"

"What do you think?"

"Hello, Mr. Nuñez. My name is Andy and I'm calling from Waterhouse Collec—"

"I know who this is, Andy. And I'm sorry, I really am, but I can't pay you guys a cent. You can call all you want, but it ain't happenin'. Capisce?"

"I'm calling from Waterhouse Collections," the voice continued, unfazed. "How are you doing today?"

Oscar's temper flared, but he tried to control himself. Andy would have the upper hand if he lost his cool. "Peachy as pie. What the hell is this, a recording?"

"No, sir." For the first time, Andy sounded flat. Not offended, but cheerless. "First of all, let me take this opportunity to inform you that your overdue balance of thirty-six hundred dollars and six cents from—"

"Yeah guy, you told me already. You got something new for me or not?"

Silence. Oscar looked at his phone and watched the seconds count up on the call timer. A full ten seconds passed before Andy's soothing voice returned. "First of all, let me take this opportunity to—"

Oscar ended the call.

"What a freak."

Andy called again the next day, but Oscar didn't answer. He noted the phone number—312-3351. Local. Nice touch. Makes it look like the chicky you met last night at the bar is calling. Waterhouse Collections had their shit together.

The phone buzzed with a received message and asked if he wanted to listen to it now. He pressed yes, entered his pin, and listened. It was Andy.

"Hello, sir or madam, my name is Andy and I am calling from Waterhouse Collections for one Oscar Nuñez with an exciting chance to save money. First of all, let me take this opportunity to inform you that your overdue balance of thirty-six hundred dollars and six cents from Credit National, N.A. has been transferred to Waterhouse . . ."

This guy's a broken record, Oscar thought.

". . . Collections for handling. As such—"

He hung up and the next day, when Andy called at one o'clock, he didn't answer. He deleted the message without listening. And every day went the same for a week. 312-3351, always at one. He eventually put the phone on silent. No one else had called in that time anyway.

During that week he tried to paint, to forget it all, but as with Grimm Desires, he couldn't. His brush and canvas were sworn enemies.

He finally gave up trying and considered taking a few nights away from the apartment to re-establish his mojo. He hadn't been out since he and Susie split. Back then, he was little more than a hobo selling paintings on the corner of Fifth and MLK. She took notice of his work one day, and before long they were chatting about their favorite artists. She was stunning, confident, and way out of his league. But something kept her talking, and Oscar managed to seal the first date by giving her a simple painting of a rose. It turned out that she promoted artists for a living, and in a matter of months she took him from street art to solo exhibits. She even helped him win an award from the Painter's Guild—a bronze statue of a paintbrush that now collected dust on his mantel. But, as relationships often go, theirs headed south. Susie blamed his obsession with work. Oscar thought his passion was what attracted her.

Often, when he thought about her, it wasn't of their relationship or the bitter breakup. He stuck to the infallible details, elevating her in his mind: her jade eyes; the way she snorted when she laughed; the birthmark on the back of her hand that was little more than a freckle.

He grabbed the phone and noticed seven missed calls and seven messages. Not that he needed to check to know, but they were all from 312-3351. He checked in case one of the calls happened to be from Susie. They hadn't spoken in over three months, and he knew hope was a masochist's way of self-inflicting pain, but he couldn't help thinking it was her. There was *always* a voice saying maybe . . . just maybe.

Sometimes he wondered if hope was the only thing getting

him out of bed. Anxiety crept into him as he wondered how long that would hold out. Then a darker question surfaced. What would happen when hope wore off?

The light from his phone blinked in a silent ring. 312-3351 flashed on the screen. It's almost six o'clock, he thought. Odd.

His thumb hovered over the accept button and curiosity urged him to push it. Why was Andy calling at a different time? An upward counting call timer replaced the accept button.

00:01, 00:02 . . .

He held the phone to his ear and listened to the empty line, half expecting to hear heavy breathing. He glanced at the screen. 00:26. He slowly put his ear to the receiver. Still nothing. Thirty seconds without a peep. The only reason Oscar knew someone was on the other end was because the call hadn't disconnected.

His heart pulsed in his temple, and he jerked the phone away as if the person on the other end might hear it. He felt silly. What the hell was he afraid of? It's just a guy on the phone. Time to man up.

"Who is this?" he asked in a stern impression of confidence.

"Good afternoon, sir, would Mr. Nuñez be available?"

His bravado withered beneath Andy's creepy, upbeat tone. "This is he."

"Great. First of all, let me take this opportunity to inform you that your overdue balance of thirty-six hundred dollars and six cents"— it was the same song and dance, but something seemed different— "from Credit National, N.A. has been transferred to Waterhouse Collections for handling. As such, we are willing"—Andy's voice held a bitter subtext—"to negotiate a lowered lump-payment as settlement or a payment plan with a lower interest rate. Choose or there *will* be consequences."

Oscar froze. Did he hear the last line right? "Um . . . excuse me?"

"You heard me, Oscar."

Oscar was speechless. Questions and outrages swirled in his mind, but he couldn't pin them down. He wanted to be angry. He wanted to tell Andy to shove that polite attitude right up his ass. He wanted to do a million things, but couldn't.

"Waterhouse Collections isn't your run-of-the-mill collection agency, Mr. Nuñez. We're a bit more . . . *eternal* than that."

"Eternal?"

"Yes. You can think of us as the *final* collections agency. Except our business model isn't structured around money." Andy chuckled. "The CEO of Waterhouse Collections is more interested in the acquisition of souls. But don't fret, Oscar, The Boss is reasonable. He doesn't expect you to come up with so much cash on short notice. If you lack the funds for repayment, your debt can be settled by simply dirtying your soul with blood." He paused and time halted. "What is your reply?"

Oscar didn't have one. The words were there, but something was holding them back. But what?—fear? confusion? *humor*? Was this guy serious? He checked the timer. 01:51. He stared at the screen until it reached 02:00 and hung up.

No, not humor, he thought.

The call came at nine in the morning the next day.

He hadn't slept. It bothered him that the calls were coming at random times now, but he was relieved to have today's call out of the way so early. He could relax, forget, and maybe get some painting done. He did a mental check for the little light inside. The light was always on and was always one of two colors. It represented the itch for creation he felt within and decided whether he was in the mood to paint. The light was almost always green, but it had been a blaring red lately.

And then inspiration struck and the light burned a mighty green. What better way to express life's contradictions than to paint a crosswalk light with both 'Walk' and 'Don't Walk' lit?

He hustled to his office and began. Brush met canvas and the old frenzy took over. As he dabbed and slashed and eased in details, the image developed as if it was already on the canvas and he merely had to wake it up.

The sun faded in the apartment as the hours stretched, and Oscar soon found himself shirtless and drenched in sweat. His arm ached, his head swirled, and a sense of euphoria settled on him as he stepped back from his painting. The word 'Walk' shone with an inner brilliance, like a beacon drawing the viewer in. The eye naturally moved down to the words 'Don't Walk,' which were set in a deep, blood-filled red. The bottom of each letter ran slightly as if bleeding. Below the sign, people crossed the street in both directions as speeding cars closed in from the left and right.

He decided the piece was wall-worthy and scanned the apartment for the perfect spot. Other than the higher reaches, most of the walls already featured his work. He practically lived in a gallery.

Before he could decide, his phone began flashing. Dread swelled. He cursed and leaned his painting against the wall.

To his amazement, 312-3351 wasn't the number displayed. Instead, the screen read: Susie Pendergrass. Oscar almost forgot how to breathe.

He answered, "Susie?"

"Hello, Oscar. How . . . have you been?" She sounded tired, as if she'd woken in the middle of the night to call.

"Fine, fine. Working like mad. You?"

"Me? Oh, I'm not . . ." She paused. In the background, behind the faint hum of an open line, Oscar thought he heard clicking—a fingernail tapping a desk. "I'm not sure why I called."

"I do. I know why. I'm a mess, too. Ever since—"

"Oscar?" Her voice sounded dreamier than ever.

"Yeah?"

"Don't fret." That phrase turned his blood to ice.

"Wha—"

"If you lack the funds for repayment, your debt can be settled by dirtying your soul with blood."

The line went dead.

Oscar balked, stared at his phone, dumbfounded, and turned it off.

He ran to the kitchen and furiously washed his hands, scrubbing the paint from around his fingernails. Nothing made sense anymore. A million and one questions swarmed in his mind, each fighting for voice over the others. As he started his second lathering, a shrill ringing erupted in quick bursts. He froze. Impossible. But there it was—the phone turned off, but the speaker squawking its tinny ring anyway, mocking him, playing his nerves like a steel drum.

Oscar took tenuous steps toward the phone. He yearned for it to go to voicemail, but after ten rings he realized that wasn't happening. Not this time. Something told him it never would; no matter how long he ignored it, it would ring and ring and ring and ring and—

He picked up the phone. The screen was bright and clear, fully powered. It was Andy.

He popped the back off the cell and removed the battery with a palsied hand. The ringing ceased and the backlight died. He dropped the pieces on his bed and sprawled out next to them, burying his face in a pillow. The event played in his mind over and over as he toyed with the idea that maybe he hadn't turned the phone off after all. Stress was getting to him, making him forgetful, maybe even a little loopy. He closed his eyes and, after a while, fatigue dragged him into sleep.

When he woke, hours or minutes later, the first thing he did was check his phone. Still disconnected and useless. He pushed himself from bed and staggered toward the kitchen. The shelves of the fridge were bare. Mustard, canned pears, vegan sausages growing a vegan fuzz, a half-can of soda, and Indian take-out from last week.

As he reached for the pears, a confident knock thundered from his front door.

His first instinct was to jump under the bed. Run, hide, scream. Memories of his first conversation with Andy flooded his mind, and he realized the fearful anticipation of this moment had been there all along. "We'll just have to visit his residence," he had said in that polite tone. But it wasn't politeness, was it? No, Oscar realized he had misinterpreted Andy. The tone didn't come from some dedication to customer service or a caring nature. He proved that last night. What Oscar heard in Andy's voice was a remorseless certitude that everything would end up as Andy wanted. He spoke with the confidence of someone who could foresee the future, and that twisted Oscar's perspective of things. These weren't collection calls from some nut who took his job too seriously; they were more like calls of destiny . . . or doom.

The knock came again, no more or less forceful than before. Oscar didn't need to look. The way each connection of fist against wood seemed polite yet unavoidable told him all he needed to know.

It was Andy.

Oscar went to the door and checked the peephole, keeping his face as far away as possible. What he saw was beyond astonishing. The man who stood on the other side held his hands together in front of his black suit. He was bald, thin, and radiated a serene intensity. He was also the man in Oscar's painting.

He reeled, stumbling backwards from the door. He hit the floor with a crash and scooted away in panic.

The phone rang, loud, sharp, and unmistakable. Oscar flipped his head toward the sound, toward his bed, and saw the three pieces of the phone still scattered by the pillow. The back and battery lay next to a flashing screen.

His Adam's apple swelled, cutting off his oxygen. He wanted to call the police, but his phone was possessed. He wanted to run, but Andy had him trapped.

Andy knocked again and spoke just loud enough to be heard through the door and over the ringing. "Good afternoon, sir, would Mr. Nuñez be available?"

It was as if he had X-ray vision and knew Oscar was only a few feet away.

"Go the fuck away," Oscar screamed.

"Mr. Nuñez, your debt *must* be settled."

Oscar scrambled to his feet and searched his cramped apartment for a solution. He had no idea what he was looking for, but when his eyes fell on the bronze Painter's Guild award, he knew he found what he needed.

The knocking not only continued, but gained in frequency until it filled the silent spaces between the ringing.

He held the award by the thick paintbrush and test-swung it so the diamond-shaped base acted as a bludgeon. It was heavy enough to do serious damage, but light enough to swing quickly.

He thought about Andy's hounding phone calls and the sickening way he spoke. He thought about the week of not being able to paint and the effect it had on his morale; then the stress those persecutions had brought on. All the sleep he lost. Everything. This flowed into the problems outside his debt and Andy. Susie, for one. Suddenly, his problems with her and his career and life in general all became Andy's fault.

In that instant, an idea formed. He knew a way to make the phone calls and knocking stop; a way to get his work back on track; a way to get Susie to come home. It all came together in one simple thought.

*Kill Andy.*

Oscar walked to his bed and looked at the phone. He knew, just like all the other times, who was calling. 312-3351. He just wanted the reassurance that he was making the right decision. He didn't even care that a picture of Andy's bald head and knowing grin now accompanied the number. He wasn't letting that freak scare him anymore.

Oscar moved to the door and grabbed the handle. "You want my reply?" he shouted. His hand squeezed the knob in anticipation. If he didn't pull the door and swing just right, Andy might dodge the blow. He checked the peephole. Andy stood in the same pose as before. "All right, you got it."

With one single motion, he flung the door open with his left arm and brought his right down in a chopping motion. The downward arch added to the speed of his swing, and he connected with a heavy thud. Red mist sprayed and the award tumbled from his hand. The momentum carried him forward, and he collapsed into a heap on the floor with the unmoving body.

Oscar pushed himself away, uncertain of Andy's condition. He doubted the man still lived, but he had to be sure. If this guy could make a disconnected phone ring, then what else could he do? Oscar fumbled for the award, held it over his head with both hands for the final blow, and started to swing—

He stopped.

What had he done? Blood stained his white shirt and a red stream trickled down the body, forming a puddle on the hardwood. Oscar let the award slip from his hand. It landed on his leg, but he didn't care. Not anymore. Nothing would ever matter again.

The person lying dead in front of him wasn't Andy. Not at all. This person had long, mahogany hair, dark, enticing skin, and a birthmark on the back of her hand that was little more than a freckle.

She had come back. . . .

But how? Where was Andy? He'd been standing outside, knocking. It was him. The man from the painting. ANDY. That lunatic. How'd he do it? How? HOW?

Andy's voice echoed in his mind. ". . . your debt can be settled by simply dirtying your soul with blood."

And he had.

Oscar died there and then. His physical body went on living, but for all intents and purposes, Oscar was dead.

The phone rang. His subconscious directed his hand to his pocket. He didn't realize he had hit "accept" or even that he was holding a phone. Everything was dull now. Andy's sweet voice spoke, cordial as ever, knowing that things had turned out the way he wanted them to.

"Good evening, sir, would Mr. Nuñez be available?"

"Uh-huh," some detached part of Oscar mumbled.

"Great. Our records show your debt as settled. Thank you for your prompt repayment. On behalf of the Waterhouse family, it was a pleasure doing business with you. Goodnight."

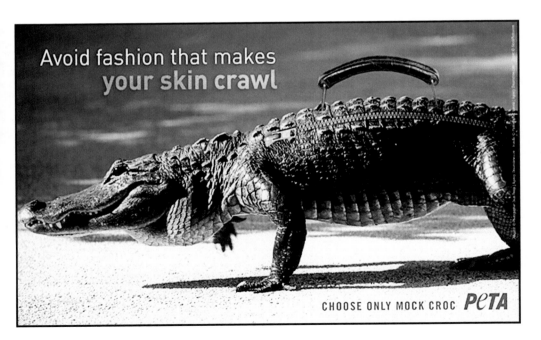

"...this film is enjoyable, and any fan of Ackerman
should pick up a copy for their library."
--TheoFantastique

"Forry was one hell of an influence to several generations...
you should see this film."
--James Robert Smith
(author, *The Flock*)

"Really a fascinating piece of work..."
--Marc Scott Zicree
(author,
*The Twilight Zone Companion*)

"If Famous Monsters of Filmland
was an important part of your life...
you need to see this."
--Ray Garton
(author, *Live Girls*)

# THE ACKERMONSTER CHRONICLES!

The Forrest J Ackerman Story

A Film by Jason V Brock

# The Group:
## Bradbury, Matheson, Beaumont, Nolan

### By S. T. Joshi

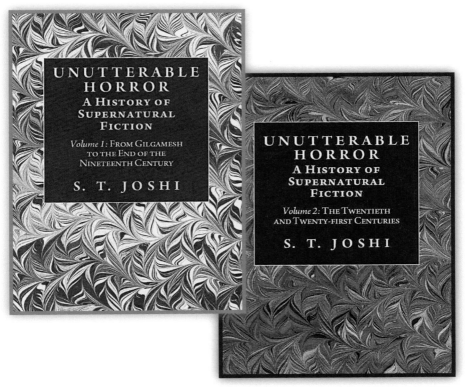

*Excerpted from* **Unutterable Horror: A History of Supernatural Fiction,** *PS Publishing, 2012*

In the 1940s and 1950s, a remarkable group of writers, mostly based in California, effected a revolution in supernatural and non-supernatural horror literature as dramatic as that engendered by H. P. Lovecraft and his compatriots a generation earlier. This group—called, blandly enough, "The Group," and consisting chiefly of Ray Bradbury, Richard Matheson, Charles Beaumont, and William F. Nolan, with other, lesser figures such as George Clayton Johnson and John Tomerlin, several of whom, to our great good fortune, are still with us—all worked seamlessly in the genres of supernatural horror, crime/suspense, science fiction, and fantasy. In some senses this genre-switching and genre-blending was a result of market forces: the demise of the pulp magazines (*Weird Tales* finally

collapsed in 1954 after thirty-one years of existence) and the emergence of the digest-sized science fiction magazines (*Fantasy & Science Fiction, Galaxy,* and many others) created a sudden absence of a market for pure supernaturalism and a need to present weird fiction in the guise of science fiction or psychological suspense. The end result was that these writers, all acquainted with one another and often exchanging ideas dynamically, fostered a modernisation of the supernatural by appeal to science as well as an appeal to the mundanities of contemporary life in America, with the result that much of their work features a social criticism of the increasing blandness and conformism of their time.

Chronologically speaking, Ray Bradbury (1920–2012) should probably be regarded as the pioneer in the midcentury shift of supernatural horror from the flamboyant cosmicism of Lovecraft and his colleagues to the mundane social realism that in some ways continues to dominate the field today. Bradbury's letter to the editor in the November 1939 issue of *Weird Tales* briefly praises Lovecraft's "Cool Air," and he retained a lifelong devotion to the exotic prose-poetry of Clark Ashton Smith's fantastic tales; but his own work, while being richly prose-poetic in its own way and deftly fusing fantasy, supernatural horror, psychological horror, and a delicate character portrayal not often found in weird fiction, is as different from Lovecraft's Cthulhu Mythos or Smith's tales of Zothique and Hyberborea as any literature could well be.

And yet, Bradbury's devotion to the pulps compelled him to publish much of his early weird work in *Weird Tales* and its rivals, beginning in 1942, and these tales were quickly noticed by August Derleth, who was always on the lookout for promising new work to publish with Arkham House. His identification of Bradbury's talent is one of his most astute observations, and his publishing of Bradbury's first volume, *Dark Carnival* (1947), is a landmark both for its author and for its publisher. That single volume—or, perhaps more accurately, the extensive revision and reordering of that volume in the later collection *The October Country* (1955)—could be said to have all but single-handedly initiated a new and vibrant trend in weird fiction.

What distinguishes Bradbury's work from that of many of his predecessors, contemporaries, and successors—aside from the sheer inventiveness of his imagination and his immense gifts of language and story construction—is his uncanny ability to construct weird scenarios that serve as powerful symbols or metaphors for central human concerns. Perhaps the most obvious—but nonetheless effective—instance of this trait is the somewhat later story "The Dwarf" (*Fantastic,* January–February 1954), which utilises Bradbury's patented carnival setting. Here the dwarf of the title is obviously a stand-in for Bradbury himself, as he writes pulp detective stories (Bradbury wrote extensively for the detective pulps as well as for the weird and science fiction pulps). Ralph, the operator of the hall of mirrors at the carnival, switches mirrors so that the dwarf looks, not bigger, but even smaller than his actual dimensions: a more transparent symbol could scarcely be sought for Bradbury's own insecurity as he was transitioning from a pulp writer to the greater stature he sought as a mainstream writer.

Several other stories deftly probe abnormal psychological states in either a supernatural or non-supernatural manner. Of the former sort is the chilling tale "Skeleton" (*Weird Tales*, September 1945), in which a man develops a shuddering horror of his own skeleton: "A skeleton. One of those jointed, snowy, hard things, one of those foul, dry, brittle, gouge-eyed, skull-faced, shake-fingered, rattling things that sway from neck-chains in abandoned webbed closets, one of those things found on the desert all long and scattered like dice!" (*OC* 68). As a result of this bizarre affliction, he loses weight—whereupon he thinks that his skeleton is trying to starve him. The supernatural element here is a bit adventitious—a strange physician, Dr. Munigaut, removes the man's skeleton, rendering him a jellyfish-like creature—but the psychological analysis remains acute. A purely psychological horror tale is "The Next in Line" (first published in *Dark Carnival*), in which a woman visiting a remote Mexican town becomes terrified by thoughts of mortality—especially when she learns that the town digs up graves if the survivors do not continue to pay a fee for their maintenance. This story achieves an acme of physical horror at the thought of death and its aftermath.

Other stories continue the exploration of abnormal psychology. "The Wind" (*Collier's*, 5 August 1950) tells of a man who thinks the wind is after him: he is under the impression that it absorbs the intelligence of those it kills, thereby growing increasingly more powerful and dangerous. In a clever supernatural twist, the man hears the laughter of a friend outside—but no friend is there.. . . Also effective is "The Night" (*Weird Tales*, July 1946), in which a boy's terror of a ravine at night metamorphoses into a general terror of human loneliness. (It becomes evident that August Derleth borrowed heavily from this tale in "The Lonesome Place.") "Fever Dream" (*Weird Tales*, September 1948) also seems on the surface a tale of psychological horror—a boy suffering from scarlet fever thinks that his hands have been taken over by the fever, to such a degree that at one point he tries to choke himself—but features a clever supernatural twist at the end.

Bradbury quickly developed a remarkable insight into human character and motivation, and also the skill to adopt weird quasi-supernatural scenarios to express it. Consider "The Jar" (*Weird Tales*, November 1944), an unforgettable etching of the dreary hopelessness of rustic life. A man named Charly buys from a carny a jar containing

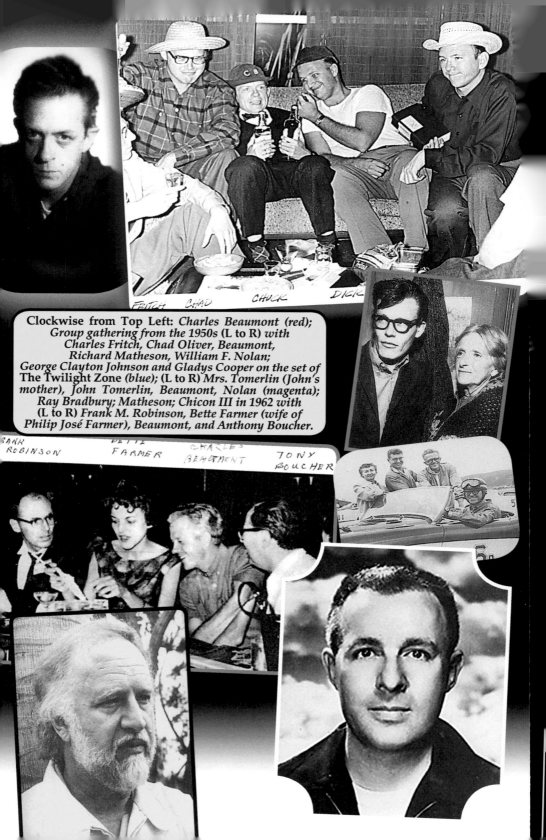

FRITCH    CHAD    CHUCK    DICK

**Clockwise from Top Left:** *Charles Beaumont (red);
Group gathering from the 1950s (L to R) with
Charles Fritch, Chad Oliver, Beaumont,
Richard Matheson, William F. Nolan;
George Clayton Johnson and Gladys Cooper on the set of
The Twilight Zone (blue); (L to R) Mrs. Tomerlin (John's
mother), John Tomerlin, Beaumont, Nolan (magenta);
Ray Bradbury; Matheson; Chicon III in 1962 with
(L to R) Frank M. Robinson, Bette Farmer (wife of
Philip José Farmer), Beaumont, and Anthony Boucher.*

FRANK
ROBINSON    BETTE
FARMER    CHARLES
BEAUMONT    TONY
BOUCHER

what appears to be some strange entity preserved in formaldehyde. He becomes the talk of his wretched community with the possession of this grisly object, even though the carny later admits to his wife that the object is a fake. Refusing to believe it, Charly kills his wife and places her head in the jar. There is an unparalleled poignancy in Bradbury's depiction of a man who has nothing in his life except the attraction of what might or might not be in a jar. "The Lake" (*Weird Tales*, May 1944) is also extraordinary poignant in depicting a man's remembrance of his adolescent relationship with a twelve-year-old girl who had drowned. Does she come back from the dead to finish a sand castle the two of them had begun decades ago? We never learn the answer to that question, but the portrayal of bittersweet young love has never been bettered.

Bradbury's later work has (probably justly) been criticised as at times maudlin and sentimental, but early in his career he could produce tales of remarkable grimness, even of bitter cynicism. Probably the chief among them is "The Small Assassin" (*Dime Mystery*, November 1946), which was, incredibly, actually submitted to *Good Housekeeping* but was rejected because the editors rightly maintained that it would prove offensive to young mothers! This immortal tale of a young couple who come to believe that their own new-born baby is trying to murder them is a flawless instance of the kind of "mundane horror"—horror emerging from the seemingly bland events of ordinary life—that Bradbury and other members of The Group championed. As David Leiber, the father of the child, states to a physician:

"But suppose one child in a billion is—strange? Born perfectly aware, able to think, instinctively. Wouldn't it be a perfect setup, a perfect blind for anything the baby might want to do? He could pretend to be ordinary, weak, crying, ignorant. With just a *little* expenditure of energy he could drawl about a darkened house, listening. And how easy to place obstacles at the top of stairs. How easy to cry all night and tire a mother into pneumonia. How easy, right at birth, to be so close to the mother that *a few deft maneuvers might cause peritonitis!*" (*OC* 141)

The story progresses with enormous skill from psychological horror—at the outset we are merely led to believe that the baby's mother is merely a victim of post-partum depression—to actual supernaturalism.

Just as grim in a different way is "The Crowd" (*Weird Tales*, May 1943), in which a man comes to realise that the crowd that appears to gather at car accidents and other disasters are, in many cases, the same people—and the crowning horror is his awareness that they are in fact dead. Bradbury is somewhat less successful at humorous treatments of the supernatural, as in "There Was an Old Woman" (*Weird Tales*, July 1944), in which a woman refuses to believe that she is a ghost. "The Man Upstairs" (*Harper's*, March 1947) is a half-comic vampire tale of no great

distinction.

Bradbury of course quickly achieved enormous celebrity as a science fiction writer with the publication, in rapid succession, of *The Martian Chronicles* (1950), *The Illustrated Man* (1951), and *Fahrenheit 451* (1953). A number of the stories of this period powerfully fuse horror and science fiction. Perhaps the best of them is "The Fog Horn" (*Saturday Evening Post,* 23 June 1951), the basis for the film *The Beast from 20,000 Fathoms* (1953). This story of a lighthouse keeper who comes upon the last surviving prehistoric creature who thinks that the lighthouse's foghorn may be the call of its long-lost mate is inexpressibly touching:

"All year long, Johnny, that poor monster there lying far out, a thousand miles at sea, and twenty miles deep maybe, biding its time, perhaps it's a million years old, this one creature. Think of it, waiting a million years; could *you* wait that long? Maybe it's the last of its kind. I sort of think that's true. Anyway, here come men on land and build this lighthouse, five years ago. And set up their Fog Horn and sound it and sound it, out toward the place where you bury yourself in sleep and sea memories of a world where there were thousands like yourself, but now you're alone, all alone in a world not made for you, a world where you have to hide." (*Stories* 269)

"The Veldt" (*Saturday Evening Post,* 23 September 1950; in *The Illustrated Man*) is more chilling but perhaps somewhat less successful. The story broaches the notion of virtual reality: in the future, homes are now equipped with walls featuring moving images that display landscapes triggered by the thoughts of the children occupying them. In this case, the children repeatedly think of an African veldt with dangerous lions in the background. Later, the children lock their parents into the room, where they are killed—not by the lions coming to life, but by the parents somehow entering the image of the veldt on the wall. Ingenious as this idea is, the plausibility of the conception leaves something to be desired; and the general symbolism of the tale—a satire on permissive parents and unruly children—seems a trifle mundane. More purely science fictional, but perhaps among the most chilling stories in Bradbury's entire oeuvre, is the brief and celebrated "There Will Come Soft Rains" (*Collier's,* 6 May 1950), an imperishable depiction of a house that continues to operate automatically after what appears to have been a nuclear holocaust.

Of Bradbury's novels, only *Something Wicked This Way Comes* (1962) needs to be considered here. In a sense it is a successor to *Dandelion Wine* (1958), a fix-up novel that somewhat clumsily stitched together a number of Bradbury's short stories into an affecting depiction of the nostalgia of summer as seen through the eyes of a small-town boy. Bradbury, whose understanding of the psychology of adolescent boyhood is perhaps unmatched in literature, and whose ability to evoke the aching nostalgia of long-lost childhood is also second to none, brings both qualities to the fore in a novel of genuine terror. *Something Wicked* takes place in Green Town, a transparent metaphor for the town of Waukegan, Illinois, where Bradbury spent his own boyhood.

*Something Wicked* focuses on two teenage boys, Will Halloway and Jim Nightshade, the latter born on Halloween and the former the day before Halloween. In the week before their birthdays, a carnival—Cooger & Dark's Pandemonium shadow Show—comes to town. One senses at once that something is awry: carnivals never come to the town after Labor Day; the carnival arrives on a train at 3 A.M.; as it progresses, a calliope is playing—but no player is visible. Further bizarre manifestations occur, the most notable of which is the remarkable power of the merry-go-round or carousel to increase or decrease one's age depending on whether it goes forward or backward. (This idea was derived from the earlier short story "The Black Ferris" [*Weird Tales,* May 1948].) Mr. Cooger rides the carousel eighty or ninety times, with the result that he is hideously aged:

The eyes were mummified shut. The nose was collapsed upon gristle. The mouth was a ruined white flower, the petals twisted into a thin wax sheath over the clenched teeth through which faint bubblings sighed. The man was small inside his clothes, small as a child, but tall, strung out, and old, so old, very old, not ninety, not one hundred, no, not one hundred and ten, but one hundred and twenty or one hundred and thirty impossible years old. (75–76)

But these horrific scenes are only the surface phenomena of the much deeper purpose of the carnival. As Will's father explains:

"All the meannesses we harbor, they borrow in redoubled spades. They're a billion times itchier for pain, sorrow, and sickness than the average man. We salt our lives with other people's sins. Our flesh to us tastes sweet. But the carnival doesn't care if it stinks by moonlight instead of sun, so long as it gorges on fear and pain. That's the fuel, the vapor that spins the carousel, the raw stuffs of terror, the

Left to Right: *Writer William F. Nolan, editor/agent Forrest J Ackerman, and author Ray Bradbury at a signing in the 1950s*

excruciating agony of guilt, the scream from real or imagined wounds. The carnival sucks that gas, ignites it, and chugs along its way." (148–49)

What *Something Wicked This Way Comes* is really about is the

ability to resist those desires that we know to be impossible (such as the desire of Miss Foley, the teacher, to regain her lost youth) or self-destructive. It is also about boyhood, the bonds of young friendship ("Oh, Jim, Jim. . . we'll be pals forever" [213], Will says at the end), and the developing relations between father and son. It is at once the culmination of Bradbury's utilisation of the carnival motif—a motif that fuses light-hearted play, secretive darkness, fantasy and illusion, magic and trickery—and of his evocation of nostalgia and adolescence. It is written in perhaps an excessively self-conscious prose-poetry, but its elements of terror and wistfulness have rendered it immensely influential on subsequent weird writing.

Bradbury's ability to use weird motifs as metaphors for profound human concerns allowed him to shift easily from the pulp market to slicks like *Collier's* and *Saturday Evening Post*, while his hugely popular works of science fiction helped to raise that genre in critical esteem and to elevate his own work to the level of an American classic. It is a bit sad to note that the best of his work had largely been written, with rare exceptions (like *Something Wicked*), by the late 1950s. Bradbury, more than most authors, has written far too much and has also in some senses believed his own press and become a self-consciously literary author. His later work is sadly melodramatic, even maudlin, and little that he has written since the 1960s is of any account. But his early work has made an imperishable impression on the fields of science fiction, fantasy, and supernatural horror, and his undoubted talents will establish him as a writer close to the stature of a Lovecraft or a Poe.

Richard Matheson (b. 1926) is as different a writer as two Californians working in the same genre(s) could possibly be. Deliberately eschewing the prose-poetry of Bradbury, Matheson developed a flat, mundane, Hemingwayesque style that is frequently effective in conveying the subtle incursion of the bizarre into the ordinary lives of ordinary Americans; but on occasion, this excessive spareness renders his conceptions difficult to swallow. Although Matheson did publish two stories in *Weird Tales*, they are not among his most distinguished, and he did his best work in the weird/supernatural vein in stories published chiefly in the burgeoning digest-size science fiction magazines of the period. Matheson also wrote a considerable amount of non-supernatural or psychological suspense work, some of which borders on the weird.

Matheson's work offers definitive proof, as if it were needed by now, that the heritage of both supernatural literature and horror film was casting a pronounced influence upon the literature of this and subsequent periods. Several of his earlier stories are conscious riffs on prior work in the field. "Blood Son" (1951), about a boy who wants to be a vampire, contains patent references to both the novel and the film

*Dracula*. "Lover When You're Near Me" (1952) is a science fiction story based on the premise of Robert Hichens's "How Love Came to Professor Guildea." Even the late story "Button, Button" (1970) is a variant of "The Monkey's Paw," and one wonders whether Matheson is even aware of the borrowing.

In other stories, Matheson fashions deliberate take-offs of well-known supernatural motifs, as in the well-known "Witch War" (1951), where the poltergeist abilities of young girls are harnessed to fight wars. His two *Weird Tales* stories may be of this sort: "Slaughter House" (July 1953) is a rather tiresome account of a revenant, written in a poor "Victorian" style (as Matheson himself has labelled it [*CS* 2.48]) that is ill-suited to his talents; "Wet Straw" (January 1953) is a routine story of supernatural revenge.

Several of Matheson's best stories are interesting fusions of psychological and supernatural horror, at times lapsing into science fiction. One of the most powerful of his early tales is "Mad House" (1953), in which a man, Chris Neal, who seems constantly enraged at life feels that the inanimate objects in his house are conspiring against him. A physician, influenced by Charles Fort, believes that Chris's anger is itself causing these bizarre events and that it may kill him without the presence of his wife, Sally, who is "acting as an abortive factor" (*CS* 1.194). When she leaves, the objects in the house become actually animate and induce Chris to kill himself with a razor. Somewhat similar, but resolving itself non-supernaturally, is "Legion of Plotters" (1953), in which a man believes there is a conspiracy on the part of the rest of humanity to drive him insane by constantly irritating him, to the point that he finally snaps and stabs a man on a bus who had been sniffing loudly.

Matheson is at his most effective in establishing mundane scenarios that veer off into the bizarre. Consider "The Curious Child" (1954), in which a man finds that he does not know where he lives or works, and finally ends by not even remembering his own name. An unconvincing science fiction conclusion dealing with time travel does not mar the nightmarishly unnerving quality of the overall narrative. Similar is "The Edge" (1958), where a man named Arthur Nolan recognises Don Marshall as an old friend, although Don does not know who he is; Arthur then goes home and finds that his own wife fails to recognise him. In stories of this type Matheson again is able to present effective non-supernatural variants: "The Children of Noah" (1957) deals with a traveller stopped for speeding in a small town in Maine and, after repeated humiliations that lead him to be kept in jail overnight, discovers that the townspeople are going to eat him. In "The Distributor" (1958) a man moves into a placid suburban neighbourhood and by simple acts

sows discord among his neighbours. Matheson wrote in a note on the story that "that's what true evil would be like. It's not monsters and devils and all that. It's what happens every day in your own neighborhood" (CS 2.444)."Prey" (1969) is another nightmarish story of a Zuni fetish doll that comes to life in a woman's apartment.

Matheson is also clever at incorporating humanity's inveterate fear and unease at new technologies. In this sense, "Long Distance Call" (1953) is a prototypical story. An elderly woman, Elva Keene, finds that her phone is constantly ringing, but no one responds when she answers. In later calls, a man does respond, but he evidently cannot hear Miss Keene's increasingly frantic words. The story contains a clever double twist: it is not merely that, as the operator discovers, the phone calls are coming from the cemetery; it is that, in the final call that concludes the story, the man states ominously, "Hello, Miss Elva. I'll be right over" (CS 1.399). The celebrated "Nightmare at 20,000 Feet" (1962) should be discussed in this context. This well-known story of a man on a plane who believes—rightly, as it happens—that a gremlin is seeking to bring the plane down is really a parable about the advance of technology beyond the powers of human beings to absorb it, and the concomitant feelings of helplessness it engenders.

Several of Matheson's stories, however, suffer from his mundane prose and from implausible scenarios. In "Disappearing Act" (1953) the tokens of a man's identity disappear one by one, but the narrative is unconvincing. "Old Haunts" (1957) could have been a poignant story about a man who revisits his college and comes upon younger versions of himself; but Matheson's mechanical prose fails to engender the nostalgia inherent in the plot—something that Bradbury or even Rod Serling could and did engender in analogous tales. "Crickets" (1960) tells of a man who thinks that crickets are sending out messages from the dead, but the story is marred by insufficient development.

A number of Matheson's later tales show his increasing interest in the occult. Several deal with second sight or precognition. In "The Holiday Man" (1957) a man is able to predict how many people are going to die on a given holiday. Similarly, "Girl of My Dreams" (1963) tells of a woman who is a "sensitive" and has visions of the future. Her husband uses her skills as blackmail, until she takes pity on a woman whose son is going to die and warns her, whereupon her husband kills her. This story falls into what is known as the determinism paradox, something we shall find in a more celebrated work of weird fiction written several decades later: If the woman had seen the vision of the boy's dying, no act on her or anyone else's part could have deflected that result—or, rather, all actions seeking to deflect that result would have led inexorably to it; if, as a result of anyone's actions, the boy did not in fact die, the woman could not have seen the vision in the first place. In "Mute" (1962), a boy is raised by a family that does not teach him to speak, as the parents are conducting an experiment to see if he develops telepathic powers—which he does. After the parents die, his foster-parents do teach him to speak; he loses his powers but gains the familial love that has been missing from his life.

We have seen that Matheson frequently fuses supernatural and science fiction scenarios; in his tales he is not always successful, but in one novel, at least, he has produced a noteworthy contribution: *I Am Legend* (1954). The plot of this work—about Robert Neville, who fears that he may be the last man on earth who has not turned into a vampire—need not be rehearsed. The critical issue is the manner in which Matheson renders this conception plausibly. We are evidently to understand that a virus carried by dust storms has rendered everyone but Neville into a vampire; he alone is "immune to their infection" (53), because he was once bitten by a vampire bat and derived some kind of immunity in that fashion (132–33). How convincing this is can be a matter of debate; at any rate, in classic science fiction fashion, Neville spends much time at the Los Angeles Public Library looking for a "rational answer to the problem" (66) and even learning enough chemistry to identify the bacterium in a vampire's blood.

A good part of the early sections of the novel, depicting a world that is devastated and all but deserted as a result of the curious virus, reads like M. P. Shiel's novel *The Purple Cloud* (1901/1929), and I would not be surprised if Matheson were consciously influenced by it: it had been reprinted in paperback in 1946 and had appeared in an abridged version in the June 1949 issue of *Famous Fantastic Mysteries*. But the novel develops both originality and poignancy by the appearance, first, of a living dog, whom Neville spends weeks trying to catch and domesticate before it finally dies, and then of a woman named Ruth, who appears to be uninfected, although she reacts poorly to garlic. The complex interplay between the two is the emotional centre of the novel: Neville, by this time so unused to human interaction that he occasionally lapses into boorishness or even cruelty, desperately hopes that Ruth is who she says she is, and even envisions reconstituting the human race in the manner of Adam and Eve. But she is in fact a member of a small band of infected humans who have learned to survive in daylight for short periods of time, and it is this group that will establish a new society. Neville is caught, and Ruth urges him to take pills and commit suicide before he is executed. He does so, and his concluding reflections on being the last true human being on earth reach a level of poignancy and majesty that is rare in Matheson's work.

Matheson's interest in the occult is exhibited in the later novel

*A Stir of Echoes* (1958), in which a man's psychic powers reveal the dark secrets lurking behind the lives of his seemingly normal neighbours, and in the very poor *Hell House* (1971), an unwitting caricature of Shirley Jackson's *The Haunting of Hill House* (1971). By this time Matheson had virtually abandoned the writing of short stories, and his later work tends to be almost exclusively in the realms of fantasy or science fiction.

Another work that cleverly melds supernatural and science fiction motifs is *The Body Snatchers* by Jack Finney (1911–1995), first published serially in *Collier's* (26 November–24 December 1954) before appearing in book form in 1955. Set in the imaginary town of Santa Mira, California (the revised version of 1978 is set in the actual town of Mill Valley), the novel revolves around Dr. Miles Bennell, who finds that a number of his patients have come to believe that intimate members of their family are in some vague way impostors. It turns out that these individuals are in fact impostors—aliens who have come through space as pods and are able to replicate both the physical and the mental aspects of the inhabitants of whatever planet they come upon; this happens when the original inhabitants are asleep, whereupon they are reduced to a grey dust.

It has often been believed that the novel is an exhibition of Cold War paranoia and the dangers of communist spies lurking in the midst of ordinary American life; but there is very little sociopolitical commentary or implication in the novel that would lend support to such an interpretation, and it is more likely that the work is merely a rumination on the nature of humanity. The aliens lack emotions, and they cannot reproduce, so that they will be dead in five years. It is this that Miles emphasises to one of the aliens, remarking that "There's no real joy, fear, hope, or excitement in you, not any more. You live in the same kind of grayness as the filthy stuff that formed you" (183).

The popularity of both *I Am Legend* and *The Body Snatchers* is indicated by the numerous film adaptations of both: the first has been adapted three times (1964, 1971, 2007), the latter four times (1956, 1978, 1993, 2007).

Matheson and Charles Beaumont (1929–1967) were two of the most prolific writers of teleplays for Rod Serling's *The Twilight Zone*, but he also wrote a substantial amount of short fiction as well as the non-weird novel *The Intruder* (1959), about race relations in Missouri. Beaumont's work is characterised by highly penetrating analyses of character, a prose style of muted lyricism, and some powerful weird conceptions that simultaneously draw upon the heritage of supernatural literature and shine a pungent light on the social and psychological angst of the period. During his tragically shortened lifetime—he was afflicted, apparently, with a radical form of early-onset Alzheimer's, the evident result of consuming immense quantities of Bromo-Seltzer to relieve his crippling headaches—he produced a bountiful array of literary work, including screenplays and teleplays; but his stories were gathered in only three original collections, *The Hunger and Other Stories* (1958), *Yonder* (1958), and *Night Ride and Other Journeys* (1960), of which the second is almost entirely devoted to science fiction.

Relatively little of Beaumont's work is overtly supernatural, but one of these, "The Vanishing American" (1955), may be his most striking and socially relevant narrative. This plangent tale of an average office worker who gradually disappears from view is perfectly emblematic of the intellectually and aesthetically stultifying life engendered by the corporate America of the 1950s. The fact that the protagonist, Mr. Minchell, cannot see himself in a mirror evokes the similar invisibility of vampires in mirrors, but to a very different purpose. The tale ends happily, however, when Minchell throws off his staid conventionality by riding one of the stone lions guarding the New York Public Library— an act of imaginative independence that allows him to be seen by others once again.

Beaumont's other notable supernatural tale is "The Howling Man" (1960), in which a traveller, taking refuge in a German monastery, hears the appalling cries of a howling man in a cell and is soberly informed by the abbot that it is the devil. The traveller refuses to believe the abbot and sets the man free. He of course turns out to be the devil. As a tale contrasting ancient belief and modern skepticism, the tale is moderately successful, but the general implausibility of the overall narrative weakens its effect; and a happy ending—the devil is, in some unexplained fashion, once more caught at the end of the story—doesn't help.

Then there is "Black Country" (1954), an astonishing narrative that, in the manner of a jazz composition, portrays the apparent possession of a white musician's body by the spirit of his black mentor. Less successful is "Free Dirt" (1955), a predictable tale in which a miser who gets free dirt from a cemetery is later buried in it.

Beaumont's best work is in the realm of psychological suspense, where his skill at character portrayal and his acuity in the analysis of aberrant mentalities is on display. "Miss Gentilbelle" (1958) tells the seemingly simple narrative of a woman who has had an illegitimate child and, out of shame, forces the boy to think of himself as a girl; in vengeance, he later kills her. But this summary cannot begin to convey the grim effectiveness of Beaumont's depiction of the crippling effect of the mother's vicious treatment of her own son. The same could be said for "The Hunger" (1955), in which a woman, out of loneliness, deliberately puts herself in the path of a rapist-murderer.

Some of Beaumont's stories are less than successful, perhaps because the satire that he wishes to direct at some of his figures is not as subtle as it could be."Open House" tells of a man who has just murdered his wife in the bathroom but is forced to receive two friends who have arrived at his doorstep; later he feels compelled to kill them also, whereupon more friends arrive. Then there is the long and intricate narrative "The New People" (1958), in which a couple settling in a house whose previous owner had committed suicide find increasing suggestions that their neighbours are all involved in various criminal or antisocial activities culminating in a black mass. The tale proves to be highly contrived, in that Beaumont must convince us (unsuccessfully) that the young wife of the new couple is still a virgin, simply so that she can then be suitably sacrificed in the neighbours' black mass. Another story, "The Crooked Man" (1955), is disturbing for a different reason: this science fiction tale about a future society in which heterosexuality is now regarded as aberrant suggests a strain of homophobia on Beaumont's part.

"Perchance to Dream" (1958) is a remarkable fusion of psychological and supernatural horror and in some senses could be regarded as the pinnacle of Beaumont's—and The Group's—blending of genres. A man sees a psychiatrist because, as he maintains, his dreams are taking on a hideous kind of reality. The story culminates in the man's jumping out the window—but in fact the entire narrative has been a dream, and the man is found dead of a heart attack.

Some note should be taken of the work of William F. Nolan (b. 1928). In some senses his work is less spectacular than that of his friends and colleagues in The Group, and in many ways he is of greatest interest as a critic, biographer, and bibliographer of their work. Nolan compiled the first anthology of essays on Bradbury, the slim *Ray Bradbury Review* (1952), and he also wrote the later *Ray Bradbury Companion* (1975); his monograph on Beaumont, *The Work of Charles Beaumont* (1990), is an important reference work. Although best known for the dystopian science fiction novel *Logan's Run* (1967), cowritten with George Clayton Johnson and the basis for a celebrated film, Nolan has himself produced a substantial body of fiction in a wide array of genres, from supernatural horror to science fiction to crime/suspense to westerns.

The supernatural does not bulk large in his work, but some instances of it are of considerable merit. Perhaps the most notable is "The Party" (1967), in which a man who comes to an apartment where a party is going on discovers, perhaps to no one's surprise, that he has entered hell. But the merit of the story is Nolan's flawless capturing of the utterly inane and pointless conversation uttered by the various guests ("I knew a policewoman who loved to scrub down whores" [39]). Then there is

"Dead Call" (1976), in which a dead man persuades his friend to commit suicide as he himself had done ("Life is ugly, but death is beautiful" [92]); his friend does so and thereby continues the cycle. Even the science fiction tale "The Underdweller" (*Fantastic Universe,* August 1957) has its soupçon of terror: in the future, the last man in Los Angeles (or perhaps the world) lives in tunnels, continually on the run from what appear to be aliens—but in fact he is on the run from children, since the aliens who had invaded the earth years before had killed all adults above the age of six except himself. There is perhaps an influence of Matheson's *I Am Legend* on this tale, but it retains its originality because of its clever surprise ending. The retrospective collection *William F. Nolan's Dark Universe* (2001) is a worthy testament to the work of a writer whose talent and longevity deserve our deepest respect.

## Works Cited

Bradbury, Ray. *The October Country.* New York: Ballantine, 1956. [Abbreviated in the text as *OC.*]

———. *Something Wicked This Way Comes.* New York: Bantam, 1963.

Finney, Jack. *Invasion of the Body Snatchers.* New York: Dell, 1978.

Matheson, Richard. *Collected Stories.* Edited by Stanley Wiater. Colorado Springs, CO: Edge, 2003. 3 vols. [Abbreviated in the text as *CS.*]

———. *I Am Legend.* New York: Tor, 1995.

# December in the Druid Woods

The moon casts down a corpse-white radiance
Upon the grove of ancient wizard oaks,
Where through the rows, an icy wind invokes
An evensong to unknown eminence.
Gnarled limbs now animate in eerie light;
They hail a presence in their somber rows,
Their shadows flattened on the glowing snow
As if obeisant to the very night.

The wood is like a hidden world revealed,
A portal on its own primeval past—
Through which a spirit, since those times concealed,
Now moves namelessly, ineffable and vast;
Supernal in its cold nocturnal grace
And silent as the starry vault of space.

# Astral Hierarchy

At twilight come the minor moon
To float in skies of purple wine,
And desert spirits walk attuned
To subtle prodigies and signs
Beneath the glowing minor moon.

Then rising is the second moon—
It looms behind the minor sphere,
And night is litten as at noon
Awhile, as midnight's atmosphere
Lies mute beneath the second moon.

Then over all, the major moon
Arises like a queen of Hell;
Weird crimson light illumes the dunes,

And all seems in a wizard spell
Beneath the glowing major moon.

# The Eremite

*"We have seen the black suns*
*Pouring forth the night."*
                    —*Clark Ashton Smith*

On moonless nights when stars are crystal clear
And shadows lie down softly, black and calm,
I leave my unlit hut and raise weird psalms
In praise of blacker gulfs beyond the spheres,
Then wait until the world is quietest
To walk with voiceless entities unseen
Who hear my hymns from where they roam between
The known dimensions and the alien rest.

A hermit of the outer wastes, I stand
In reverence of what the darkness brings.
My mantras nullify the lakes of light
That flood from golden temples of the land,
And prophets fear the pious songs I sing—
The songs of black suns pouring forth the night.

# A Vessel for Black Waters

Out in the wasteland in the days before
The solstices, I journey to the caves

Which hold monastic bones in hidden graves
Beneath the table of a windswept moor.
The ceremonies that I here perform
Were well-known once, but long-forgotten now—
Except by few who share a sacred vow
To see this world by prophecy reformed.

Attuned to distant voices here entombed,
I am an empty vessel, mute and still,

Through which the spirits speak and guide my quill—

This way an elder wisdom is exhumed
From scriptures long-since lost in holy wars—
And wise men call these books I write grimoires.


—*Wade German*

# The Echo

By Michael Aronovitz

*May*

J.F.K. is dead. Judy Garland, Osama bin Laden, King James, Chaucer, Hitler, Shoeless Joe Jackson, Nostradamus, all dead, like a trillion others. So am I, but don't ask if I've seen your long-lost great uncle or anything. It's not like that. There's just foliage out here; vague images and dark outlines in the passing windows, a lot of roadway.

I drive a '95 Nissan Sentra, and it's an absolute shitbox. Members of my family tease me about it; the pitted back bumper, the broken driver's side door handle that makes you lower the window and claw out to flip up the exterior release, the lack of a floor mat on the passenger side, the worn felt seat cushions marbled like old dough.

Oh, and don't fret over the fact that I refer to my wife and kids in the present tense. I engage in this practice only because I think I am trapped in a moment that keeps being played out as if in live time, and my family is no more concerned about me than they were in terms of their "yesterday" or the day before that. And though I cannot be utterly sure in terms of hard proof, I am fairly certain that I am indeed deceased because I don't get hungry anymore. Moreover, I can only recall universalities. I know that killing is wrong, that getting a girl pregnant before you marry her can put a real dent in your plans, that The Who were always better than the Beatles, if not in terms of cultural impact, then by a standard of showmanship and instrumentation, but I don't remember what I had for dinner last night (if there is such a thing as an "evening" for me any longer). As I alluded to before, I know I have kids, but can't recall how many. I know my wife is a pale brunette, but I can't recollect her laugh. I know she has sun freckles dusted across her cleavage, a nondescript suburban ass, and Mediterranean cheekbones she accents with lavender blush, but I can't remember her maiden name. My whole life, or past life if you will, has been reduced to wallet-sized black-and-whites, faded and out of order.

Thing is, I don't miss it. My life. Because even though it seems I am stuck for eternity in this shitty charcoal gray Nissan, there is also a feeling about me (or in me) that I am in transit to a destination. Now, please don't interpret that as something spiritual, as if I am on some cosmic pilgrimage to meet the Almighty. I mean that the feeling about me (or maybe imposed on me) is that I am on my way to work, or the

Crate and Barrel, or the driving range for a quick bucket, or the Lord & Taylor because I forgot to get Mother's Day garbage, and it doesn't feel anything like eternity. The window is open with my elbow up on the rim, I'm squinting slightly, and the sky is that pale broad canopy of the lightest blue that fills us all with hope and longing: leisure images of sailboats inching along sun-spangled waters, traveling carnivals, picnics, barbecues, graduations, promises.

Here's the thing. I can't exit the vehicle without dire consequences.

The first time it happened was quite by accident, pardon the pun, when I rear-ended a big dude in a black Dodge Ram, silver diamond grid contractor boxes bolted to both sides of the back bed, ladder rack on the roof, trash barrels and rusted steel drums filled with rakes and hoes and pole tools and shovels all surrounding a black pockmarked roofing kettle. I'd been cruising along and had just passed an area where the roadside sound barriers flanked the near spread of woodland like the walls of some majestic fortress, and I had sort of realized in the back of my mind that I hadn't seen a road sign in awhile. It was the first inkling I'd had that something was odd about this journey, and the first hint that maybe I'd been on this road for longer than what I might have considered "normal"; but just as I started to focus on the fact that I'd been driving without noticing the passage of time, a green sign flashed by, bolted to an overpass, and I realized I'd missed another one, and then traffic before me had come to one of those sudden standstills, and I hit the brakes and screeched the tires.

I skidded, swerved a bit left, and plinked his back bumper. An insignificant little nudge, a Boston kiss.

"Fucking moron," I heard. Couldn't see him. The back window was tinted jet black, but I saw his arm from out the driver's side window, flannel cut on an angle high up at the shoulder in a makeshift short sleeve, bicep hair, beef-bull forearm. The arm went straight up, and then his index finger curved. He jabbed the affair toward the area up and over the roof, toward the breakdown lane. It was an order, and he wasn't kidding. The car in front of him moved forward a bit, and he pulled over, tires making chock 'n' gravel sounds. I followed, stopped, put it in park, kept it running. My heart was thudding a bit and my face was ashen, or at least it felt that way. And I couldn't find my information in the glove compartment. It was a mess of papers, envelopes, expired insurance cards, parking passes, old directions printed off Mapquest, dashboard flyers to identify me as a parent for summer camp pick-up, and I couldn't even remember what I was supposed to be searching for in the first place. Did he need my owner's card? My license? My social security number?

I reached out through the open window, flipped up the handle, and got out of the car.

Everything changed. I wasn't on 476 or 95 or the Northeast Extension anymore, and it wasn't spring. It wasn't daytime either. It was late fall, you could tell because there was that smokehouse tang in the air as if someone had been burning leaves, and the trees all around me were bare, crooked, and spidery, making crisscross shapes before a low moon. We were on a dirt road cutting through the forest, and the pickup had its blinkers on, leaning slightly right because he'd pulled into a bit of a ditch.

There was a rather brisk wind on my face, and I had not brought out anything from my glove compartment. I walked forward; sure, I was going to get a lecture, or maybe even a punch in the eye. I was sweeping apologies together in my head, trying for the right flavor, and couldn't decide between the half-jest "sorry about that," or the sincere, "Hey friend, my fault, what can I do" kind of thing.

His door opened, and a leg thrust itself out, work boot clapping down to the dirt, jeans with cuff-frays coming behind the heel. He pushed out, gripping the upper door rim, and he had to duck to get out because he was that big, and he was muttering, ". . . learn to drive in a fucking girl's room . . ."

And he stood and he was turning toward me, and he pulled at his crotch to move the underwear a bit, and he had a chain going from his wallet to his belt, and a chest like a grizzly and a long chin-beard and a big bulb of a nose and wood chips in his hair, and he was shaking his head as if he was going to teach this little bastard a lesson, and then he looked up and he saw me and his mouth dropped open. He slumped a bit, shoulders curling in and withering, knees knocking in toward each other as though he'd just been whacked in the nuts.

"Uhh . . ." he said. He fumbled back for the open doorway and almost missed, still staring at me, measuring my approach, scrambling sort of sideways for the sanctuary of the truck.

Then I saw it—what scared him. It was only for a split second, and then it was gone, there in his back window, jet black and kicking up gleam from the moon, and I only saw it out of the corner of my eye because I was so focused on his odd retreat, and it was only a flicker because it changed when he broke eye contact. For that one second, it was a creature from some haunted lagoon or lake or swamp, dead, damp vegetation draped over its skull as if dragged up from the bottom of dark waters, fingers long, pointed, water-rotted skin hanging off the bones in tatters and shreds.

It was my silhouette in his back window, and I know it was me because it was mimicking my advance, I could see it at the periphery of my vision, both hands extended out like "what the heck" in response to his cowardly crawl back into the cab, and he broke eye-lock, and I looked at the black outline directly, and it was just me in there now, short hair, pudgy face, I could even see my glasses with the moon reflected in the bottom rim of each lens.

I somehow knew that the rotted figure in the glass had been an image he'd picked up from some TV special he saw when he was six, after he snagged his sister Melinda's Ranch Doritos and tiptoed down the basement even though it was past his bedtime and if Daddy caught him he'd warm up his behind something good. I saw the original horrific images washing over his face in pale lines and shadows just as clearly as I saw the flash forward to his wetting the bed for a year, lying in his own sour dampness with the comforter pulled over his head, breathing all cut and shallow through the little porthole he'd made for his mouth.

The pickup pulled off in a roar, kicking up dirt and road grit.

I blinked, and it was spring again. I was doing a lazy sixty-three miles per hour, and the sky opened before me in that panorama of oceanic crystallized blue. There was sloping acreage to the right, wheat or rye moving with the pattern of the breeze, and on the left there was a long meadow with antenna towers in the background. There were cars around me, but the occupants were forms, vague outlines, shapes.

And no road signs. When I concentrated and focused, bore down the way my dad used to tell me to do in Little League when I couldn't find the strike zone, I'd see something ahead, that familiar rectangular green with the white outline and the white block letters, and then I'd get distracted at the last minute by a deer crossing sign, or a plane flying low overhead, or a truck passing too close.

After some indeterminable amount of time, I pulled into a Howard Johnson's to get directions, to get a handle on this, to convince myself that what happened with the contractor was illusory, and that, finally, I wasn't the creature from the black lagoon.

I didn't get further than the parking area.

Originally, the structure had seemed a familiar, charming little piece of commercial Americana, offset from the highway by a grand sort of rotary, restaurant at the far edge, sprawling golf course in the background. Across the way was an antique furniture store and a glass crafter, both a short walking distance from the shopping center with the Wegman's and the Giant. But when I stepped out and shut my door, I realized I had been mistaken about the surroundings. Everything was gray, and to the left across the highway was an abandoned warehouse, windows darkened, weeds at the perimeter growing out of the cracked cement tire bumpers. Past the motel dumpsters on the far right side, a swarm of cattails and yellow grass led to an area of marsh and tangled woodland. To the right of the place was a rusted cyclone fence with old trash blown in at the bottom, and beyond that, a drainage ditch and an abandoned quarry, dozers parked up on the mounds, and I remembered that the parking lot seemed full when I entered, yet now stood empty for all but a maroon minivan with a soccer magnet in one corner of the back window and a Garfield toy with foot suckers in the other.

I walked up to the vehicle and noticed that my forearms had run over with goose bumps. It was starting to rain, slanted darting drops, and the clouds moving across the sky were running thin shadows along the asphalt.

In the sideview mirror I could see the woman in the driver's seat, designer sunglasses propped above her forehead, auburn hair in a ponytail, severe eyebrows, delicate face—beautiful like glass, a look of general superiority and disinterest.

"Excuse me," I said."Could you tell me where I am, please?"

I honestly believe she was about to turn toward my voice and acknowledge me, but a piercing scream erupted from the back seat. I didn't have a good angle to get a look inside past the lady's shoulder, but when I backed off a half-step I could see through the glass it was a toddler in a car seat, struggling, scratching at his harness, staring at me with wide, rolling eyes.

With Mom occupado, I bent to look in her sideview and saw the strangest, most frightening thing looking back at me on an angle.

I was a playing card, a Jack I think, and I couldn't tell if I was a heart or a diamond, but I knew for sure I was one of the red ones. My face was elongated, skull-like, shaped like the "Scream" mask, but the eyes were brilliant and savage, close-set and piercing, the drawn lines around the mouth sitting deep and carved like judgments. I was holding a flaming scepter, and my hair was a nest of wriggling snakes.

I stumbled away from the vehicle, out of the kid's sightline, and I was driving again, back in the burst of landscape unfolding into the bosom of flawless blue sky, warm and mindless, a vacant baseball field on the right, a red barn, a silo, grazing cows.

The boy's name was Jason MacGonigle, and his mother had been trying to teach him to play "Go Fish" while the tile man was laying a mosaic pattern on the floor in the sunroom. It was the Jack of Hearts, and while the African prints in the living room were a comfort, animal shadows like the ones in his story books, this robed nightmare with the skinny face and the big fire-stick had hideous black eyes that followed him even when he pushed it across the table and told Mommie he didn't want to play anymore.

I knew that he dreamed about the Jack of Hearts that night, and that the dream character was far worse than the playing card itself, elongated, fluid, and reptilian, a Disney cartoon gone horribly wrong, and the thing slithered through the cracks outlining the closet door and wore the shadows like a cloak, waiting for Jason to close his eyes so he could rise tall above the bed and claw his dagger-like fingernails straight into the boy's once rosy cheeks, squeezing and squelching up fistfuls of bloody ribbons that lay in hot spatter across his straining bone knuckles.

So you see now that I am everyone's nightmare. I wonder what I did to earn this title, but my past life is a blur. I do know that I am on a real highway with real people who don't have a clue as to my presence, not really. But how often do we really notice who sits next to us at a red light, or cruises in the neighboring lane at seventy-plus? Looking would be rather impolite, like staring at someone in an elevator when we all know the rising or falling floor numbers are a mandatory study.

Plainly, this is my hell, I suppose. I am to stay on this road for eternity, and if I veer off of it, or cause some sort of accident that disrupts my journey, innocent people, real people will pay. This is all a private outdoor prison that is secured by my morals, go ahead, go figure, chew on the irony.

I tried driving off the road and aiming for a tree once. It was one of those humongous oaks that had an L-shape cut out of the branches to let a power line through, and I got close enough to see two knots in the bark, and I put my hands in front of my face, just to get beeped at for my trouble. You see, just before impact I was "sent back" to the two-lane thoroughfare I had been driving on all along, and suddenly I realized that I had merely drifted a bit over the double yellow. Instinct came into play, and I jerked the wheel to hard right just in time to avoid oncoming traffic—another irony, since I had just tried to kill my already dead self.

I've tried driving off bridges, causing head-on collisions, making dangerous 360 turns in heavy traffic, all failures. Nowadays I pull one of these just to wake myself up, for the fun of it, to remind myself that I was once a living being who wasn't stuck daydreaming for hours, years, centuries at a time, driving off to nowhere straight into the blue.

I've also caused a multitude of those minor, harmless accidents that get me "real contact," and I've scared the living shit out of more people than I can count. I do it because I have to, because being time-deprived is a torture. I do it to remind myself that even though I am stuck in this endless cycle, I'm still real.

Do my victims remember me, or am I the shadow of a dream? Am I merely a bad feeling to recover from . . . finally, the explanation for unwarranted depression?

In what seems like years ago I cut off three high school girls on the way to put in orders for prom dresses. The redhead with the turned-up nose and the ¾-moon Alice headband saw me as a cop and feared an invasive frisk outside of the car, a hard rape across the front hood, my dick a transformed billy club going down my leg, pushing a huge, blunt shape against my trousers. The ash blonde with the nose ring and practiced sour-apple pout in the passenger seat saw me as her own father, drunk again, short-sleeved dress shirt drenched with back sweat, shock of gray hair falling across his eye, punching her like a dude again and pulling her out into the brush so she could *really* get what was coming to her for acting like her mother all these years, and the little cookie in the back, rosebud lips, tiny tits, big teeth, black hair tucked behind her ears, envisioned a hillbilly with a wandering eye, one strap of his overalls unhooked and dangling, taking her by the scruff of the neck and the back of her pants and throwing her into an old van sanded down on its sides to the brown primer splotches, then belching exhaust on the way to his farmhouse basement, then a cage, and some sort of ritual that involved oily puddles, steel clamps, heavy gauge cables, and car batteries.

Of course, I retreated, but I wonder if they swapped stories, argued about my given appearance, called each other "stupid" for being so paranoid. Did they remember being cut off at all? Was my "presence" known, or just "felt"? Or, here you go . . . did I ever stop them in the first place?

I've got to live, and if I am already dead, I need to exist within this realm I have inherited. I can't ride into the blue anymore, conscious in the unconscious endlessness of a never-ending blur going pleasantly and rapidly nowhere.

The question is, what do monsters do when they finally come out of the linen closet, or the attic, or from around the corner of the woodshed? When I was a boy, I was terrified that a nameless, hooded man with yellow eyes and a steel grip was going to reach up and grab my ankle if I let it off the edge of the mattress. So what if he grabbed the ankle? What if I screamed? What if he leaned in close and breathed death into my face? What would be next? Would he ask me my favorite color? Would we talk about God? Would he tear out my throat with his teeth and put me on a road leading straight to the bosom of blue?

Time to find out. I'm going to kiss a bumper, cut off a Kia, give someone the finger. Except this time, I'm not going to walk away at the first sight of transformation in the sideview mirror. I'm going to get in the car and tell my victim to drive. Home. Into a life where the streets are named, where engines rest, and where demons, torturers, and rippers are finally granted a timeline, a purpose, a meaning, and an end.

# Kris Kuksi

## In the Realm of the Senses

### By Kaye Vincent

**Kaye Vincent:** Whether it be your drawings, paintings, or sculptures, what inspires you to turn what is in your head at that particular moment into something real that others can perceive as well?

**Kris Kuksi:** Not sure what it is. Could be an inborn trait that directs me to take my interests and relate them to the human experience. Or perhaps it could just be the idea of showing people a different view of the world. Most artists think outside the norm, and that is a good indication and drive for progression and change.

**Vincent:** You have distinctly unique styles for your sculptures, paintings, and drawings. What topics or emotions lend themselves better to a particular medium for you?

**Kuksi:** The sculptures are my passion, because I am a *builder* much more than a drawer or painter. It seems my emotions are better expressed through sculpture, and borrowing from the ready-made world of mass-produced things lend well to it. The word "composer" comes to mind more so than sculptor when describing myself.

**Vincent:** Your sculptures are so intricate. How much of it is envisioned before you create it, and when do you know when it is "finished"?

**Kuksi:** Interesting . . . The major elements are planned out and arranged, while all the secondary layers are improvised in the layout, up to the very tiniest of details. The process is about controlling chaos

---

Facing Page: Reign of Caesar
*Mixed Media Assemblage, 34"x 46"x 9", 2012*
**(All images courtesy Kris Kuksi.)**

> **Facing Page: (Top) Capricorn Rising**
> *Mixed Media Assemblage, 72"x 80"x 30", 2012*
>
> **(Bottom) Exoneration**
> *Mixed Media Assemblage, 38"x 24"x 8", 2012*

to a degree, so that everything is well placed and in balance. The pieces are finished when there are no more boring areas; when every spot is filled up with something interesting. No single edge or border is left without some interruption to give it more of a completed feel.

**Vincent:** Very interesting. With respect to painting, your portraits are incredibly lifelike. Each face has its own story. What do you seek to capture in each one? Is it something *you're* looking for, or is it something *they* are projecting?

**Kuksi:** Yes to both. What I mean is that I am after capturing a person's *soul*. When I work with someone, I photograph them and work from the photos, then work toward eliminating the 'posed' stiffness, waiting for the person to relax and just "be." That seems to allow the passion to appear, and cross over from life, to copy again on a canvas.

**Vincent:** I see. With that in mind, what qualities do you value in the relative colorlessness of your black-and-white drawings as opposed to the vibrant colors of your paintings?

**Kuksi:** Well, drawings are about the form, the texture, the mood. I would say I enjoy drawings more often, due to how color can tend to be locked into certain time periods; it can make a work feel dated. Drawings seem to be immune to this; they usually have a timeless feel to them and can be appreciated for years to come. But I could be wrong—I assume the way something is executed can make a drawing feel associated to a particular time and style as well.

**Vincent:** Interesting. So how were you trained to master these various mediums of art?

**Kuksi:** Mostly self-taught, with a few art degrees that helped along the way. Also, trips to Europe, learning Old Master painting techniques, and just being exposed to all forms of art really helped. It takes time; "creative solitude" is a must for any artist.

**Vincent:** Fascinating. What advice would you give to budding artists looking to express themselves through sculpture, painting, or drawing?

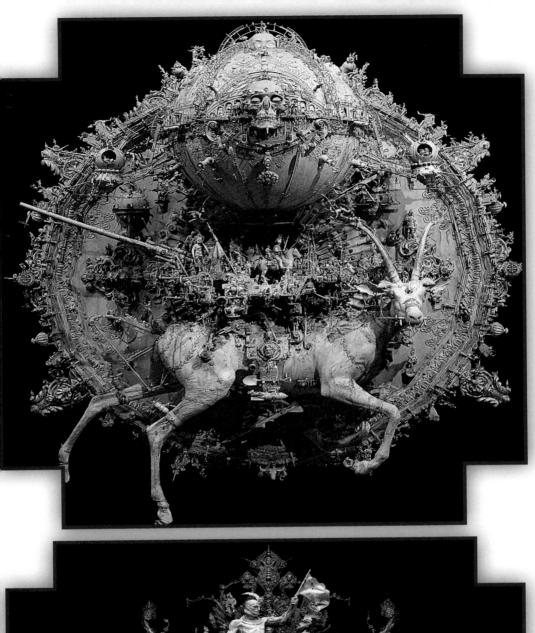

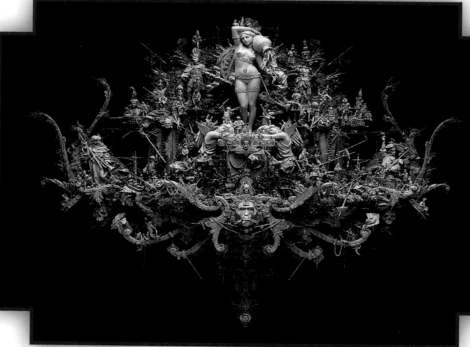

**Kuksi:** Be true to yourself—don't copy others. Following trends can lead you astray, and you'll just get swallowed up. Most importantly, *master* your medium and find your niche. Settle on a style, but always challenge yourself. And most of all, never give up.

**Vincent:** How much of your art comes from the life around you that you witness versus what you imagine?

**Kuksi:** It is split 50/50. I have a very active imagination, yet it can be formless without the structure of the material world; finding a way to bring abstract ideas into a reality that people can relate to is the challenge. It is seems that this is just intuitive, a natural artistic response to ideas and passions to create.

**Vincent:** Who were your personal artistic idols?

**Kuksi:** Ah . . . Bernini is at the top of the list. In fact, I am in Rome as I type this, and earlier today, I saw his masterworks at the Gallerie Borghese. Others include Conova, Houdon, Gerome, Leyton, and contemporaries such as H. R. Giger, Ernst Fuchs, and Javier Marin.

**Vincent:** What reaction do you like most from people who view your work?

**Kuksi:** I love the emotional response and the comments about the details. Listening to those comments while at a gallery opening emphasizes the overall respectability the viewer has, and that is what art should provoke, in my opinion. Fans keep the drive alive in me, and that kind of energy really helps create a feeling of accomplishment, of contentment.

# ++*Numinosities*++

## Things That Should Not Be—
## The Uncanny Convergence of Religion and Horror

### By Matt Cardin

Recently I gave an interview to the entertainment editor at the local daily newspaper in Waco, Texas, about the third installment of an annual horror film festival that I created down here a couple of years ago. The festival's theme this year is "Horror and Apocalypse," and one of the questions posed to me during that interview was an iteration of a question that I'm always asked whenever I talk about my long-running focus on the intersection of horror with religion, philosophy, and psychology: "What's the connection between horror and the apocalypse? What do they really have to do with each other?"

This came just a few days after I was interviewed for *Expanding Mind*, the radio program hosted by Erik Davis and Maja D'Aoust, and devoted to exploring "the cultures of consciousness: magic, religion, psychology, technology." A large part of that one involved a discussion of why religion and horror should emerge as centrally related to each other in my thought and writing. This in turn came not long after my friend and fellow idea-driven horror writer T. E. Grau asked me something similar while interviewing me for his blog. It also came up when I talked to the Lovecraft News Network and to John Morehead of Theofantastique. Why horror-and-religion, always spoken as if in the same breath? Why these two together? How do you see them as connected? What led to your dual interest in both and your authorial tactic of using each to talk about the other?

The more I'm asked these questions, often by people who are themselves deeply invested in a similarly cross-fertilized creative career of exploring the very same thematic intersection, the more my answer, however long and involved it may be, tends to boil down to the same short and semi-rhetorical response: "How and why *not*? How are horror and religion, not to mention philosophy, psychology, and spirituality, *not* directly related, fused, intertwined, bound together in a synergy and a symbiosis so total and profound as to make the one not even discussable in the absence of the other?" To me, the connection is so obvious, so blatant, so patent, that I truly have to struggle to understand and communicate with those who don't see it. (Such people, I hasten to added, are almost never my interviewers, the majority of whom know full well the deep connection in question and are living it out in their own thoughts and lives, and are only asking me about it in order to grease the wheels of the conversation.) But those who don't see it are legion, those for whom the very idea of talking about horror—literary, cinematic, you name it—in relation to religion is shocking, if not authentically anathema. And this very fact, I think, says something important about the religion-horror nexus itself, and about the respective qualities and meanings of both horrification and religious experience.

In point of fact, horror and religion have *always* been bound together in the most intimate of entanglements. Look to the ancient Sumerians: you'll find in their cosmogony the tale of Tiamat, the great chaos dragon who formed the original, primal substance of reality until her children, who were more anthropomorphic, and who were therefore the gods worshipped by humans, overthrew her. Observe that horror *came first*, before divine solace, in the most ancient creation story of which we're collectively aware. Check the ancient Egyptians, those vital quasi-neighbors of the inhabitants of the Fertile Crescent, and you'll find similar instances of daemonic monstrousness built right into their reigning theologies at nearly all points. The same goes for the ancient Greeks, some of whose creation myths involved the progressive overthrow of primal chaotic monstrousness—think the Titans, think Kronos devouring his children—in order to produce the ordered cosmos we have today.

Think of the Hebrew scriptures and their rivers of blood, not only in the heady apocalyptic visions presented in various canonical texts but in the actual cultural experience of the ancient Jews and their neighbors, whose religious practice hinged on blood sacrifice and whose lives were frequently filled with military massacres due to religious warfare. Think, too, of the awe-ful holiness of the Old Testament God, which transfers as well to the New Testament, where, echoing Isaiah, the Apocalypse of John speaks of the inhabitants of the earth shrieking and wailing as angels pour down bowls of wrath, and calling out in panic for the mountains to fall on them in order to hide them from the terrible gaze of the God who arrival announces their hideous demise.

Goya's
*Saturn Devouring His Son*

Think, especially, of those places in the New Testament where Jesus performs his miracles, or where angels appear and make announcements to humans, and the deeper point—the point about religion's genetic entanglement with horror—becomes even clearer. Because when angels appear, *people are terrified*. As the story in one of the four gospels has it, when an angel descends to roll away the stone covering the entrance to Jesus' tomb, the centurions standing guard pass out in terror. When Jesus walks on water or heals the sick or drives out a demon, the response of the multitudinous onlookers is not, "What a wonderful thing this is! Praise God! I'm so thrilled!" No, far from being filled with joy and a sense of divine benevolence, they are—and the Koine Greek of the New Testament is very precise here—described as being filled with dread, awe, terror, trembling.

Most pointedly, the Gospel of Mark, which is held by most Bible scholars to be the earliest-written of all the gospels, and therefore to represent a more direct and less textually and theologically elaborated tradition of early Christian teaching, ends on a note of divine terror stemming from what is universally touted as the greatest of the Christian miracles and the very founding event of Christianity itself: the resurrection of Jesus. The ending to the book that most people grew up reading for the better part of two millennia, the one featuring instructions from Jesus about drinking poisons and handling venomous snakes, is actually recognized by scholars today as a tacked-on affair that was added later by some unknown hand. The book in its more ancient form ends with two women going to Jesus' tomb to anoint his corpse with oil, only to find him gone. A man (or angel) greets them and announces that Jesus is not there, that he is risen. The women "fled from the tomb, trembling and bewildered, and said nothing to anybody, because they were too afraid." And that, as they say, is that. The earliest-written gospel—a word whose etymological meaning of "good news" seems most curious and dubious in such a context—ends right there, on a distinct note of supernatural dread.

Examples of similar tropes and trends from different religious traditions around the world could be multiplied at length, revealing a trajectory of uncanny religious horror arcing its way through human history and finding its way in particular to us Americans via the channel of our Puritan forebears with their witch- and demon-haunted worldview of perpetual hell-spawned threat. Observing this, the point becomes clear: that something fundamentally disturbing, unsettling, *uncanny*, lies right at the heart of religion itself, as evidenced in the darkness infecting the religious and spiritual traditions of the human race since the dawn of recorded history (and therefore, presumably, since prehistoric times as well). And it comes out most pointedly in those religious contexts where the very idea, let alone the manifestation, of the supernatural itself is framed and experienced as fearsome, as terrifying and horrifying, as something that confronts us with a proto-Lovecraftian sense of metaphysical revulsion at the revelation of "things that should not be."

So why, then, should people today still find it necessary to ask about the connection between religion and horror? When it would be more reasonable to ask if they have ever *not* been connected, why do so many of us moderns find it odd or shocking to hear their deep linkage called out and explicitly identified?

Perhaps—and here I may simply be indulging my own temperament and mistaking it for insight, or perhaps I may really be onto something (a judgment I will invite the reader to make for him- or herself)—perhaps it has to do with an unconscious recognition that only a few have ever named aloud, a recognition that is simultaneously implicit and explicit in all those great biblical images of a wrathful god whose transcendent nature is categorically *other than* the natural world, so that, even though his nature is technically termed "holiness," it emerges in human experience more as a tremendous, awe-and-dread-inspiring eruption of supernatural nightmarishness that is fundamentally corrosive both to the world at large and to the human sensibility in particular. In other words, perhaps it has to do with a psychologically subterranean sense of unsettlement at the notion that the divine itself, not just in its conventionally demonic aspects but in its intrinsic essence, may be fundamentally menacing.

Lovecraft noted something exactly like this when he wrote in *Supernatural Horror in Literature* that "There is here involved [in the phenomenon of supernatural horror fiction] a psychological pattern or tradition as real and as deeply grounded in mental experience as any other pattern or tradition of mankind; coeval with the religious feeling and closely related to many aspects of it." Ten years earlier, the theologian and philosopher of religion Rudolf Otto wrote in his now-classic book *Das Heilige* (translated as *The Idea of the Holy*) of a stage in the history of religious experience that he posited as preceding, both psychologically and historically, the familiar divine dread of the "higher" traditions. He termed this earlier experience "daemonic dread" and "numinous dread," and described it as something that "first begins to stir in the feeling of 'something uncanny,' 'eerie,' or 'weird.'" Even more, he argued—in words that fully deserve to be presented in italics—that *"It is this feeling which, emerging in the mind of primeval man, forms the starting point for the entire religious development of history."* Also worth italicizing is Otto's contention that *both the human religious traditions and the age-old tradition of telling ghost stories and other stories of supernatural fear stem from this same primordial category of experience.*

If Otto is even close to right, and if Lovecraft is even marginally accurate, and if the whole record of human religious experience tells us anything for certain about who we are and what we're like in the deepest layers of our selves, then religion and supernatural horror, more than just "going together," in some strange sense *are each other.* You can't have one without the other or the other without the one. If you try to think and talk about religion, let alone to have a religious experience, then horror is never far off, in precisely the same manner that the experience of dreaming always comes with a shimmering shadow of nightmare that hovers at its boundaries and might invade the dream world at any moment to tip it over into awfulness. If you read or watch a supernatural horror story, then religion is embedded right there in the midst of the metaphysically fearsome goings-on, regardless of whether or not it is overtly mentioned.

What's shocking, in short, is not that the two things should be presented and talked about in tandem, but that anybody should ever have thought to separate them in the first place. How that separation occurred in popular thought is an interesting story in its own right, but it's one for another time.

# +Dark Side of the Moon+

## The Quiet Horror of

### By Paul Bens

It's 1975 and British Producer Gerry Anderson, best known for his Supermarionation television series *Thunderbirds*, has just launched his newest project, *Space: 1999*, a live-action science fiction spectacular that would become the most expensive series of its time. Taking its cue more from *2001: A Space Odyssey* than the then cult favorite *Star Trek*, *Space: 1999* starred Martin Landau and Barbara Bain, fresh off their stints on the wildly popular *Mission: Impossible*; Barry Morse, much respected from his time on *The Fugitive*; and an impressive cast of British and Australian supporting actors including Prentis Hancock, Clifton Jones, Zienia Merton, Anton Phillips, and Nick Tate.

The staff behind the scenes was impressive as well. Cambridge-educated writer Christopher Penfold would guide the series through its first sixteen episodes and, together with Irish poet and science fiction fabulist Johnny Byrne, would be largely responsible for capturing the epic feel of the series in those formative days. What appealed to Penfold was the storytelling possibilities of the premise. "We weren't afraid of big ideas," he explained in a 2002 interview. "It was what drove us on from day to day; it gave us a huge sense of excitement."

Added to the mix were the best directors British television had in Charles Crichton, Raymond Austin, and David Tomblin, as well as an enviable guest cast of some of the finest British actors around: Christopher Lee, Peter Cushing, Margaret Leighton, Joan Collins, Roy Dotrice, and Judy Geeson.

With a budget of more than a quarter million dollars per episode and boasting special effects the likes of which had never been seen on the small screen (courtesy of *2001: A Space Odyssey*'s Brian Johnson), the series debuted to critical acclaim when it finally hit the small screen. *Time* magazine declared that the series was "ingenious . . . an Arthurian space fantasy," and

Images from *Space: 1999* (Clockwise from Top Left): Horror staple Christopher Lee as the pacifistic Captain Zantor; Game of Thrones' Roy Dotrice as Commissioner Simmonds, entombed in "Earthbound"; Brian Blessed tells the Alphans they have found Shangri-la while John Shrapnel's Captain Jack Tanner warns them off; Tony Cellini's dragon waits for him to return in the Lovecraftian "Dragon's Domain"; Peter Bowles as the sadistic Balor in "End of Eternity"; Giancarlo Prete is haunted by his own ghost in "The Troubled Spirit."

the *Wall Street Journal* stated: "It is the most gorgeous, flashy sci-fi trip ever to appear on TV." But the praise was short-lived.

No less a figure than Isaac Asimov publically criticized the series for its central plot point: that a nuclear explosion would hurl the moon out of the Earth's orbit rather than destroy it. Notwithstanding that science fiction has a long history of suspension of disbelief (it is fiction, after all, not fact) in order to propel a continuing series, the criticism only increased. Most interesting, however, was that the most critical of comments seemed to center on the fact that *Space: 1999* wasn't *Star Trek*, the then lone-wolf of science fiction television. It didn't matter that *Space: 1999* was never designed to be like *Trek*. *1999* was about near-future, not the twenty-third century, and, unlike *Trek*, the residents of Moonbase Alpha were not in control of their own destiny: they had no ship for interstellar travels, no advanced weaponry, no five-year mission to explore. The central point when comparing the two series seemed to be missed. They were as different as apples and oranges, really, and the difference is, in retrospect, noted in the pilot episode when Bain's Dr. Russell tells Koenig, "We're looking for answers, Commander; not heroes."

Ultimately, the heavy criticism seemed to prevail, and when the series was prepped for second season, ITC Entertainment (the corporation syndicating the series) demanded massive changes. *Trek* producer Fred Freiberger was brought on board to help Americanize the show, and a large chunk of the supporting cast was unceremoniously jettisoned. Reaching back to his *Trek* roots, Freiberger created a resident alien named Maya, portrayed by Catherine Schell, who, unlike the stoic Spock, had a pixie-esque sense of humor and the ability to transform herself at will into any living creature. The focus would shift from the heady — almost metaphysical — science fiction stories of the first season to ones more focused on action and adventure.

While the changes were jarring (and largely unexplained), fans embraced the second season and the new additions to the cast, especially Schell's infectious and sexy Maya. But when the numbers didn't add up, the series was shuttered in 1977 despite fan outcry and a fervent campaign for a third season.

It's been almost thirty-five years since the series went off the air, but the fan base is still as loyal as ever. Starting in 1978 and continuing for the last three decades, devoted fans have gathered at conventions in order to celebrate the show, meet the stars, and raise money for various charities. Over the years, a vibrant cottage industry of officially licensed merchandise has even taken root and flourished, bringing new canon to the *1999* world. For the last ten years, Mateo Latosa's Powys Media (*http://www.powysmedia.com*) has published a line of wildly successful novels based upon the series, and Drew Gaska's Blam! Ventures (*http://blamventures.com/space-1999/*) is bringing the series into the graphic novel world with several highly anticipated releases. In fact, Powys and Blam! both launched their latest projects at *Alpha: 2012* (*http://www.alpha2012.net*), the latest in a long

*Barbara Bain, Barry Morse, Nick Tate, and Martin Landau face the mysteries of the "Testament of Arkadia."*

line of *Space: 1999* conventions held in Burbank, California, on September 14–16, 2012.

Earlier this year, ITV, the current owner of the *Space: 1999* franchise, took fans by surprise when it announced that the series would be re-imagined as *Space: 2099*, to be produced by American producer Jace Hall, the man responsible for ABC's recent *V* remake. While Hall's refusal to confirm whether the central premise of the series will be retained has caused massive concerns for fans, the announcement has certainly reignited interest in the series.

It is the year 1999 and the moon has become a waste dump for Earth's spent nuclear fuel as well as a launch platform for various deep-space missions, all coordinated from Moonbase Alpha, an impressive international science center constructed in the crater on the near side of Luna. The problem is, people are dying up there and no one seems to know why.

Enter Commander John Koenig (Landau), assigned by Earth politicians to find answers and clear up the mess while at the same time getting a highly anticipated (and political) deep-space mission off the ground. Guided by Dr. Helena Russell (Bain) and Professor Victor Bergman (Morse), Koenig decides to cut through the politics and solve the very serious issues facing him. But when the nuclear waste disposal areas explode in a freak nuclear accident, the moon is propelled out of the solar system, leaving a ragtag group of survivors to fend for themselves in the deepest reaches of space.

That was the launching point, the aspect of the series that managed to garner so much criticism. But like any sci-fi television show, it was a tool, used to facilitate the telling of some fantastic—and, oftentimes, very dark—stories. Given the intense resurgence of interest in the original series, it seems an ideal time to re-examine the classic elements of *Space: 1999*, those aspects which helped garner such a devoted fan base. Despite the heavy criticism,

the series does, in retrospect, seem ahead of its time, but with roots that can be traced back to some of the darker speculative fiction as well as classic science fiction television series like *The Twilight Zone* and *The Outer Limits.*

In "Earthbound," the third of the episodes to be broadcast, politician Commissioner Gerald Simmonds (Roy Dotrice, *Game of Thrones*), who had found himself inadvertently marooned on Moonbase Alpha, meets a particularly gruesome ending, one that harkens all the way back to Poe.

When a ship en route to Earth lands on the Moonbase, the Alphans discover a race of aliens in deep stasis, and, in their attempt to awaken the group, inadvertently kill one. The other pods, which are essentially see-through coffins, come to life, and when the leader of the alien race (horror staple Christopher Lee in a brilliantly restrained performance) rises from his bed, it is a very Dracula-esque moment. With Lee's gravitas, those first moments of silence make us certain he will take retribution for the death of his comrade. But the writers take a more interesting approach, playing against Lee's well-established horror "type."

Lee and the rest of the Kaldorians hold no ill will, seeing the death for what it was: a terrible a mistake born of ignorance, nothing more. Rather, they are a pacifistic race on a long journey to Earth, where they hope to be welcomed. Given that one of the aliens had been killed, Lee magnanimously explains, there is room for one of the Alphans to join the seventy-five-year voyage.

The sniveling Simmonds takes this news to heart, suggesting to Koenig that they eliminate the Kaldorians so that more Alphans can return to Earth. It's a nice switch for sci-fi: the alien race the pacifistic; a human, the evil aggressor. Koenig rejects Simmonds's plan outright, deciding instead that the individual joining the aliens would be chosen by Main Computer.

Not content with his chances in a lottery, Simmonds takes hostages, including Lee, to ensure that he is the one to return to Earth. However, the

**Deadwood's *Ian McShane*, zombified in "Force of Life."**

good Commissioner does not give Lee enough time to attune the stasis pod to his human physiology. (Lee isn't particularly forthcoming, and, in some interpretations, rather devious in his omission.) Simmonds falls into a deep slumber, and the ship leaves Moonbase Alpha far behind.

Only a few hours later, however, Simmonds awakens thinking that he has come to the end of a seventy-five-year journey. He tries to contact Earth through the portable communication device carried by all the Alphans. Only when Earth does not respond does Simmonds realize not only that is he nowhere near Earth, but that he is trapped in the stasis chamber for the remainder of his life. The visual of him pounding against the sides of the coffin, like a moth in a bottle, is chilling; the horror for both Simmonds and the audience is jaw-dropping.

Back on the base, the Alphans hear Simmonds's screams for help, knowing they can do nothing. In the end, it is revealed that Main Computer had indeed chosen Simmonds, the only person on Moonbase Alpha who did not serve a useful purpose.

"Force of Life," written by Byrne, is essentially a zombie story; however, it is one with a humanistic twist. An amorphous alien entity infects Anton Zoref (*Deadwood*'s Ian McShane), a well-liked technician, who, after the encounter, finds himself desperately in need of warmth, of energy in any form. Unfortunately for his friends, some of this energy is found in their bodies, and when Zoref touches them, all the heat is drained from their bodies.

After each absorption of energy, the Anton Zoref everyone admires slowly fades away, his quest driving him to a singular purpose. He becomes a member of the walking dead, human in form but stalking those in the base, draining the energy supplies that sustain the community. Director David Tomblin's impressive use of Hitchcockian camera angles, fish-eyed lenses, and slow motion gives the episode a true sense of terror; but the pathos with which McShane portrays Zoref makes the story an interesting amalgam of horror and heartbreak.

Tomblin was wise not to turn Zoref into a monster, knowing that real horror often resides in that which we know, what is every day and normal. It's the person next door. Throughout the episodes, Zoref looks as he always had, masking the true danger within him; it is not until the third act that the technician is transformed into what we would see as a traditional zombie, a grotesquerie, as the Alphans try to keep him from reaching a nuclear reactor by shooting him with a laser. Zoref merely absorbs the energy but in the process is immolated from the inside out. His charred remains continue on and, when he reaches the reactor, the true nature of the alien being is utterly transformed.

Tomblin also directed another standout episode in "The Infernal Machine," guest starring the remarkable Leo McKern (*Damien: Omen 2, Rumpole of the Bailey*) in a dual role. A strange spaceship approaches the base, and a voice calls for assistance in gathering necessary supplies, a benign

enough request. When the Alphans board the ship, they find only an old man, Companion, who knows nothing of the request. It turns out that the ship itself—a sentient AI known as Gwent—summoned the Alphans; and Gwent, it seems, has an ulterior motive.

As the episode progresses, Koenig, Russell, and Bergman realize that Companion is dying and that Gwent, for all his knowledge and power, has never lived alone. When Companion dies, McKern's performance as Gwent is stellar: a mix of heartbreaking sadness the machine feels for his friend, the childlike fear of abandonment, and terrifying determination as he turns his sights on imprisoning the Alphans as his new companions.

At the denouement, it is learned that Companion had long ago created Gwent, infusing his own personality, the sum of all his knowledge and foibles, into the omnipotent machine. As Gwent is "dying," after being defeated by the Alphans, he admits all that he is and is not:

"I misjudged you. My experience over these years, traveling the universe, alone, blind, dependent on Companion, has left me untrusting, suspicious, cynical, perhaps even paranoid. You see, having built this, yes, machine, to preserve my personality, I discovered too late its inherent weakness. I need . . . company. None of us exists except in relation to others. Alone, we cease to have personalities. Isolation. Do you understand?"

As weakened and as frail as Companion had once been, Gwent ultimately chooses to release the Alphans and then does something remarkable. This . . . machine . . . commits suicide. It's an expert turn on the topic of artificial intelligence, the search for perfection, and what constitutes "life." Certainly, other science fiction works had expounded on the subject matter—especially that of a living, intelligent machine—but here the hubris and foibles of man are exquisitely intertwined in a way that, especially for the time, was unheard of. A machine that needs company? A machine that feels all that we do and commits the same sins? A decade and a half later, *Star Trek's* Data would aspire to be more human. Had he met Gwent, he might have reconsidered that dream.

In Penfold's "The Guardian of Piri," the Alphans are seemingly delivered from their odyssey when a beautiful young woman offers them the perfect life, one without cares or strife. However, perfection is not all that it is cracked up to be, and Koenig realizes that his people are truly being left bereft of the need and desire to attain, to move forward and become something more. They are reduced to blissful ignorance, little more than a vegetative state. Touching on issues of cultism, it's an examination of the dichotomy of man who very often pursues that which will doom him.

The nature of man is also examined in "The Full Circle," in which the Alphans encounter an odd time warp that regresses them to their most basic, primitive state—that of cave men. The use of non-traditional music and the sharp direction by Bob Kellett keep this episode moving at a brisk and tension-filled pace and begs the question of how much man has really changed in 40,000 years.

In the very *Twilight Zone*-esque "The Troubled Spirit," Byrne crafts a ghost story in which a man is haunted by his own murderous ghost, a ghost intent on avenging its own murder . . . which hasn't yet occurred. Director Ray Austin, the second most utilized director of the series, sets the tone exquisitely from the very opening scene. Intercutting between a rare musical concert and a séance in another part of the base, the tease is a series of long tracking takes intercut with methodical dolly-shots, a brilliant counterbalance to the frenetic and non-traditional sitar score by Jim Sullivan. The result is a haunting tone and pace that Austin maintains for the duration of the episode as he plays not only with the visuals but also with sound (and the lack thereof). The result is a stunning chiaroscuro of sight, sound and story.

In Penfold's "War Games," the Alphans are given a glimpse of the dangers of acting out of fear and ignorance when their base is all but destroyed because of hasty and uninformed decisions made by Koenig. "You have . . . no future. You carry with you the seeds of your own destruction," says the leader of an alien race that has launched a brutal counter-attack on the base. "You are a contaminating organism . . . a fatal virus . . . a plague of fear."

Four years before Robert Wise utilized essentially the same story device in his feature film reboot of the *Trek* TV series, *Space: 1999*'s Byrne's wrote "Voyager's Return." Using the inspiration of the real-life *Voyager* missions, then in development by NASA, Byrne crafted a morality tale and a study in the need to atone for sins, intentional or not.

Back on Earth, the *Voyager* craft was designed as both an unmanned scientific space probe and as a friendly calling-card: "Greetings from the people of planet Earth," the spacecraft announces when it approaches each new star system. But the *Voyager* has a complex and controversial background, one that evokes fear as the craft approaches.

The ship was designed to use a normal propulsion system when near potentially populated worlds, and the more advanced and deadly Queller Drive when traversing the empty reaches of space. An accident on Earth when the ship was being developed killed thousands of people, including a number of relatives of those on the base; yet the ship was ultimately launched. And now it has come back, with the gift of years of remarkable data stored within it and an imminent threat as the Alphans realize the Queller Drive is malfunctioning and will destroy everything in its path, including the Moonbase.

The race is on to find a way to countermand the probe's primary instructions. Knowing he is the only one who can solve the situation, Dr. Ernst Queller, designer of the drive, breaks cover of the assumed name given him for his own protection. A brilliant scientist, Queller has been living an unassuming life on Moonbase Alpha, working alongside those who had lost so many because of his invention. But now the stakes are incredibly high, the pressure to succeed unimaginable. It turns into an episode that

evokes the context, tone, and regret inherent in Robert Oppenheimer's quotation of the *Bhagavad Gita*: "Now, I am become death, the destroyer of worlds." In the end, Queller makes the ultimate sacrifice for the Alphans and for his own soul as a race of aliens whose worlds have been devastated by *Voyager* descends upon Moonbase Alpha seeking retribution.

Charles Crichton was the director most often utilized on the series. Largely responsible for the look and tone of the first season, Crichton directed 14 of the 48 produced episodes—many of them the most highly regarded—including the aforementioned "Earthbound" and the haunting "Death's Other Dominion."

Inspired by James Hilton's 1933 novel *Lost Horizon*, screenwriters Anthony Terpiloff and Elizabeth Barrows, as well as director Crichton, stick largely to the concept of that novel, but then throw in an unexpected twist, making the episode particularly memorable. The moon comes across an ice world, Ultima Thule, upon which is living the remaining crew of a lost expedition from Earth. The survivors are in remarkable health and the leader of the group, Dr. Cabot Rowland (Brian Blessed, *Flash Gordon*), explains that, due to the mysteries of time and space, they have been living on Thule for hundreds of Earth years and are immortal. Rowland invites the Alphans to come and live with them, a proposal that is inviting despite the harsh climate of the planet.

A lone Thulean, the seemingly insane Jack Tanner, secretly warns Commander Koenig that all is not as it seems; that the Alphans should never settle on Thule. In a cavern that Dr. Rowland has kept secret from the newcomers, Tanner introduces Koenig to "The Revered Ones," members of the expedition who are now little more than living husks without minds. Tanner tenderly cares for these people, victims of Dr. Cabott's medical experiments; experiments of which Tanner is the sole, lucid survivor.

It seems that though Rowland has painted Thule and immortality as a wondrous thing, the Thuleans have discovered that living forever destroys the desire to live, each day becoming a monotonous exercise in futility and hopelessness. Dr. Rowland, however, sees things differently, viewing immortality as a boon once they manage to escape the bonds of Thule, and he has desperately been trying to discover the secret of immortality. The Revered Ones were volunteers, those who either believed in Rowland's vision or those who assumed that immortality could be "cured" once the secret was known. In reality, the arrival of the Alphans represents a new herd of research subjects, people Rowland can use rather than endanger what is left of his own community.

Charmed by Dr. Rowland, his romanticized view of the situation, and the promise of eternal life, the rest of the landing party convince Koenig that the issue of whether to settle on Thule should be put up for a vote on Alpha. Koenig reluctantly agrees, and Dr. Rowland agrees to go with them to explain his proposal. But, en route to Alpha, in a shocking turn, it is revealed that Dr. Rowland and Thule—like Lo-Tsen and the mythical

Shangri-La—can never be separated.

Peter Bowles (*The Legend of Hell House*) turns in a chilling performance in another of Byrne's scripts, "End of Eternity." When the Alphans discover a nearby asteroid that registers an internal chamber and atmosphere, they investigate, blasting their way in. There they discover Balor, on the brink of death due to injuries the Alphans unintentionally inflicted; yet, by the time they get him back to Alpha, the alien's wounds have miraculously healed. Balor explains that he is an immortal and had been imprisoned in the asteroid by his own people, who found his claims of the degenerative nature of immortality to be heretical. Yet something doesn't quite sit right with his story.

In the chamber that once surrounded Balor were hundreds of paintings, all depicting great physical horrors inflicted on people. After Balor manipulates an Alphan into beating John Koenig nearly to death only to heal Koenig's wounds, Balor's crimes become all too evident. A voyeuristic sadist, Balor intends to use Alpha as his personal playground, bringing each of them to the brink of death or, better still, having them turn on each other, only to regenerate their flesh so that the games may continue on for eternity.

The episode was already treading on dicey ground with sadism, but the overt violence utilized in the beating of Koenig—though tame by today's standards—was too unyielding in its realism. The sequence was ultimately edited down to more acceptable primetime standards. Still, the episode had moved into uncharted territory and had asked the question of how one kills that which cannot die. The solution is one Ridley Scott would later utilize to great effect in *Alien*.

Cannibalism and the exploitation of the poor, weak, and infirm are topics touched on in "Mission of the Darians," which explores what mankind will do in order to survive. When the Alphans come across a fifty-mile-long space city, it is discovered that the inhabitants are all that survive of a doomed world. Led by the charming Joan Collins (*Star Trek*), the Darians explain that they are attempting to rebuild their race, using the bodies and the DNA of those who have passed away. But far beneath the lovely living quarters of the upper Darian social structure are those less fortunate: the indigent, the ignorant, the malformed, who are sacrificed in an almost ceremonial fashion. It's a nice exploration of the manipulation of the uneducated and the immense power of religious imagery to benefit the rich and powerful at the expense of the lower classes. It is a theme that in this day and age of the 99% still has resonance.

The penultimate episode of the first season harkens all the way back to the Crusades for its inspiration and mixes it with a healthy dose of Lovecraft's Cthulhu Mythos. A loose retelling of the legend of St. George and the Dragon, Penfold's "Dragon's Domain" takes on a mythical feel as astronaut Tony Cellini finds himself faced with a real-life nightmare from his past.

Years before being placed on Moonbase Alpha, Cellini had been commander of the doomed Ultra Probe, a long-distance mission that stumbled upon a graveyard of ships in deep space. Cellini makes the fateful decision to investigate what appears to be the lead ship and, because of his decision, a demon is unleashed and his crew is devastated, each member devoured by a multi-tentacled beast—part octopus, part dragon—that spits their corpses, stripped of flesh, from its steaming, gaping maw.

Cellini escapes the graveyard—the episode's version of R'yleh—and survives the long journey back to Earth, only to be confronted by a skeptical scientific and political community. It seems that the Ultra Probe's black box does not corroborate Cellini's story, nor does any of the physical evidence in the Ultra Probe command ship. It is deemed that Cellini bungled the mission and, either by deliberate act or inadvertent mistake, killed his crew.

It is a mission that has haunted Cellini and now, with nightmares reawakened, he finds that the moon is approaching that very same graveyard. He knows the dragon only sleeps deep within those ghost ships; it lies dormant, waiting for his inevitable return. Cellini becomes obsessed with a need to confront his nightmare, to avenge his crew's deaths, to once again find his sanity. Cellini comes face-to-face with the dragon, and the other Alphans must confront their own preconceptions and judgment of his metal stability. It is far easier, it seems, to find a man insane than believe in monsters, a theme that would later be touched on briefly in *Aliens*, where Ripley, lone survivor of a similarly doomed mission, is confronted by an equally skeptical community.

The series didn't only deal with dark themes. Spirituality, fate, and destiny also got equal play in impressive ways. In "Collision Course," written by Terpiloff and directed by Austin, John Koenig has an almost religious encounter with Arra (Margaret Leighton, *Alfred Hitchcock Presents*), Queen of Etheria, who convinces him to have faith and maintains that instead of colliding, the moon and her world will simply touch in a moment of cosmic evolution. "Our two planets have met in the body of time for the great purpose of mutation," Arra explains. "We shall change utterly and the change will reverberate through the galaxies and universes of eternity. You and I are two vital drops in the boundless ocean of Time. We have met with purpose. We must not fail our destiny." When asked what will happen to the Alphans when the worlds collide, Arra responds, "Your odyssey shall know no end. You will prosper and increase in new worlds, new galaxies. You will populate the deepest reaches of space." All John Koenig must do is nothing. Yet his fellow Alphans don't quite see it that way as the mammoth world comes closer to a collision course.

In "Black Sun," the Alphans find their moon being drawn into the crushing forces of a black hole. Again, the mystical elements of the universe take over, this question of faith and destiny hanging over them. How the Alphans each deal with their inevitable deaths is a mastery of writing, acting, and filmmaking . . . a montage of quiet moments: a game of chess, a bottle of brandy, the quiet strum of a guitar. But instead of being crushed, the Alphans have an encounter with a being, God if you like. "Why have I never talked with you before?" Professor Bergman asks. And in a move that was quite controversial at the time, a female God responds, "Because of time. You think at what you call the speed of light. In eternity, I have no hurry. I think a thought perhaps, in every thousand of your years. You are never there to hear it."

The final episode of the season, "The Testament of Arkadia," again touches on the origins and destiny of man when the Alphans discover a dead world that not only seems to have been the point of origin for life on Earth, but also one that comes to life again once the Alphas set foot upon the soil. It would seem that the Alphans are home, and a few of them want to stay.

Despite all the criticism, the ratings for season one of *Space: 1999* were respectable enough for ITC to greenlight a second season, but not without some provisos. The budget would need to be cut, dictated Abe Mandell, president of ITC and the man who had put together the initial syndication deal for season one. And, more importantly, it would have to appeal to a wider audience, namely an American one. Fred Freiberger, who had produced the final seasons of *The Wild, Wild West* and *Star Trek* (and who would produce the final season of *The Six Million Dollar Man*), was brought in, and the changes he instituted were considerable.

Barry Morse, who had portrayed Victor Bergman in the first season, either left of his own accord (Morse claimed that once he heard Freiberger's plans, he told the producers, "I'm going to go play with grown-ups now") or was the victim of a contract dispute (according to ITC executives). Most of the rest of the cast was disposed of as well, with Nick Tate and Zienia Merton brought back at the very last moment, the former due to his popularity with fans and the latter, according to some sources, at the request of Bain.

Freiberger reached back to his stint on *Trek* and created Maya (Catherine Schell), a resident alien who could molecularly transform into any living creature for an hour at a time, and added the character or Tony Verdeschi (Tony Anholt) as a love interest for the new character. The romantic relationship between Landau and Bain's characters—subtly present in the first series—would also be more overt.

Christopher Penfold had departed in the first season, and while Byrne remained, he was disenchanted with the changes Freiberger was instituting, later stating: "I'd simply given up and wanted to finish my commitment precisely to the requirements of Freddie." The focus was now on action/adventure and interpersonal relationships, as opposed to thought-provoking science fiction.

New ideas and new writers certainly brought new blood and excitement; and, initially, fans were impressed with what amounted to a brand-new show. But in the end, perhaps the second season's greatest flaw

was the jettisoning of the identity of the first season—so carefully cultivated by Penfold and Byrne—in an attempt to ape what it was not. . . *Star Trek*. Ultimately, a series of weak scripts combined with the massive budget cuts reflected on the screen and, despite a devoted fan base and extreme enthusiasm for the characters played by Schell and Anholt, *Space: 1999* was canceled after that second season.

Yet, over the last thirty-five years, fans of *Space: 1999* have remained as devout as any group of fans ever has. For me, *Space: 1999* was truly a show ahead of its time. The deep themes and the thought-provoking stories that propelled the first season are all hallmarks of quality sci-fi and hold up extremely well even today. Other shows have explored such territory since to great critical and financial success.

With the resurgence of interest in the series, perhaps it is time to rediscover *Space: 1999* and re-examine it with a more even hand. Perhaps some will realize that the early criticisms were unjust; that the dark, mythical, and ethereal qualities of this iconic series were vastly ahead of its time . . . and exactly what sci-fi fans crave today.

# Captivities, or, Béla Lugosi, 2031

By J. J. Steinfeld

In the middle of yet another night of confinement, immediately after Lyxvyx woke from a not unpleasant dream about watching *Mother Riley Meets the Vampire* on the large-screen TV in his and Woxgoxot's luxurious apartment overlooking the river, he heard words through the walls. Earthling words, not all that clear but still audible, even if he could not fully understand them. Two voices conversing. It was Woxgoxot's voice he wanted to hear, but he could not be sure if it was hers or Haxteckul's. Haxteckul had arrived on Earth many years after them, wanting to return almost from his first day on Earth to their home planet, Gyrzgylx, but perhaps he had been also caught. In Lyxvyx's latest dream, he and Woxgoxot were both wearing beautiful capes he had sewn, as had become part of their nightly ritual watching old films on DVD and feasting on the glorious strength-revitalizing Earthling blood. The capes were copied after the one worn by Béla Lugosi in *Dracula*, a film they had watched innumerable times at home and actually seen at a movie theatre when it first appeared, in 1931, a hundred years ago.

Lyxvyx has often heard sounds through the walls during his confinement, sounds that could change from moment to moment, or day to day, but sounds whose sources were unknown to him. Sometimes animal sounds, other times machine sounds, at times sounds that were a jumble of animal and machine sounds. Now it was words, and he wanted them to be Woxgoxot's: "Found out . . . limited rations . . . we must find another place . . ." Lyxvyx could only assume it had to do with the changes in the sky outside. Or that there were more vehicles than usual going down the street. Old vehicles, like those he remembers from films he saw long ago— *how many years since I'd seen a film?* he thought. One of the interrogators, not long after his capture, said his impressive DVD collection of Béla Lugosi

films, indeed all their DVDs, had been destroyed, and Lyxvyx had cried, something that would have been impossible in his former condition or on Gyrzgylx. Lyxvyx had developed a great fondness for watching Earth films, especially those that dealt with what the Earthlings imagined to be vampires. It was as he and his love of a hundred years on Earth, Woxgoxot, were watching for the fifth time that night, an old Béla Lugosi film, sharing the richness of an Earthling, the poor helpless soul still able to gurgle out a few words, that they were caught and separated. Woxgoxot was explaining to the man that it wasn't like in the movies, that he wouldn't have immortal life or even die; but he wouldn't remember a thing that had happened in the room, and all his senses would be somewhat impaired, and for at least a week would suffer from a horrible flu. Woxgoxot was sounding almost apologetic when a squad of Protectors burst into their apartment and doused them with the paralysing concoction.

"Vat do you vant?" he had shouted out at the beginning of the raid, caught by surprise and dangerously using Béla Lugosi's thick Hungarian accent, forgetting he needed to continue to fool Earthlings. He had never known where they had taken Woxgoxot, but the sounds through the wall has given him some hope. Woxgoxot adored Béla Lugosi even more than he did, if that was possible. On Gyrzgylx, she was his superior and had selected him for the life-prolonging mission to Earth. Few of the vampires on Gyrzgylx—or at least what was analogous to the Earth concept of *vampire*—were eager to go to Earth, but the supply of blood was thought to be limitless and Gyrzgylx was on its last legs, in the words of the Earth phrase he had learned.

When he dared to look between the crack in the dark curtains, at the outside, the outside that was forbidden to him, he saw the colors were different, tampered with. More debris in the streets, but there was no sign of anyone, except the shadows that were driving the vehicles. Keeping them confined in small, retrograde rooms, keeping them alive but in a weakened state by synthetic blood—this was how the Earth authorities studied those they captured from Gyrzgylx, or, as the Earthlings called them, vampires, even though there was no word in their language for vampire. But through seeing the Béla Lugosi films, he soon learned that they were similar to the Earthling conception of vampires as needing blood. Those on their planet had been sustained by blood, either animal or Gyrzgylx, for thousands of years.

For the longest time, Lyxvyx thought a family of Protectors were in the apartment next to his, but now he's not certain. He sees them in the corridors, but who can tell unless you touch them, and the merest touch would result in a worse confinement than he has now—the worse getting worse hardly makes sense, he thinks, still after a hundred years not all that comfortable with Earth thinking and words—not even a crack between the curtains to look out at the sky with its changing colors, no corridors to wander. Who knows if it is true, but the only way to tell the difference between a Protector and one of the Earthlings or Gyrzgylx captives is in their genital area, which supposedly feels metallic, a compartment where their electronic workings are housed. Lyxvyx wonders why the government scientists would put the controlling devices there, but maybe it is a peculiar sort of joke.

Humor, along with dreams, he knew were an acquired taste, and he laughed slightly. Isn't that the thought, walking up to a suspected Protector and squeezing their genitals to determine identity, Lyxvyx thinks. If metal, a Protector who could worsen your confinement, or if softness, one like an ordinary Earthling, who might beat me senseless for my brazen inquiry— again, worse than worse. And does it matter anymore? Synthetic, tasteless blood food is delivered to his door every third day, three days' worth each time, beautifully organized in packages he puts outside his door before the next delivery, everything is kept clean and organized, and he can walk for an hour a day around the entire floor of this building, the corridors are spacious, it's just that he cannot go a floor above or a floor below. The already constrained, blood-denied captive doesn't want to ask what the punishment for that would be.

Lyxvyx knows that if he attempts to speak to anyone in the corridors, his punishment would be swift and severe: the removal of his tongue. He has seen the tongueless ones, both as captives on his floor, and earlier a few who had been released, having drunk some of their blood. Lyxvyx is resigned to not going outside again. He just wishes he could remember his crime, even if in a dream from which he wakes in a terrified sweat. Lyxvyx has forgotten—or had erased—so much. He could remember the Béla Lugosi films, they were more real than so many of his other Earth memories. He thought of the times he and Woxgoxot would spend long hours watching the films, usually with a good supply to drink. It was not difficult to lure visitors into their apartment for the prospect of good food and drink, and whatever else might toy at the imagination. Lyxvyx and Woxgoxot were, after all, attractive in human terms, movie-star attractive wouldn't be an inappropriate description of the two, and they had more than learned the Earthling ways of sex. And the lure of the luxurious—Lyxvyx and Woxgoxot had marvelous gambling instincts and had methodically accumulated large sums of money over the years

betting on sporting events—could never be underestimated. And a more intangible attraction, their passion for Béla Lugosi films, also seemed to be a lure for some, but that had not been incorporated into their acquisition of Earthling blood until the advent of DVDs. They also had an ample supply of music and books and artwork that had been used through the years as lures. Restored films such as *Béla Lugosi Meets a Brooklyn Gorilla, Scared to Death, The Body Snatcher, Zombies on Broadway, The Return of the Vampire, The Devil Bat, Island of Lost Souls,* and *Dracula.*

Praise be to Béla Lugosi, the greatest Dracula of all time, praise be to *Dracula,* the greatest vampire film of all time, 1931, the year they had arrived on Earth. If he could only be sure, extract the revitalizing, strengthening blood, he would be able to outwit the Earthlings, perhaps find his love, but he doesn't want to flee their planet. He wants to return to the film-watching, the excitement of dreaming and strengthening himself by drinking Earthling blood. He wants to be with his love on this strange planet. He liked dreaming, something he was able to do only on Earth— and dream about the old films he and Woxgoxot had watched on DVD years ago. Every film Béla Lugosi had appeared in between 1929 and 1956 that had been restored and remastered for video; most of them they had seen at movie theatres when they first appeared, including the classic of all classics, as Woxgoxot liked to call it, *Dracula,* in the year he and Woxgoxot had arrived on Earth. In fact, in the back of the theatre they were able to have a nourishing drink from a man who told them he was willing to try anything once, and received a kiss from Woxgoxot that he could never have imagined in his most lecherous dreams. They had gone to the film not long after Lyxvyx and Woxgoxot had won one of their first sporting wagers, a hefty bet on a 20-1 long-shot horse most felicitously named Fast Count.

He is considering speaking out loud today, his lips close to the wall, all the walls in his room. What will they hear between our walls? What will it accomplish? He doesn't know what punishment speaking in one's confinement would bring. Not like speaking to someone in a corridor. No, such an act couldn't be subversive. But would he be talking to another in confinement, or one of the Protectors who find those who need to be confined? He should be thankful, but he wants to hear more words. He wants to converse with those in the rooms next to his. He wants again to see a Béla Lugosi film. He tries to imagine Béla Lugosi on his planet, a celebrity of unimaginable proportions. He had technique, star quality, he captured what it was to be an Earth vampire. And to Lyxvyx, caught in his bloodless captivity, Béla Lugosi had the heart and soul of the most noble blood-drinking resident of Gyrzgylx.

". . . expiration of understanding . . . adequate sustenance . . . how can a death be so defined . . ."

Lyxvyx believed he must keep everything recorded in his head: the colors of the sky, the words he hears, the deliveries of his food, his strolls up and down the long corridors, descriptions of those he saw in the corridors

. . . He may have a chance to converse with someone, to share what he has seen. His confinement classification does not permit any writing or recording and communication devices. Bad enough he has been denied any Earthling blood, he has not seen a screen of any sort as long as he has been here, and he has difficulty determining how long that has been. Lyxvyx speculates he must have been in a suspended state for a lengthy time before waking here, in this room, the animal and machine sounds coming through the walls. At first he tried to understand the sounds, and to believe they had a language he compiled a dictionary in his head, thinking he heard certain sounds repeated, those sounds corresponding to certain words, the words in a certain order, offering messages to him. Foolishness or delusion. More likely, treachery of the mind. Lyxvyx had long ago stopped wondering what his crime had been, apart from being who he was, doing what was most natural to him. Enough to know he had committed a crime; his confinement classification attests to that unequivocally. Why quibble with the unequivocal? He feels himself smile at the thought. How long would he have to be on this planet to truly absorb the Earthling sense of humor?

"I love you," Lyxvyx said at the wall, at first softly. Love was one of their most valued words, and he had learned to say it to Woxgoxot. Before they had been captured and taken from their transplanted lives, Lyxvyx had told Woxgoxot he loved her more than the life-strengthening blood, she still trying to comprehend this Earth-word. In time, she too embraced the word, told Lyxvyx she loved him. Now he is saying that word *love*, a little louder each time, dozens of times, until he is saying the words as loud as he can. He recalls that when he first arrived on this planet, he had a strong voice, the beautiful Hungarian accent he learned from Béla Lugosi films, and he and Woxgoxot only used in private, not willing to draw any unnecessary attention to their identities, but he has not spoken during the time of his confinement, or had a single drop of the precious Earthling blood. Soon enough he will find out if there are Protectors next to him or others in confinement, who still want to converse. Yes, that will be their escape, small conversations between walls. Perhaps if they take him elsewhere, he will squeeze hard as he can and see how the metallic compartment feels. He has heard the horrifying stories, but he had never felt a metallic compartment. For now, all he can do is think about his confinement, imagine what was before, Woxgoxot and he watching a Béla Lugosi film, drinking the life-revitalizing blood, viewing films in his mind, imagining what is on the other side of the walls, no need to indulge in exactness and precision, no need at all. If he could get his strength back, he would find and free his love and they would assume changed identities and start a new life on Earth. If he could just have one Earthling to give him the desired, life-prolonging, strengthening blood, he could easily break down the wall. Next time he was in the corridor, he would grab one of the others, grab one and drink to his heart's content.

# ++*Alternate Words*++

## *Examining Weird Fiction*
"Episode One: In which Doris Gets Her Oats"

### By Sam Gafford

So just what the hell is "weird fiction" anyway?

It's a question that really only seems to bother writers and critics. Well, maybe booksellers as well, because they need to know where to put all the books. But it's not something that really occurs to those of us who are fans and readers of the genre. Why? The answer is similar to the infamous definition of obscenity given by U.S. Supreme Court Justice Potter Stewart in 1964: "I know it when I see it."

We don't really need to have it explained to us or partitioned or compartmentalized. We know "weird fiction" when we see it. It doesn't matter if it's vampires, zombies, werewolves, Cthulhu, or Leatherface (with a chainsaw in the parlor), or something else, we know what it is.

And, thankfully, it's all around us.

Now I could sit here and amaze you with my knowledge of the history of "weird fiction." I could talk about how this genre has basically existed since human beings first told themselves stories around a fire at night. But you know all about that already, don't you? Just like you know all the major writers and all the essential texts. You've done your homework. You've read Lovecraft and Poe and the modern writers but, like some gnawing hunger, it hasn't been enough and that's why you're here . . . to learn still more.

Weird fiction is one of those things that just goes back and forth. Some years it's popular, other years it's kinda forgotten, but it's always there . . . lurking in the corner. Many critics have made connections between the popularity of weird fiction (or "horror" as they like to keep calling it) and national uncertainty. Certainly when a society is feeling nervous about the future it becomes easier for it to accept such concepts. The '70s was a time of great social unease after the devastation that was Watergate and the economic recession. Perhaps it's not so surprising that weird fiction began to gain in popularity during that time and hit a peak in the 1980s that it has yet to reclaim.

But the problem with anything reaching high levels of popularity is that you get an awful lot of junk as well. Theodore Sturgeon's Law of "90% of everything is crap" certainly holds true in this field and especially in the '80s when basically anyone with access to a typewriter was pounding out dreck as quickly as possible in order to cash in on the boom before it died. These were the endless mass-market paperbacks with names like "The Whatever-ing" that still make up the bulk of the horror paperback sections in used bookstores today.

Part of the problem is the fact that what makes *good* weird fiction is completely subjective. There are those who think that the latest zombie opus is the greatest thing ever written by anyone, *anywhere*. The fact that I find zombies to be boring, uninteresting, and completely drained as a genre is beside the point. To them, that is the epitome of what "weird fiction" should be, and that's perfectly fine. Weird fiction *shouldn't* be the same thing to everyone all the time, because what scares people isn't the same for everyone all the time.

Not to mention the fact that our outlook changes over time as well.

The stories that scared you as a child have little power over you as an adult. Similarly, the tales that unnerved you at twenty will not have the same impact when you read them at fifty. Trust me, I've tried. At twenty, *H. P. Lovecraft*'s cosmic indifference resonated with me precisely because I was a young adult with feelings of insecurity and insignificance. Today, while those feelings haven't entirely gone away, the things that affect me have gotten more personal in nature. My cosmic outlook has dwindled to an individual focus. Long since resigned to man's universal insignificance (and, thus, my own), I find myself more concerned with the here and now and those things that threaten my personal well-being. Life has a way of changing your viewpoint so that the things you thought were important fall away while other concerns, which you never bothered with before, take center stage. So you seek out new stories that reflect that change and speak to you in entirely new and different ways.

Which is my roundabout way of saying, dear reader, that we may not always agree on what makes weird fiction. To you, it may be zombies. To another, it may be psychotic slashers. Still a third might state that it's *Lovecraftian* horrors. All these answers, and many more, are exactly right. It is that diversity that makes weird fiction such an astounding genre.

There is literally something for everyone in weird fiction. You can be like myself and prefer the classical authors like Lovecraft, Machen, Poe, Blackwood, and Hodgson. Or you can embrace newer writers like Kiernan, Barron, Ligotti, and others. Your focus can be individual like Stephen King or cosmic like Lovecraft. Your tastes can run from literate to modern.

In many ways, this genre we know as weird fiction is even more powerful than mainstream literary fiction. Despite the often fantastic backgrounds or plots, the stories in the end are about people and their struggles against not only horrors, but also themselves. Like it or not, horror is a part of life. We experience horror on virtually a daily basis, whether dealing with work, stress, or relationships. Fear invades everyone's life even if we don't recognize it. Is fear of a giant Cthulhu entity that much different from fear of illness or cancer? We deal with our fears through reading weird fiction and, in this way, we come to grips with it and hopefully overcome it.

In the end, there is no definition of weird fiction because we create it ourselves. It is many different things to many different people and each one is as valid as the rest. So if anyone ever asks you, "So just what the hell is 'weird fiction' anyway?", just smile and say, "I know it when I see it."

# Man-Eater

By Rahul Kanakia

For several days the widow Ajanta had known that another tiger-catching expedition was coming. She directed the village in moving their livestock out into the fields so that no cows or goats would be caught by the gunfire, then she cleared a large empty space in front of her hut—a site where the grass had already been beaten down by the passage of so many tiger-catching expeditions and so many wild celebrations by the ever-victorious tiger.

When the jeeps finally arrived, she saw that there was something strange about this expedition. The men were not blowing on their horns and hitting at passersby with sticks. They were sitting still and upright. When the last car stopped, she saw why: this expedition had brought along a foreigner. He was a tall white man with red hair, wearing blue jeans and a shirt with a pebbled surface.

The jeeps excited everyone's interest for a moment, but the village was accustomed to expeditions by now. After a few moments everyone returned to work. Up on the embankment that kept out the sea at high tide, women were dragging nets through the water and emptying their catch—thousands of tiny larvae—into shallow pans. They picked through pans, extracting the one or two prawn seeds that would sell for a few rupees to the shrimp farms. Beyond the embankment, men in small boats were struggling to pull a few fish from the water. Out under the *sal* tree, dozens of children ranging from six to fifteen years old were scratching at slate tablets and waiting to see if their teacher—who lived in the block capital—would decide to show up today.

The village headman bustled over, offering tea and biscuits and Coca-Cola and whiskey, but the foreigner was staring at Ajanta, who was hanging up her washing. She saw the white man's eyes stray over to her well, and then up to the solar panels strung up atop her thatched roof. She saw the understanding enter his face. She wondered if the tiger would let this one live.

The foreigner gestured to the smallest and oldest of the khaki-suited men and said, in English, "Mr. Das, look here at this woman's roof. She's taken a tiger payout, hasn't she? Can you talk to her for me? I want to know which member of her family was killed by the tiger."

"This is not certain," Mr. Das replied. "Perhaps money came to her from a shrimp pond, or from an inheritance, or a microloan. India has many schemes to aid those like her."

"The Tiger Protection Fund knows that thirteen people have taken payouts in this village—the highest of any place in the project area. Just ask her, please."

"No, no, not a good idea," Mr. Das said. "These villagers worship the tiger. They do not like us to catch him."

"If that was true," the foreigner said, "then the tiger population would be much larger. I wonder how many tigers these villagers have killed?"

The widow hadn't understood any of the preceding conversation, but she knew they were talking about her. She said, in Bengali: "Why did you bring him?"

Mr. Das replied, very rapidly, "This man has come to watch us and make sure that none of our trapping efforts are harming the tiger. You must tell the tiger he cannot hurt this man."

"If I said that, it would only make the tiger angry," she said. "Gwadar detests all those who scorn the gift of the tiger death."

But for those who sought the tiger death, the price was also heavy. When Ajanta's husband asked for the tiger death, four years ago, Gwadar took away most of the government money and left her with only enough to dig this well.

In broken Bengali, the foreigner interjected, "The tiger death? No, no, no tiger death. You lose family? Bring money. We pay blood price. No revenge on tiger."

The foreigner's exhortations were interrupted by a loud roar and then a single gunshot. The women on the embankment got up and fled, dragging their nets and pans with them. Mr. Das sprang up and started shouting. The foreigner stood still and quiet. One jeep disgorged its men. They were holding tranquilizer guns and nets. The rest of the men stayed where they were.

Mr. Das shouted, "He is near! Ready yourselves. Do not bother with his men. Aim at the tiger!"

One of the jeeps started up and rolled off down the street in the same direction from which it had come from. Two more followed it. Only one jeep was left. Mr. Das and the four remaining men stood with their dart-guns ready.

Officer Das shouted, "Gwadar! You must come out and surrender yourself. You will not be harmed. We only wish to return you to the forest. Even the Tiger Nation wishes you to return. Your own brothers have assisted us in tracking you. You must go home. Please allow this to be a peaceful transaction."

Eighteen men crawled up over the embankment and leveled their assault rifles at the tiger-catching crew. The four stalwarts dropped their dart-guns. One of them wrestled the gun away from Mr. Das.

When the tiger appeared, he was sopping wet. He must have swum here from the forest. The tiger prowled the length of the embankment, then skittered down the side of the embankment with no greater noise than that of two pebbles tumbling down a hill.

Gwadar padded over to the foreigner, and nudged the man with his head. "I am pleased to finally see a member of the illustrious Tiger Project," Gwadar said, in English. "Would you please come inside, Mr. de Kooning? We have much to discuss."

The tiger turned and walked into Ajanta's cottage. She sighed and dropped her washing back into its bucket.

Ajanta was boiling *chai* over the cookstove in Bani and Kanchan's cottage. She'd displaced them just as Gwadar had displaced her. Ajanta had sent her oldest son make sure that every household was cooking for tonight's feast, and she'd sent her youngest son to the next village to steal a goat—a loss that would be attributed to the depredations of the tigers—for Gwadar himself to slaughter and consume.

When she was leaving the hut with the pot of tea, Ajanta was stopped by Bani, who was holding the arm of her fourteen-year-old daughter Rupa.

"You must speak to him now," Bani said. "There can be no more delays. Rupa has talked to you many times. How can you have any more doubt that this is her own choice? The moneylender keeps coming to us with more demands. He will throw us out by next month if we do not bring him the money."

"Maybe it is better to be thrown out," Ajanta said. "The tiger will take nine out of every ten rupees the government gives you for Rupa's death. You will be left with sixty thousand rupees maximum."

Immediately, Ajanta knew she'd made a mistake by saying the number. "Sixty thousand!" Rupa said. "That would be more than enough. You *must* tell him we are worthy of the tiger death."

"You have a beautiful daughter," Ajanta said. "You have fed her and clothed her and spent at least sixty thousand rupees on her. This is foolish maths. Do not do this. Go to the city. She will make money as a worker."

"I know what kind of work it is that girls her age do in the city," Bani said. "You should not be discouraging us. Look at how well you've done."

Ajanta sighed. She had loved her husband Tushar. But when he'd come home from Kolkata with broken and useless legs, he'd

done the only brave thing. The irrigation supplied by the well had allowed her to raise large crops even in dry years and to gradually become the wealthiest person in this village. But she had been lucky. Usually the remaining money was lost to swindlers from the district capital who descended on the families of tiger victims with sweet words that spoke of so many possible uses for the government money.

"Fine," Ajanta said. "I will speak to Gwadar."

When she entered her hut, Officer Das, the foreigner, and the tiger were all sitting on her bamboo mats. The foreigner was smiling.

"You are truly something unique," the foreigner said, in English. "I can't believe that I am looking at one of the last of the wild tigers."

Gwadar said, "My brothers do not think I am unique. They think I can be dispensed with. They don't approve of my activities."

"But how many of you are there, really?" the foreigner said. "The Indian government tells us that your population is over seven hundred, but we do not believe that the official estimates can be correct."

"We don't have even a tenth of that number," Gwadar said.

"How will you survive?" the foreigner said.

"Will you miss us?" Gwadar said. "I hear that America has thousands of tigers. I have seen them, in the movies. They look like strong soldiers and cunning detectives and brave wilderness explorers."

"They're domesticated things," the foreigner said. "They are born in breeding pits to fat mothers who've traded their freedom for the government's money. The tiger cubs spend years learning to cradle a pen in their clumsy claws. They are held in slavery by a system they cannot understand—one that constrains them to live in thirty-square-meter apartments when they should be ranging across hundreds of kilometers; one that forces them to eat cooked meat from a cold plastic wrapper instead of gorging on fresh kills; one that forces them to restrain their instincts every moment of every day, on pain of summary execution by the jackbooted thugs of animal control. They look nothing like you. They're pathetic, twitching things. Many run to fat. Others are losing their fur because of stress. All have anxiety, depression, alcoholism, social phobias and other mental disorders caused by their unnatural living circumstances. They call every human being 'sir' and jump to do the bidding of even the lowliest man. Americans treat them with contempt, and it's hard to blame them. Those tigers are fallen beings; they've lost the grace and beauty that nature gave them."

The tiger stretched out its neck and laid its head on the foreigner's lap.

"I am sorry to hear about the plight of my distant cousins," Gwadar said. "We still keep to the old ways here. I was born in the mud. I stalk my prey every day, and I kill it fresh. I sleep outdoors and range over the whole of this district."

"You hunt sick old men," Officer Das muttered in Bengali.

"And then make their widows buy you fat cows and goats to eat."

"No," the foreigner said. "I cannot believe that you are the source of all the tiger-related deaths in this district. It must be fraud: the villagers are faking tiger involvement in order to get the payouts. We knew it. We must find some way to bring this program under control."

"Would you really blame me if I sometimes had to kill a man?" Gwadar said. "They come to the forest and poach my game, so I am forced to come here and take their animals. Then they get angry at me and I must defend myself."

"Then . . . you truly caused all these deaths?" the foreigner said.

Ajanta waited for a break in their foreign babble and then offered them tea. When the foreigner waved her away, she waited silently in the corner.

After a few moments the tiger said, "I have to protect myself."

"But you can't stay in the forest?" the foreigner said. "Why do you come into their villages? Surely you see how your presence only leads to more violence?"

"They beg him to come," Officer Das said.

The tiger looked up at the forgotten forestry officer. "Quiet," said the tiger, in Bengali. "Do you need money so badly that you've decided to beg for the tiger death? Speak another word and you shall receive it."

Officer Das opened his mouth and then closed it.

"Whatever is happening, our project is not working," the foreigner said. "We can see that. Attacks by tigers have skyrocketed since we began trying to forestall revenge attacks against your kind by making payments to those who suffer from tiger-related injuries. But from what you tell me, the tiger population is continuing to decline. And now you are also saying that the villagers are still trying

to attack you? I think that my organization will need to re-evaluate our involvement. Please, won't you tell us what it is that you need from us in order to build yourselves up again? We can provide you with breeding females to re-wild. We can give you the money and technical support to police the borders of your forest. We can give you anything. The world will spend any sum to protect you! The seventy of you are  the largest and most cohesive tiger population in the wild. The conscience of the world will not allow you to be destroyed!"

The tiger's ears had perked up. It raised its head. The foreigner said, "What is it? What's happening?"

As the tiger paced the edges of the hut, Ajanta heard the whirring of helicopters. The tiger nodded at her. She ducked outside.

The tiger's men were gone. They'd taken shelter in the huts. The villagers had run back into the paddies.

The helicopter was painted in green colors but lacked other insignia. It flew low over the water.

"Your brothers," she whispered into the hut.

The helicopter came up over the village. The sound was earth-shatteringly loud now. It sounded like a fleet of tourist boats with their motors running. The tiger padded out of the hut. The foreigner stood in the entrance, but Officer Das pulled him back.

An amplified voice rang out. "This is your last chance, brother," it said in Bengali. "We cannot allow you to continue in this way. Submit to the government's tiger-catching squad and allow them to bring you home."

Gwadar shouted something, but it was drowned out by the noise.

Officer Das said, "That voice. It's Chintil, the eldest. He's the leader of the tigers."

"Don't move," the helicopter said. "Allow the officers to bind you up. If you come home, you won't be harmed."

The helicopter had moved some distance off and it was a little quieter, but it had swung about sideways, and Ajanta could see the gun covering them from its side door.

Gwadar roared: "You'd kill one of your own brothers? You'd kill the largest, the strongest, the most virile amongst you? You'd kill the finest tiger left in the world?"

"You've cost us too much, brother," the amplified voice said. "Every time you kill a man, the government tells us that we must allow them to chop down some of our trees, or run around the forest in front of more tourists, in order to allow them to recover the costs of the payments. But even that is no longer enough. You are a monster. The money to satiate you . . . it is not possessed by any of us. Cease this

madness. Come home."

Gwadar turned to reenter the hut, but then he fell. There was a streak of blood on the ground near one of his hind paws. He got up, tried to walk, and collapsed. The helicopter's gun flashed again.

Ajanta ran, and jumped up onto the tiger. She lay on top of the thrashing beast and hoped that he wouldn't rip off her head with a

delirious paw.

She screamed, "Come, come, those are tigers in the helicopter. Our deaths will be tiger deaths!" But between the groans of the tiger and the noise from the helicopter, she didn't know if anyone heard her.

Then there was someone else next to her. Rupa was holding onto one of the tiger's flanks. They held on for long, loud moments. Ajanta got

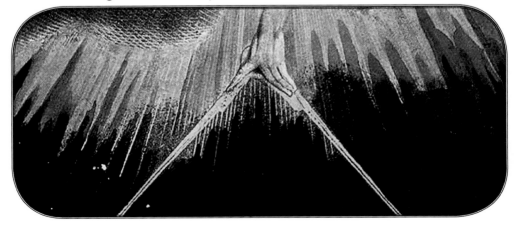

the impression that she was surrounded by dozens of other villagers.

Rupa emitted a long sigh. Somewhere above, the foreigner was shouting. Ajanta was covered in blood. Was it Rupa's, Gwadar's, or her own? Then, between one moment and the next, Ajanta could hear again. The noise of the helicopter was getting softer.

Bodies shifted atop of her. The tiger groaned, and bucked, and threw them off. It lashed out with a paw as they fell to the ground, and Ajanta was hit with a spray of blood. There were two dozen villagers surrounding the tiger. Down by its hindquarters, poor Rupa was lying on her stomach with blood pouring out of the red mass that had been her back. Next to Ajanta, a villager was bleeding out from a cut throat. On the other side of the tiger, one of her neighbors was groaning and holding the bloody scraps of his shirt to a wound in his side.

The tiger was bucking and thrashing and screaming. They drew away from the mad creature. One of its hind paws was a matted mess of blood and flesh, and more blood was leaking from a hole in its side. The tiger issued a long, keening sound from far back in its throat.

"Careful," said Officer Das. The forestry officer was beside her now. He was holding a dart-gun. "I'll tranquilize Gwadar and take him back in our jeep. There is a veterinary officer at the forest outpost only fourteen kilometers from here."

Officer Das took aim with the gun. Ajanta pulled it away from the startled officer and clubbed at him with the rifle-stock.

"No!" she said. "Gwadar is ours!"

"Stunning. Heroic," the foreigner said, in English. "They risked their lives. They threw themselves between the bullets and his claws. I've never seen anything like it. You were right. They really do worship the tiger."

"You'll testify that you witnessed all these deaths?" Ajanta said to Officer Das.

The tiger had fallen again. "Bastards," he growled. "I'll tear their throats out. Well, what are you all waiting for? Go find Dr. Kapoor. He's in amongst my men. He'll be able to bandage me."

"I can't let Gwadar escape again," Officer Das said.

By this time, the tiger's men had come out of their huts. The armed men circled warily around their injured leader.

"Why did you not protect him?" Ajanta yelled at the wavering men.

The lead man said, "The helicopter would have—"

She shouted again, "Gwadar, your men have been hired by your brother! They betrayed you! They are coming to kill you!"

The delirious tiger snarled and struck out at the lead man. The tiger grabbed him by the throat and brought him down. The rest broke and ran for the boats they'd moored on the other side of the embankment. They were so quick to abandon their leader that Ajanta wondered if they actually had been paid to betray him.

Officer Das's four men were still trussed up in one of the huts. When Ajanta came upon them, Das was trying to free them. She clubbed him again, and the little man went down.

The village was split by a roar.

"He is ours now," Ajanta said. "We will keep him safe. You and your foreigner should go to the district capital. You tell them about the three of us who have died. You bring us our money."

"But . . ." Das said.

She raised the dart gun, and he scampered off.

She had the villagers load his men, still trussed, into the jeep. The tiger was calmer now. He was lying there, gently moaning, curled up around the bodies of Rupa and the bandit he'd once commanded.

The foreigner was standing a few feet away, next to Officer Das. When Ajanta walked up to him, the foreigner said, in English, "He was attacked by his own kind and saved by ours. I see now the damage we've done. Our payments only disordered these peoples' traditional beliefs. We thought that the indigenous people were the main enemy of the tiger. Now I see that these villagers are the tiger's main source of protection. When I get back, I'll recommend that we re-evaluate our approach and stop trying to substitute traditional practices with financial incentives."

Officer Das said, "You don't understand. They don't care about the tiger. The money is important to them. It's very important . . ."

Then Das looked at Rupa's body. "Maybe you're right," the officer said. "Maybe the villagers are the only ones who truly care for the tiger. We'll discuss it on the way back."

"But he needs medical care," the foreigner said.

"He'll receive it," Das said. "There is an animal doctor just near here. We'll stop and find him and send him back. The tiger will be returned to full health."

Ajanta was paying no attention to them. Her mind was full of plans. She'd need to coax the tiger into one of the huts, where they could hide him if his brothers came back. She'd need to treat the wounds, but hopefully they would heal badly, and the crippled tiger would be dependent on the village from now on.

The foreigner and Officer Das were walking away. "Make sure you tell them about the deaths," Ajanta said. This time the tiger would not get his portion of the government money. The village would keep it *all*. Maybe Ajanta would even take a little bit off the top from Kanchan and Bani's portion. They didn't deserve to profit so immeasurably from

sacrificing their daughter.

"Waiiiit," the tiger groaned, in English. "Don't leave me." The foreigner stopped. The tiger said, "You must protect me!"

Ajanta leaned close. "Don't trust the white man," she said, in Bengali. "Is it just chance that the first time a foreigner arrives is also the first time that your brothers have been able to find you? Your brothers are slave to the foreigners. Your brothers dance for them in the forest. They wanted to sell you to America, to dance."

The foreigner leaned in close. "What do you want from me?" he said. "I'll give anything."

The tiger lashed out with a paw. Officer Das pulled the foreigner back just in time. The two of them ran to the jeep. The tiger let his head fall into Ajanta's lap. She stroked Gwadar's head. She interspersed her orders to the villagers with whispered repetitions of "You will be fine, this will all be fine" to the tiger.

"I've studied tigers all my life," the foreigner said. "And I've always longed to have the sort of bond with one of them that this woman seems to have achieved without effort."

As Officer Das drove his jeep away, Ajanta looked up and saw the foreigner staring back at her. His eyes were full of tears.

Ajanta looked at the corpses all around her. These were her neighbors. She'd known them since birth. And now each one of them was worth half a million rupees. This tiger could make money with a swipe of his paw. They could have as many tiger deaths as there were people with wives and husbands and children who deserved to become rich. If the world thought that a tiger's life was worth more than a human's, then why should Ajanta argue?

Then she remembered the weary, exultant face of her husband. Tushar hadn't told Ajanta that he was going to visit the tiger. If he had, then she hoped she would have stopped him; she hoped she would have told him that a man—even a crippled man—was worth more than a well.

Now she had a chance to ensure that no one else would ever have to make that choice.

In her lap, the tiger's eyes were closed. The jeep was out of sight now. She slowly lifted the dart-gun, balancing the heavy object in one hand. She tried to breathe as softly as possible. As she leveled the gun at the tiger's face, its eyelids opened. She fired the dart into the tiger's wide-open eye.

The villagers watched as the tiger tore open Ajanta with a swipe of his paw and then collapsed. They buried the tiger in a distant field, but kept the bodies of their neighbors, in case the government men wanted proof of what had happened. Then they went back to their fields and their fishing boats and waited for the money to arrive.

A Biannual Journal of the Macabre, Esoteric, and Intellectual...
Fiction & Poetry: S/F - Dark Fantasy - Weird - Magic Realism
Nonfiction: Thought - Criticism & Analysis - Interviews - Reviews
Audio/Visual: Art - Film - Music - TV - Comics

# Reviews & Analysis

*Dan O'Bannon's Guide to Screenplay Structure*
By Dan O'Bannon with Matt R. Lohr
*Foreword* by Roger Corman, *Afterword* by Diane O'Bannon
Michael Wiese Productions, 2013
ISBN: 978-1-61593-130-9
264 pgs; Trade Paperback; $26.95 US
*www.MWP.com*

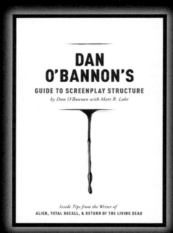

Dan O'Bannon should be a household name to anyone that has seen a film in the last thirty-odd years. Sadly, this is not the case, but many of the films that he either wrote, co-wrote, or directed certainly are: *Alien, The Return of the Living Dead, Dark Star, Total Recall, The Resurrected.* These are but a few examples of a uniquely creative mind; a mind that was not only exceptional intellectually, but also willing to challenge, to experiment, to push boundaries artistically.

In their new book, *Dan O'Bannon's Guide to Screenplay Structure,* O'Bannon and Lohr have set out to document the process and the rationale behind why screenplays that work make satisfying and successful films (irrespective of whether or not they are blockbusters financially), while others simply don't. During that analysis, the duo explore many classic works, and O'Bannon gives much in the way of "behind-the-scenes" insight about the Hollywood mindset. As he points out in his introduction, O'Bannon's chief concern here is not to overcomplicate the situation, but rather to educate writers about a simple, yet powerful, set of principles that he discovered by way of his own personal search for the reasons behind successful cinematic efforts. It is not a book of "do's and don't's," or a set of rules to follow that will guarantee success at the box office (as a collaborative institution, filmmaking is too difficult a process to document the reasons why brilliant ideas fail, while inane movies become top grossers), nor is it a book designed to teach screenplay formatting and etiquette.

Instead, this book is about one thing: structure, and why a certain story structure has revealed itself to be not only the gold standard for cinema, but also a useful story-propelling engine. Granted, one must have ideas for plots and characters, but with those elements in place, the next step is the structure at the core of the story. Here is where the magic of the book comes to the fore, and the authors do a great job of not only laying down who the major educators in the screenwriting field are, but documenting why the O'Bannon approach is at once similar in some aspects (such as the methodologies promoted by Robert McKee and Syd Field), yet also superior. It is worth noting that, while these authors have all contributed works of varying usefulness and skill, no one has ever written a book like this, as none of these other writers/educators has had the track record of Dan O'Bannon (compare the filmography in this book with the others, if they even have one in theirs!).

With a thoughtful foreword from the influential director Roger Corman, O'Bannon and Lohr deliver the goods. Written in an accessible, engaging style, the book is dryly amusing, fascinating, and easy to read. For the hardcore scripting and analysis set, there are multiple opportunities (by way of written exercises) to stretch out their reasoning skills, as well as chances to flesh out their own personal ideas and stories. Here the book excels, and it will likely be the foundation of a series of classes taught by the co-author.

Unfortunately, O'Bannon passed away before he could see his vision of this book come to fruition. Lohr, along with Mrs. O'Bannon, have given the world a gift by shepherding this important and valuable contribution to the history and theory of cinema to the public. It is among the finest books on this topic I have read (no small number, including all the ones so expertly critiqued in this volume), and I feel certain that many will feel the same way; I can easily imagine this becoming required reading at film schools all over the world, which is as fitting a legacy as any creator can strive for: to be remembered, and to help others in the process. Highly recommended.

—*Jason V Brock*

*Mutation Nation:*
*Tales of Genetic Mishaps, Monsters, and Madness*
Edited by Kelly Dunn
Featuring: Roberta Lannes, Maria Alexander, and others
Rainstorm Press, 2011
ISBN: 978-1-93775-802-8
198 pages; Paperback $14.95

In her Introduction, editor Kelly Dunn credits *The True History of the Elephant Man: The Definitive Account of the Tragic and Extraordinary Life of Joseph Carey Merrick* by Peter Ford and Michael Howell for a life-long fascination with professes her fascination with mutants, not as mere spectacles, but through which can be found an examination of humanity, both disturbing and reaffirming.

As Dunn's first fiction anthology, she does a commendable job of putting together a selection of fine stories. None of the stories disappoint, and many are surprisingly beautiful in their surreal depiction of love and empathy.

Ed Kurtz's contribution, "Angel and Grace" starts the book with a tale that seems to be of an expected subject matter (backwoods mutant twins shackled in the cellar with a mother that will do anything for them) but with a plot and style that is unexpectedly interesting. "Queen of Hearts" by Helen E. Davis is a strange story about growing extra organs and ends in a very odd place. Jarret Keene's "Swanson" employs a favorite mutation trope—radiation—to spin a quirky account of a robot created to care for his master (the latter often requesting to be served a TV dinner) thereby giving the robot the nickname for which the story is titled. A fun read.

One story, which haunted me for days after reading it, was "Compatible Donor" by JT Rowland. The auspicious protagonist falls victim to his superhuman ability to self-heal, even after having multiple organs harvested. Always a perfect match for any recipient, he becomes a priceless commodity on the black market.

"Nickelback Ned" treats us to a variation on the "boogie man." Author Maria Alexander opens with a childhood rhyme, setting the tone for her protagonists to return to their hometown to face down the villain. Owing some to Stephen King's *It*, Alexander provides a more concise and convincing plot leaving the reader to imagine what might happen next. "American Mutant: The Hands of Dominion" by Barbie Wilde explores exploitation and evangelism with a twist of come-uppance that is sublime.

Stephen Woodworth's "Menagerie of the Maladapted" is one of the best entries in the book. The future Los Angeles, scorched by the effects of climate change, provides a compelling backdrop for the introduction to a story about evolution that keeps the reader thinking long after. My personal favorite, "The Dream in a Box" is a gorgeous story about a caretaker longing to escape her charge. Having the pleasure of reading other stories by Wendy Rathbone, she is certainly one to watch in an emerging genre of magical realism meets dark fantasy and horror.

*Mutation Nation* is recommended for those who crave depth and beauty from the dark and wondrous strange.

—*Sunni K Brock*

## Conspiracy of the Planet of the Apes
By Andrew E.C. Gaska
With Illustrations by: Jim Steranko, Matt Busch, Patricio Carbajal, Colo, Dave Dorman, Erik Gist, Lucas Graciano, Scott Hampton, David Hueso, Joe Jusko, Ken Kelly, Timothy Lantz, Leo Leibelman, Miki, Christopher Moeller, Andrew Probert, Brian Rood, Sanjulian, Chris Scalf, Tom Scioli, David Seidman, Dirk Shearer, Barron Storey, Mark Texeira, Daniel Dussault, and Chandra Free
Archaia Entertainment, LLC, 2011
ISBN: 978-1-93639-336-7
272 pgs; Hardcover; $24.95 (list)

"Beware the beast Man, for he is the Devil's pawn. Alone among God's primates, he kills for sport or lust or greed. Yea, he will murder his brother to possess his brother's land. Let him not breed in great numbers, for he will make a desert of his home and yours. Shun him; drive him back into his jungle lair, for he is the harbinger of death."

—The Sacred Scrolls

Though author Pierre Boulle considered his 1963 novel *La planète des singes* to be one of his lesser works, this wry, sci-fi parable garnered critical acclaim upon publication and lead to one of the most beloved franchises in motion picture history: *The Planet of the Apes*.

With its subtle social commentary, 1968's *The Planet of the Apes* (penned by Michael Wilson and sci-fi god Rod Serling) was a box-office and critical success, leading to four more features, two reboots, two television series, and a countless number of comic books and graphic novels. In its original incarnation, the *Apes* films garnered a devout following as each movie built upon the cannon which had come before, each film more inventive and thematically complex than the prior (well, at least up until the final film, *Battle for the Planet of the Apes*). A lot of the credit for this can go to screenwriter *Paul Dehn* who served up thoughtful science fiction in films two through four, and didn't pull any punches or talk down to his potential audience. Unwell at the time of the ill-advised fifth film, Dehn was replaced by John and Joyce Corrington (*The Omega Man*), two writers who later admitted to never having seen any of the prior Apes film before writing that film. In many circles, the loss of Dehn's unique perspective was a major factor in the shuttering of the original franchise.

The fan base for Apes is devout and not one to suffer fools lightly. Tim Burton's 2001 reinvention—which abandoned all the hallmarks of the series in favor of an uninspired action story—was largely rejected by fans. 20th Century Fox' 2011 reboot, *Rise of the Planet of the Apes,* was more warmly received, but it largely jettisoned both subtlety and the brilliant origin story laid out in the earlier *Escape from the Planet of the Apes* and *Conquest of the Planet of the Apes*.

It is entirely coincidental that Drew Gaska's illustrated novel *Conspiracy of the Planet of the Apes* landed on store shelves just as *Rise* was hitting motion picture screens, but its arrival could not have been any better timed for those fans hungry for more of the original Apes philosophy. Officially licensed by FOX, *Conspiracy* is not a movie tie-in adaptation. Rather, it is a return to the Ape City as envisioned by Wilson, Serling, Dehn and producer Arthur P. Jacobs, and manages, rather brilliantly, to be both a loving tribute to the original vision and a careful expansion of the cannon that fans have come to know (and protect) so well.

Taking place during the events of the original 1968 film, *Conspiracy* wisely explores a number of minor characters from that picture to tell a story that, prior hereto, has gone untold. And in the process, Gaska manages to weave together a coherent continuity between the original films, filling in holes and solving huge inconsistencies.

Our story follows what happened to astronaut John Landon after

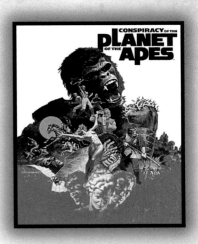

his and George Taylor's spacecraft crashes into a planet where Apes rules and man is subjugated. Separated from Charlton Heston's Taylor, we follow Landon and see the events which lead to his demise in the form of a pre-frontal lobotomy. Though the Taylor character is jettisoned early in the novel, Gaska does give us enough time with the crew of Liberty 1 to set up the personal dynamics as Landon, Taylor and astronaut Thomas Dodge begin their long trek across the desert. Heston's Taylor is as smug and overbearing as he appears in the film (Gaska perfectly captures Heston's vocal cadence and hubris). It seems our hero Landon is not a fan, Taylor's cynicism and brashness annoying and abrasive. It doesn't help that Taylor shows no desire to return to earth, nor any sadness about the loss of fellow astronaut Maryann Stewart who perished long before Liberty 1 was lost in the alien sea. Conversely, Landon has many regrets about the loss of Stewart, a woman with whom he'd had a long professional history (as part of the prior Juno/Mars mission) and a torrid extra-marital affair.

Marooned and dealing not only with the loss of Stewart but also the realization that his entire family back on Earth is long since dead, Landon feels his hatred of Taylor blossom as the trio traverses the Forbidden Zone. Taylor clearly sees himself as the Alpha male, the one man who will tame and conquer this brave new world with or without his fellow astronaut's cooperation, a fact he makes abundantly clear when he takes charge of the only weapon between them. Or perhaps it is simply Landon being paranoid. Or is it something more. . . something within the Forbidden Zone which makes him consider the voices in his head telling him to "Kill your enemy." Surely, Landon is losing his grip on reality as he begins hallucinating, reliving scenes from his past life, especially those involving Maryann.

When a gorilla security force hunts a group of humans in a now iconic cornfield scene, Landon is separated from his fellow astronauts and, after some initial "intake" procedures, is secretly given to a chimpanzee, Dr. Galen, who—unlike his colleague Dr. Zira has questionable scientific methods, largely informed by a desire to rise politically within the scientific branch of Ape society. Finding himself unable to speak and, ultimately, without control of his own mind, Landon must find a way to communicate and escape or suffer a terrible fate. . . a fate we know is inevitable.

Gaska is clearly a fan of the original film franchise, but make no mistake. . . *Conspiracy of the Planet of the Apes* is not a piece of fan fiction; rather, it is an lovingly and artfully constructed work of fiction. Gaska's prose is fluid and easy and his dialog is smart and realistic, the latter a particularly tricky situation given that the potential audience knows the voices of many of the characters before they even crack open the book.

Wisely, Gaska did not venture into a mere retelling of the first *Apes* film and those who are looking for major appearances by Taylor, Zira and Cornelius may be disappointed as they appear in little more than "cameos." Instead he focuses on relatively minor characters and creates outstanding backstories for each of them, stories that have a direct bearing on events that transpire in the sequel films.

Landon, of course, is the first of these minor characters and, at first glance, he is a tough character to love. His dislike of Taylor and his mourning of Stewart play a huge part in his early personality, resulting in numerous internal dialogs that are alternately angry and, at times, whiny. He feels almost off balance and the reader is left to wonder how this seemingly unstable man was ever chosen to be an ANSA astronaut. But there is a method to Gaska (and Landon's) madness at work here as it slowly dawns on the reader that Landon seems unstable because his mind is truly not his own. For deep in the Forbidden Zone are a group of mutants who are all too aware of the presence of the Liberty 1 crew and the potential threat they represent. By the time Landon start hallucinating, the reader realizes the mutants are in control here and they will do with Landon as they see fit.

The influence of the Mutants is a device Gaska also masterfully uses to solve a major problem of any novel that takes on a story within the time frame of the original movie. . . if Landon talks, doesn't that invalidate the shock the Apes express when Heston's character shouts "Take your stinking paws off me you damn, dirty ape"? By having the mutants controlling Landon, preventing him from speaking lest he rile up an army of Apes, Gaska creates a plausible reason for Landon's silence while remaining faithful to the film.

One of the most difficult tricks in fiction is having a lead character mourn someone who has died "off screen" as Landon does. The reader won't know this person who is being mourned; they won't feel the loss because they never "knew" them. Gaska again utilizes the mutant's control of Landon's mind to solve this potential problem, creating one of the most legitimate uses of literary "flashbacks" I have seen to date. This way, we meet Stewart and understand what the loss of her means to our hero and, in the process, Gaska creates an engaging "B" story in which he can explore a piece of *Apes* lore that never went beyond a mere mention in the films. . . the Juno/Mars mission. And it's a rich backstory he weaves here with intrigue and deception of its own.

Another minor character that receives great treatment in *Conspiracy* is Milo, the chimpanzee scientist played Sal Mineo in the third film, *Escape from the Planet of the Apes*. For those unfamiliar with the films, the planet of the apes was destroyed at the end of the second film when Heston's character detonates The Holy Bomb, leaving screenwriter Dehn is a quandary when studio execs called for another film. How, exactly, does one do another *Apes* film when the entire planet was destroyed? Quite simply. . . that tried and true sci-fi staple. . . time travel. But Dehn put his spin on it with a clever role reversal. This time, *Apes* would return to Earth when humans still ruled supreme: 1973. As it turns out, the young and inventive Dr. Milo found and salvaged Liberty 1 and he, along with Zira and Cornelius, escaped the destruction, entered a time warp and ended up back on earth.

Unfortunately, in the film, Dr. Milo is killed before the end of the first reel. Again, Gaska finds fertile creative ground to plow in *Conspiracy* and Milo becomes a full-blooded and uniquely charming character in his own right. Gaska gives us the story of the resurrection of Liberty 1 and again gives us answers the filmmakers never could.

In that third film there is also a character named Dr. Otto Hasslein, played with brilliant malevolence by Eric Braeden. As revealed in *Escape,* Hasslein is adamant that the *Planet of the Apes* should never be allowed to come to be; yet he unwittingly becomes, in essence, the father of the Apes' evolution into masters. Although the Hasslein character never rises above that of a "cameo" in *Conspiracy,* his presence is felt throughout the novel and, thereby, Gaska creates a palpable underlying tension that rings utterly true to the franchise.

Gaska also focuses on other minor and not so minor characters in the franchise. The gorilla military leader General Ursus (James Gregory in *Beneath the Planet of the Apes*) and the orangutan Dr. Zaius (Maurice Evans in the first two films) appear prominently in the novel, Gaska capturing their voices exceptionally well. Dr. Galen, a minor character in the films, is front and center and chillingly (if not blindingly) evil, and Marcus—another member of the military and virtually unnamed in the films—becomes a rich, central character as well.

Gaska has clearly done his homework and doesn't just rely on his own memories and impressions of the *Apes* films. He digs deep, sometimes referencing characters or events in the television series,

comics and even promotional material from the original films. And he ties it all together with great skill, filling in all the missing pieces of the puzzle. It is, in fact, interesting to this reviewer that no one in the long, storied history of the franchise has ever attempted to tell the story that Gaska delivers so well.

There are a few minor flaws in the novel that I would be remiss not to mention. While the flashback to the Juno/Mars mission are well done and mostly interesting, Gaska tends to focus a bit too much on the relationship between Landon and Stewart rather than the possible "conspiracy" aboard the vessel. There's only so much "pining" a reader can take and this does, at times, result in a drag on the pacing. The resolution of the conspiracy theory is a bit predictable, as well. I was looking for something more directly related to the main story. That having been said, however, the final scene of the Juno mission provides one of the most Dehn/Serling moments in the entire novel. . . a very, very nice touch.

Another flaw is one over which Gaska has little control, a problem that plagues the film franchise as well. . . and that is the fact that the Apes and their society are always far more interesting than their human counterparts. Such is the case here. As well as Gaska has drawn Landon, I found myself anxious to get to the next Apes experience. But, again, I don't know that any writer could overcome this fact.

On the production side, the novel could have benefited from one more pass by the copy editor. Though not overwhelming, there are some typos, a paragraph break mid-sentence and a few misused words ("prostate" substituted for "prostrate"; "NASA" substituted for "ANSA"). The volume is, however, beautifully bound and printed on high-quality, glossy pages with over 30 full-color illustrations and 20 black and white illustrations by some of the hottest graphic artists around. For *Apes* collectors, this will make a stunning addition to their collection and could easily be priced higher than the $24.95 list price. For non-*Apes* fans, it's a beautiful addition to their libraries.

In the end, Gaska reveals himself as a skilled storyteller and a masterful juggler. With his attention to detail and extensive knowledge of the franchise, he not only puts forth a highly entertaining work of science fiction, but also weaves a discordant and often contradictory history into a highly logical summation. Most importantly, however, Gaska stays true to the vision and tone first birthed by writers Boulle, Serling and Dehn by delving deep into the political, religious and sociological aspect of Apes society and holding the Ape mirror up to humankind. A welcome addition to the *Apes* franchise.

*—Paul G. Bens, Jr.*

## Edgar Allan Poe's *The Conqueror Worm*

Adapted by Richard Corben (writer, artist, inker, colorist)
Lettering by Nate Piekos of Blambot
Dark Horse Comics, November 2012 (one-shot)
$3.99 US

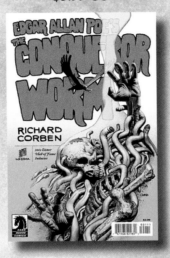

It's been some time since I've been exposed to the poem that serves as the inspiration for this illustrated re-imagining. Richard Corben's vision of a morbid classic work enhances my appreciation for Poe's skills, and has burned some vivid horrific images into my memory that I'll always recall when thinking about *The Conqueror Worm*.

Those who share an interest in illustrated adaptations of classic horror works are already familiar with the extensive catalog of Corben, who has been writing and drawing comics since mid-1960. His most definitive body of work would be found amongst the black-and-white pages of old *Creepy*, *Eerie*, and *Vampirella* magazines, and later glorious full color in *Heavy Metal* magazine. Corben was recently inducted into the Will Eisner Hall Of Fame (at San Diego Comic Con in July 2012), and deservedly so. *Ragemoor*, his recent Dark Horse collaboration with writer Jan Strnad, mines the Lovecraft mythos for its origins with a frightening tale of a living castle nurtured on blood. You may expect to see an extensive review on this site in the future, webmaster permitting.

Utilizing theatre imagery, *The Conqueror Worm* by Poe is a metaphor for limited human existence and the unavoidable death that waits for all. At the time of its first publication in 1843 the common perception was that underground worms would eventually find the buried treasures in wooden cemetery coffins, and would bore and eat and flourish in the forms within without respect for former background or legacy. A

meal is a meal.

In the poem, an audience of angels views the play that affirms the tragedy of "Man," performed by mimes responding to some controlling off-stage puppetry. Using this as a framework, Corben elaborates on the theatre setting/ puppet show and adds a background story of arrogance, greed, betrayal, lust, murder and deception. To help us transition between scenes, he adds a narrator in the form of Mag the Hag, a hooded crone of dark nature that reminds of the prophetic witches of Shakespeare's *Macbeth*. Perhaps not so coincidentally the central character, Colonel Mann (ha!), comes across some worm-ridden remains and quotes from *Hamlet* (with another reference to worms).

Set within the nineteenth century and apparently in the American West (Arizona?) the jealous, greedy and self-centered Colonel Mann meets some actors curiously wandering around in the desert. In the back of his mind, he wonders if they were witness to his recent bloody activities. Some deceitful wordplay engages between all parties. Through alluring music and hand puppetry, the male-female pair invites him to attend a special performance ("a play upon man's hopes and fears") just for the "dear lord" and his "honored guests." Colonel Mann then gathers his relatives together and suggests they attend the play in order to ease their mind of concern for the whereabouts of some recently missing family members. The commentary of his conservative and staid family members as they view the shocking and ominous performance lends a bit of humor to the otherwise grim proceedings.

Corben pulls lines directly from Poe's poem and cleverly incorporates them into his story at various points in the narrative. Wisely, the entire text of *The Conqueror Worm* is reprinted in the back pages for reference. Both poem and comics adaptation are worth several reads back and forth to fully appreciate how much Corben has elaborated and enhanced the original work in masterful fashion.

The inclusion of a sketchbook with artist notes and initial drawings also helps reinforce the power of this adaptation. For example, it explains how a condor in the poem appropriately became a turkey vulture in the comic. Looking for the absolute #1 single-issue story among the best of 2012's comics? Look no further than right here. If H. P. Lovecraft were a comic artist, he would have produced something like this. I highly recommend it.

—*Michael J. Clarke*

*Dark Directions:*
*Romero, Craven, Carpenter, and the Modern Horror Film*
By Kendall R. Phillips
Southern Illinois University Press, 2012
ISBN: 978-0-80933-095-9
$29.95; 215 pgs

"Whatever the fates of their more recent efforts, all three directors remain remarkably influential. The most obvious manifestation can be seen in the flood of remakes emerging from the back catalogue of these directors. There is, of course, always something lacking in remakes—a sense of treading over ground that has already been visited and often in more intriguing ways—but the sheer volume is striking."
—from the conclusion to *Dark Directions*

This book is a fascinating attempt to examine the corpus of three well-regarded genre directors: George A. Romero (*Dawn of the Dead*), John Carpenter (*Halloween*), and Wes Craven (*A Nightmare on Elm Street*). Though an "academic" work, the writing style is crisp and engaging, stripped of the all-too-frequent pomposity of the majority of such tomes.

In addition to this refreshing approach, Phillips brings numerous novel ideas to the fore with respect to the oeuvre of these filmmakers, some of which I disagree with, but most of which I found thoughtful and meritorious. The analysis of (arguably) the most important of this triumvirate, George Romero, was particularly interesting and is alone worth getting this volume. Recommended.

—*Kaye Vincent*

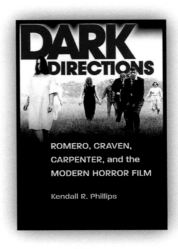

## *Dreams* and *Visions*
Both by Richard Lupoff
Hippocampus Press, 2012
ISBNs: *Dreams* 978-1-61498-039-1; *Visions* 978-1-61498-038-4
*Dreams*, Paperback, 257 pages; *Visions*, Paperback, 268 pages
$20.00 each

Recently, the prestigious Hippocampus Press issued two collections by writer Richard Lupoff, *Dreams* and *Visions*. Lupoff is a model of science fiction writing: His work can be ultra-funny; it can be craftsman-like additions to subgenres of the field; it can occasionally be among the best examples of the short story form (I didn't say science fiction short story—I said short story with Hemingway and Borges in competition); his work can be fan-fiction.

Lupoff followed what used to be "the" path of becoming a science fiction writer. First he had his magic moment: He read a story that altered his psyche. In his case it was Ray Bradbury's "Mars Is Heaven." Then he wrote for fanzines, while working at places where science fiction became fact (IBM). Then he published a Hugo-winning fanzine (*Xero*). Along the way, he wrote a great biography of Edgar Rice Burroughs (*John Carter of Mars*).

Then he wrote some wonderful novels beginning with *One Million Centuries* (1967), followed by *Sacred Locomotive Flies* (1971) and *Into the Aether* (1974). One of the best fantasies ever written, his novel *Sword of the Demon* was nominated for the 1977 Nebula Award. Finally in 2012 he fulfilled his life dream of collaborating with me on a short story, "Splash." Lupoff never actually said that was his life dream, but some things are better unsaid.

Lupoff is a master of voice. The work in these two collections demonstrates his work from 1969 (height of the New Wave), "A Freeway for Draculas," to a Holmesian pastiche in the 2003, "The Adventure of the Voorish Sign." We get to see approaches as variable as the lesbian porn (er um *racy*, that's the ticket) of "Dingbats" (2005) to autobiography as SF in "Cairo Good-Bye" (2010) to Western Cthulhu Mythos in "Petroglyphs" (2007).

His range is huge.

At times, when I was thinking about this review, I was looking for authors to compare Lupoff to. Dick, Kuttner, Matheson, and Thurber came to mind. Lupoff matches Dick's playfulness with reality, Kuttner's social commentary, Matheson's ability to place everyman in a horrific situation, and Thurber's comic genius.

Unlike some reviews that are easy to write because the writer is a one-trick pony, this review was hard to write. It took extra time as well. When I finished the stories about a Hebrew occult detective, "The Ben Zaccheus Case Files," in *Visions*, I wrote an e-mail to a friend of mine who lives on Russian Hill in San Francisco and told him that he had to buy the book. Likewise, when I finished "The Adventure of the Voorish Sign" in *Dreams* an e-mail went off to a Lovecraft fan in Merthyr Tydfil pointing out that he had to obtain the volume. The level of craft here is better than 95% of the field, and every good science fiction library should have both volumes.

I will comment on the books individually. In *Dreams* we have sixteen stories. Among the gems are "At the Esquire," which was Lupoff's first short sale (1968), an is-it-real story worthy of P. K. Dick. "Tee Shirts" a piece of memoir made surreal. "Dingbats" (aforementioned) and the Webster Sloate Stories. The three postmodern, vaguely Lovecraftian stories, "Dreemz.biz," "Wyshes.com," and "Heaven.god," are wonderful examples of the sort of reality-context stories Phil Dick did. I heard Lupoff read "Heaven.god" at the H. P. Lovecraft Film Festival and CthulhuCon in 2010. I cried tears of happiness and called my wife minutes after hearing it. I hugged my wife and told her the world was good after reading it here—its first time in print.

In *Visions* we have thirteen tales. The highlights include the first five tales, collectively called "The Ben Zaccheus Case Files." These are a mixture of comedy and Lovecraftian horror that no one but Lupoff could pull off, featuring a Kabbalist, Abraham Ben Zaccheus, and his Irish immigrant assistant and narrator, John O'Leary. John is unschooled, funny, and brave and is as full of wonder at baseball and cars as he is at Cthulhu and the Ayin Soph.

Many writers have tried their hands at sequel matter to "The Shadow over Innsmouth." Most have failed rather badly, but Lupoff succeeds in "Brackish Waters," which deals with the Deep Ones and the Port Chicago nuclear explosion. Google it. Just like Lovecraft, Lupoff lets the real world in—the real world most people don't know about. I've dealt with "Freeway for Draculas" above. Lupoff writes a good-natured fan story in "Simeon Dimbsy's Workshop"—a tale that would have brought a smile to the thin lips of Forrest J Ackerman. In "Villaggio Sogno" Lupoff takes a page from the surrealists and produces a story from a series of dreams. "Snow Ghosts" is a fine example of the Christmas ghost tale—and is a story that should find its way into good collections of the short story, not merely SF collections.

These are good books with a solid retrospective of one of the best writers in the field. They are a good introduction to Lupoff's work, and are satisfyingly well made.

*—Don Webb*

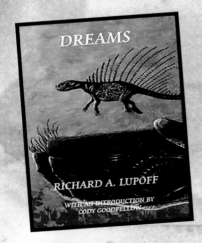

## Aftershock and Awe

By Andrew E. C. Gaska, Gray Morrow, and Miki (*Awe*);
Gaska, Miki, and David Hueso (*Aftershock*)
Co-Writer: Erik Matthews (*Aftershock* prologue)
Editor: Mike Kennedy; Art Director: Chandra Free
Creative Director and Letterer: Andrew E. C. Gaska
Designer: Anna Shausmanova; Production Manager: Scott Newman
Cover Designer (*Aftershock*): Yumi Nakamura
Cover Art: Gray Morrow and Miki (*Awe*); David Hueso (*Aftershock*)
Developed by: BLAM! Ventures LLC
Archaia Black Label, 2012
ISBN: 978-1-93639-388-6
Print: Hardcover Graphic Novel, 168 pages, $24.95 (list)
Digital Format: $2.99/Issue

It's always dicey when a publisher takes on an existing work and attempts to "re-master" it. The goal is always to bring the classic work into the new millennium and capture a new, modern set of readers while, at the same time, still satisfying fans of the underlying work. It's a path riddle with potential landmines: change too much and anger the longtime fans; change too little and that coveted new audience will be lost in translation. Luckily, Andrew E. C. Gaska, BLAM! Ventures, and Archaia Entertainment (as licensees of ITV Global Entertainment) have dodged all those problems and come out with a very good graphic novel series, *Aftershock and Awe*, based on the British cult-classic television series *Space: 1999*.

It was 1975 when *Space: 1999*—Martin Landau and Barbara Bain's first series after their stints on the wildly popular *Mission: Impossible*—premiered in American syndication. Created by Gerry and Sylvia Anderson, the series centered on the Moonbase Alpha and what happens to the 311 men and women manning it when a cataclysmic disaster rips the moon from the Earth's orbit. Drawing its inspiration more from *2001: A Space Odyssey* than *Star Trek*, it was heady stuff for the mid-1970s. And having learned from the merchandising juggernaut that *Star Trek* was then becoming, ITC Entertainment—the syndication entity at the reins—made sure that this space

epic burst onto the scene with a plethora of tie-in merchandise: Eagle Transporter models, Moonbase Alpha play sets, commlock walkie-talkies, lunch boxes, and a set of comic books inked by the late, great Gray Morrow.

The original comics—published by Charlton Media Group—are still prized by avid *Space: 1999* collectors because of the stunning artwork by Morrow and the generally well-told, albeit generic SF, stories that came three per issue. While most stories were not based on the episodes of the television series, the first issue included the story "The Last Moonrise," a 6-page condensed retelling of the pilot episode teleplay, "Breakaway." And it is this particular comic that Gaska and his team decided to tackle first when reinventing the graphic novel life of *Space: 1999.*

With *Awe*—which will be the first half of the 168-page hardcover compendium of *Aftershock and Awe* due in stores this November—Gaska and company tackle "Breakaway," the tale most familiar to 1999 fans, in a two-issue spread currently available digitally through Comixology. Gaska wisely released these issues first, as standalones, presumably to get the 1999 fan base on board with his bold, new vision, and possibly to coincide with Alpha: 2012, a *Space: 1999* convention held this past September in the Los Angeles area.

Gaska retained most, if not all, of Morrow's original artwork from that first issue and augmented it with material from a Power Records retelling. It is a deftly done reimagining, Gaska and team softening (but not wholly losing the charm of) the 1970s style coloring and bringing that artwork into the new, distinctly twenty-first-century style that graphic novel fans of today expect. The colors are bold but darkly muted when appropriate, ominous when need be. And while they stick fairly closely to the original script of the televised episode, Gaska, artist Miki, and art director Chandra Free weren't satisfied with simply recoloring or reissuing a classic work; they truly reinvented it.

Whether they are fans of the television series or just extremely good researchers, Gaska and his team add to the story with new, original artwork, new dialogue, and characters who are familiar to longtime fans but will seamlessly blend into the story for those new to the franchise. And they do it all expertly.

A two-issue arc, *Awe* adds numerous new elements to the story, and the team did its homework very well. Cleverly, each issue is given an "opening credits" title treatment that mimics in the best possible way the "This Episode" conceit that opened every episode of *Space: 1999*'s first season. Additionally, Gaska and his team have incorporated dialogue that was filmed for the pilot episode but unaired, and they also insert into the "Breakaway" storyline characters who appear much later in the television series, creating a bridge between that story and the episodes of the series that follow. What this manages to do for fans is to breathe new life into a story they can practically recite verbatim by utilizing characters whose future histories they already know: Tony Cellini, Tony Verdeschi, Shermeen Williams. This also serves to give fans a glimpse of what Gaska could offer in terms of dovetailing original stories with the existing television series canon should the graphic novel continue on past the compendium. And it isn't a clunky blend. Gaska and his team know the characters and their voices, so they feel as if they had always been in the original comics.

Another new feature is something Gaska does in an attempt to link the first season of the series to the second. Anyone familiar with the show will know that the tone and quality between season one and season two were drastically different, the latter being significantly "Americanized." In the second season, each episode started with a "Moonbase Alpha Status Report" spoken by Bain's character, Dr. Helena Russell. In *Awe*, Gaska and team draw a thread between those seasons by telling the story via alternating "diary entries" from John Koenig (Landau's character), Commander of Moonbase Alpha, and Victor Bergman (played by Barry Morse in the series), resident scientist and unlikely philosopher. For fans, this creates a continuity that was sorely lacking between the two seasons of the series. For readers completely new to the world of *1999*, it all feels exactly as if it belongs there.

*Awe* has been followed up by the first issue in a three-issue arc of *Aftershock*, and this is where the BLAM! team's creativity really gets to soar. First off is the very slick new cover artwork that utilizes all the imagery familiar to fans but gives a dark and foreboding reality to this new "series." The interior artwork and story are all brand-new, familiar features of the series woven in to make sure the new storyline stays well related to the original. Although darker in tone than *Awe*, it all fits well within both the graphic novel and television series continuity.

In an alternate reality where JFK was never assassinated and Presidents Ronald Reagan and Kim Jong Il were driven from power for causing World War III, the "Space Race" was accelerated in an effort to maintain world peace; thus, Moonbase Alpha was born. Through clever use or flashbacks and flash-forwards, Gaska, Miki, David Hueso, and the rest of the design team create the Earth—relatively absent from the television series—in that time period leading up to and beyond the accident that propels the moon out of orbit and the devastation that falls upon the Earth thereafter. Gaska creates an entire slate of characters—new to the 1999 world—and connects them through bloodlines or plot points to all the characters the fans already know. We meet Haley Carter, the illegitimate daughter of Moonbase Alpha's chief astronaut, Alan Carter. We're introduced to the smarmy Commission Simmonds (played by Roy Dotrice in the series) and learn of his earthbound life before Moonbase Alpha. We discover the dark secrets of war hero Admiral Walker, a new character whose current activities don't appear to line up with his historic reputation. Slowly a web of lies and corruption is formed, giving *Aftershock* new bite, contemporary relevance, and a very modern sensibility that shines light on the events we watched unfold in the *Awe* storyline. Perhaps the accident on the lunar surface wasn't all it appeared to be. It's political and social intrigue at its very best.

Stylistically, *Aftershock* is much darker, much more angular than *Awe,* and it is a testament to Gaska's team that they are able to pull it off, making both storylines fit together effortlessly despite the tonal shift. Again, much of this is due to the intertwining of the new storyline with that established by the television series. As an example, in both the television series and the *Awe* adaptation, Commissioner Simmonds when he arrives on Moonbase Alpha stated to Commander Koenig, "My office tried to query you on your Emergency Code Alpha One. You didn't seem to be available." It's a little detail, but Gaska zeroes in on it and, in *Aftershock*, gives us the reasoning that Simmond's *office* tried to query rather than Simmonds himself placing the call. We get backstory that not only fills in some blanks in the series continuity but also manages to propel this new story forward. Likewise, Gaska reintroduces us to the Mark IX Hawk fighter, a ship utilized in only one episode of the television series, but one for which Gaska and team have created a whole history, and it may be a sordid one. And like all good storytellers, Gaska ends each issue of *Aftershock and Awe* with a cliffhanger that makes you wonder just where he is headed with future issues.

In the end, BLAM! Ventures has come up with a winner. For fans of the television series (of which I am, admittedly, one), they've taken a story I've loved for decades and breathed new life into it through their attention to detail. This isn't a quick drive-by recreation, not some slap-ping on of a franchise name to all-new material. It's an A-class reinven-tion, and it is Gaska's respect for the details in the source material that helps him bring new canon into old and make it work exceptionally well. It's believable because the BLAM! team understands and appreci-ates the original and pays homage to it rather than simply exploiting it.

What does it mean to readers unfamiliar with the *1999* fran-chise? From a creative perspective, *Aftershock and Awe* is slick, exciting, and filled with an impressive amount of depth character and of per-spective. The artwork is top-notch; the storytelling is gripping; the ride is damn good. Do you need to know *1999* to enjoy it? Not at all. Yes, Gaska painted in a lot of material that would ring true to the fans, but he was also careful to make sure it was all seamless. Readers new to the franchise would be hard pressed to differentiate the new from the old.

So, fans . . . sit back and enjoy. And, if you're a graphic novel fan who has never heard of *Space: 1999*, give it a shot. You don't have to know the original to appreciate this exceptional work. And who knows? It might intrigue you enough that you'll want to discover what came before. I know I'm looking forward to what lies ahead.

[*A note about this review:* The reviewer read the available issues of *Aftershock and Awe* on an Apple iPad (using the Comixology app) and in advance, special print editions. The digital versions translate very well to the iPad with smooth transitions and vibrant colors. Navi-gation and download on the Comixology app is fast and easy. For the advance print issues, production values are high, with quality paper and printing.]

—*Paul G. Bens, Jr*

***Edge of Dark Water***
By Joe R. Lansdale
Mulholland/Little Brown and Company, 2012
ISBN: 978-0-31618-843-2
292 pages; $25.99 US/$28.99 CN

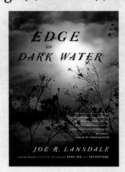

This novel presents a highly successful triple play – from Twain to Faulkner to Lansdale – who scores a touchdown. As Joe would say: "It's a pisser!"

Joe R. Lansdale is the prolific bard of East Texas, whose gutsy, outrageous style is indigenous to the area. No one can match "The Texas Kid" (as I call him) when it come to an uncompromising, no-holds-barred, in-your-face depiction of the people and places of East Texas, past and present. There is a deep love of country in every sentence of this novel, a bold river adventure along the Sabine that rivals Huck Finn's earlier travels down the Mississippi.

Lansdale has proven himself to be a hell of a storyteller, and in *Edge of Dark Water* he has a whopping good story to tell. The book compels you to keep turning the pages to find out what happens next. Lansdale is a true master of suspense. His prose is as swift as a clear-running river current and literally sweeps the reader forward.

Lansdale's colorful cast of characters includes the sharply delineated narrator, a savvy, resourceful sixteen-year-old named Sue Ellen, a guilt-ridden homosexual boy, Terry Thomas, a failed preacher, the Reverend Joy, a battered runaway wife (Sue Ellen's mama), and a vividly portrayed smart-mouth, sassy black girl named Jinx. Together, they flee from Skunk, an odoriferous stone-cold killer who wears the severed hands of his victims as a gruesome necklace.

Joe Lansdale does not flinch from overt violence, but he never panders to sick thrill-seekers; his shock scenes all ring true, without artifice.

If you want to read a novel of rare power and substance, with echoes of Twain and Faulkner, then grab a copy of *Edge of Dark Water*.

Yep, it's a pisser!

—*William F. Nolan*

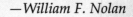

# Horror, Science Fiction, Fantasy

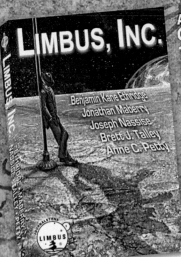

**Are You Laid Off, Downsized, Undersized?**
**CALL US. WE EMPLOY.**
**1-800-555-0606**
**HOW LUCKY DO YOU FEEL?**

So reads the business card from LIMBUS, INC., a shadowy employment agency that operates at the edge of the normal world. LIMBUS's employees are just as suspicious and ephemeral as the motives of the company, if indeed it could be called a company in the ordinary sense of the word.

In this shared-world anthology, five heavy hitters from the dark worlds of horror, fantasy, and scifi pool their warped take on the shadow organization that offers employment of the most unusual kind to those on the fringes of society.

978-1-936564-52-1  $17.95

## SOMETHING UNSPEAKABLE PROWLS THE WOODS.

Police Chief Elizabeth "Izzy" Morris enjoys keeping the peace in the small town of Kinsey in Michigan's Upper Peninsula. But when her seventeen-year-old daughter goes missing after a school dance and the mutilated corpse of the girl's date is discovered in the nearby woods, Izzy's police skills are stretched to their limits.

978-1-936564-65-1  $13.95

When thirteen-year-old orphan Penny Sinclair moves to the small town of Dogwood to live with her godmother, she expects her life to become very dull. She doesn't expect to find a strange talking fox roaming the countryside near her new home, a kindred spirit in her new friend Zoe, or the secret grove where they discover the long hidden magic of The Phoenix Girls. Learning to use magic isn't easy, though; Penny and Zoe get their magic wrong almost as often as they get it right. When something sinister threatens Dogwood, their often accidental magic may be the only thing that can stop it.

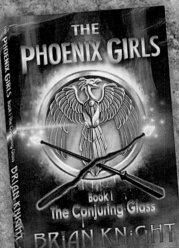

978-1-936564-72-9  $14.95

# TALES FROM WILLIAM F. NOLAN'S
# DARK UNIVERSE

**#1 OF A BRAND NEW SERIES!**

**LEGENDS ARE BORN.**

# [Namel3ss

A Biannual Journal of the Macabre, Esoteric and Intel'l

## Volume 2, Number 1: Spring/Summer 2013

Therese Arkenberg * Kalin Nenov * Michael Winegar * Shade Rupe * Triptykon/1349
Hank Shore * Sam Gafford * Bryan K. Ward * Marc Venema

## A Sneak Peak of our NEXT issue....

CPSIA information can be obtained
at www.ICGtesting.com
Printed in the USA
LVIC070424060513
332296LV00002B

★ 9 7 8 0 9 8 8 1 7 2 8 1 4 ★